'Wilbur Smith rarely misses a trick'
Sunday Times

'The world's leading adventure writer'
Daily Express

'Action is the name of Wilbur Smith's game and
he is a master'
Washington Post

'The pace would do credit to a Porsche, and the invention
is as bright and explosive as a fireworks display'
Sunday Telegraph

'A violent saga set in Boer War South Africa, told with
vigour and enthusiasm . . . Wilbur Smith spins a fine tale'
Evening Standard

'A bonanza of excitement'
New York Times

'. . . a natural storyteller who moves confidently and
often splendidly in his period and sustains a flow of
convincing incident'
The Scotsman

'Raw experience, grim realism, history and romance welded
with mystery and the bewilderment of life itself'
Library Journal

'A thundering good read'
Irish Times

THE DIAMOND
HUNTERS

Wilbur Smith was born in Central Africa in 1933. He was educated at Michaelhouse and Rhodes University. He became a full-time writer in 1964 after the successful publication of *When the Lion Feeds*, and has written over thirty novels, all meticulously researched on his numerous expeditions worldwide. His books are now translated into twenty-six languages.

WILBUR SMITH

THE
DIAMOND
HUNTERS

PAN BOOKS

First published in Great Britain 1971 by William Heinemann Ltd

First published in paperback 1973 by Pan Books

This edition published 1998 by Pan Books
an imprint of Pan Macmillan Ltd
Pan Macmillan, 20 New Wharf Road, London N1 9RR
Basingstoke and Oxford
Associated companies throughout the world
www.panmacmillan.com

ISBN 978-0-330-23380-4

47 49 48 46

A CIP catalogue record for this book is available from
the British Library.

Typeset by SetSystems Ltd, Saffron Walden, Essex
Printed and bound in Great Britain by
Mackays of Chatham plc, Chatham, Kent

Visit **www.panmacmillan.com** to read more about all our books and to buy
them. You will also find features, author interviews and news of any author
events, and you can sign up for e-newsletters so that you're always first to hear
about our new releases.

This book is for my wife and the jewel
of my life, Mokhiniso, with all my love
and gratitude for the enchanted years
that I have been married to her

His flight had been delayed for three hours at Nairobi, and despite four large whiskies he slept only fitfully until the intercontinental Boeing touched down at Heathrow. Johnny Lance felt as though someone had thrown a handful of grit in each eye, and his mood was ugly as he came through the indignity of Customs and Immigration into the main hall of the international terminus.

The Van Der Byl Diamond Company's London agent was there to meet him.

'Pleasant trip, Johnny?'

'Like the one to Hell,' Johnny grunted.

'Good practice for you.' The agent grinned. The two of them had seen some riotous times together.

Reluctantly Johnny grinned back at him.

'You got me a room and a car?'

'Dorchester – and Jag.' The agent handed over the car keys. 'And I've got two first-class seats reserved on tomorrow's nine o'clock flight back to Cape Town. Tickets at the hotel reception desk.'

'Good boy.' Johnny dropped the keys into the pocket of his cashmere overcoat and they started for the exit. 'Now where is Tracey van der Byl?'

The agent shrugged. 'Since I wrote to you she has dropped out of sight. I don't know where you can start looking.'

'Great, just great!' said Johnny bitterly as they came out into the car park. 'I'll start with Benedict.'

'Does the Old Man know about Tracey?'

Johnny shook his head. 'He's a sick man. I didn't tell him.'

'Here's your car.' The agent stopped by the pearl-grey Jaguar. 'Any chance of a drink together?'

'Not this trip, sorry.' Johnny slipped in behind the wheel. 'Next time.'

'I'll hold you to that,' said the agent and walked away.

It was almost dark by the time Johnny crossed the Hammersmith flyover in the moist smoky grey of the evening, and he lost himself twice in the maze of Belgravia before he found the narrow mews behind Belgrave Square and parked the Jaguar.

The exterior of the flat had been lavishly redecorated since his last visit, and Johnny's mouth twisted. He might not be so hot at earning the stuff – but our boy Benedict certainly was a dab hand at spending it.

There were lights burning and Johnny hit the door knocker half a dozen lusty cracks. It echoed hollowly about the mews, and in the silence that followed Johnny heard the whisper of voices from behind the curtains, and a shadow passed quickly across the window.

Johnny waited three minutes in the cold, then he stepped back into the middle of the mews.

'Benedict van der Byl,' he bellowed. 'I'll give you a count of ten to get this door open. Then I'll kick the bloody thing down.'

He drew breath, and bellowed again.

'This is Johnny Lance – and you know I mean it.'

The door opened almost immediately. Johnny pushed his way through it, not glancing at the man who held it, and started for the lounge.

'Dammit, Lance. You can't go in there.' Benedict van der Byl started after him.

'Why not?' Johnny glanced back at him. 'It is a Company flat – and I'm the General Manager.'

Before Benedict could reply, Johnny was through the door.

One of the girls picked up her clothing from the floor

and ran naked into the bedroom passage. The other pulled a full-length caftan over her head and glared at Johnny sulkily. Her hair was in wild disorder, fluffed out into a grotesque halo of stiff curls.

'Nice party,' said Johnny. He glanced at the movie projector on the side table, and then at the screen across the room. 'Films and all.'

'Are you the Fuzz?' demanded the girl.

'You've got an infernal cheek, Lance.' Benedict van der Byl was beside him, tying the belt of his silk dressing-gown.

'Is he Fuzz?' the girl demanded again.

'No,' Benedict assured her. 'He works for my father.' With the statement he seemed to gather self-assurance, drawing himself up to his full height and smoothing his long dark hair with one hand. His voice regained its polish and lazy inflection. 'Actually, he is Daddy's messenger boy.'

Johnny turned to him, but he addressed the girl without looking at her.

'Beat it, girlie. Follow your friend.'

She hesitated.

'Beat it!' Johnny's voice crackled like a bush fire, and she went.

The two men stood facing each other. They were the same age, in their early thirties – both tall, both dark-haired – but different in every other way.

Johnny was big in the shoulder and lean across the hips and belly, his skin polished and browned by the desert sun. The line of his heavy jawbone stood out clearly, and his eyes seemed still to seek far horizons. His voice clipped and twanged with the accents of the other land.

'Where is Tracey?' he asked.

Benedict lifted one eyebrow in a pantomine of arrogant surprise. His skin was pale olive, unstained by sunlight for it was months since he had last visited Africa. His lips were very red, as though they had been painted, the classical lines of his features were blurred by flesh. There were soft little pouches under his eyes, and a plumpness beneath the silk dressing-gown that suggested he ate and drank often and exercised infrequently.

'My dear chap, what on earth makes you think I know where my sister is? I haven't seen her for weeks.'

Johnny turned away and crossed to one of the paintings on the far wall. The room was hung with good original South African artists – Alexis Preller, Irma Stern and Tretchikof – an unusual mixture of techniques and styles, but someone had convinced the Old Man they were sound investments.

Johnny turned back to face Benedict van der Byl. He studied him as he had the paintings, comparing him with the clean young athlete he had been a few years before. A clear mental image in his mind pictured Benedict moving with leopard grace across the green field of play under the packed grandstands, turning smoothly beneath the high floating arc of the ball to gather it neatly, head high, and break back infield to open the line for the return kick.

'You're getting fat, Laddy Buck,' he said softly, and Benedict's anger stained his cheeks dull red.

'Get out of here,' he snapped.

'In a minute – tell me about Tracey first.'

'I've told you – I don't know where she is. Whoring it up around Chelsea, I expect.'

Johnny felt his own anger surge fiercely, but his voice remained level.

'Where is she getting the money, Benedict?'

'I don't know – the Old Man—'

Johnny cut him short. 'The Old Man is keeping her on an allowance of ten pounds a week. From what I hear she's throwing more than that around.'

'Christ, Johnny,' Benedict's tone became conciliatory, 'I don't know. It's not my business. Perhaps Kenny Hartford is—'

Again Johnny interrupted impatiently. 'Kenny Hartford is giving her nothing. That was part of the divorce agreement when they split up. Now I want to know who is subsidizing her trip to oblivion. How about it, big brother?'

'Me?' Benedict was indignant. 'You know there is no love wasted between us.'

'Must I spell it out?' Johnny asked. 'All right, then. The Old Man is dying – without losing his horror of all weakness and sin. If Tracey turns into a drug-soaked little tramp – then there's a good chance that our boy Benedict will come back into full favour. It would be a good gamble on your part to lay out a few thousand now, to send Tracey to Hell. Cut her off completely from her father – and all those nice fat millions.'

'Who said anything about drugs?' Benedict blustered.

'I did.' Johnny stepped up to him. 'You and I have a little unfinished business. It would give me intense pleasure to take you to pieces and see what makes you work.'

He held Benedict's eyes for long seconds, then Benedict looked down and fiddled with the cord of his dressing-gown.

'Where is she, Benedict?'

'I don't know, damn you!'

Johnny moved softly across to the movie projector and picked up a reel of film from the table beside it. He peeled off a few feet of celluloid from the reel and held it up to the light.

'Pretty!' he said, but the line of his mouth tightened with disgust.

'Put that down,' snapped Benedict.

'You know what the Old Man thinks about this sort of thing, don't you, Benedict?'

Suddenly Benedict went pale.

'He wouldn't believe you.'

'Yes, he would.' Johnny tossed the reel on the table and turned back to Benedict. 'He believes me because I've never lied to him.'

5

Benedict hesitated, wiped his lips nervously with the back of his hand.

'I haven't seen her for two weeks. She was renting a place in Chelsea. Stark Street. No. 23. She came to see me.'

'What for?'

'I lent her a couple of pounds,' Benedict muttered sulkily.

'A couple of pounds?' Johnny asked.

'All right, a couple of hundred. After all, she is my sister.'

'Damn decent of you,' Johnny lauded him. 'Write down the address.'

Benedict crossed to the leather-topped writing desk and scribbled on a card. He came back and handed the card to Johnny.

'You like to think you're big and dangerous, Lance.' His voice was pitched low but it shook with fury. 'Well, I'm dangerous too – in a different sort of way. The Old Man can't live for ever, Lance. When he's gone I'm coming after you.'

'You frighten the hell out of me.' Johnny grinned at him, and went down to the car.

The traffic was solid in Sloane Square as Johnny eased the Jaguar slowly down towards Chelsea. There was plenty of time to think; to remember how close they had been – the three of them. He and Tracey and Benedict.

Running together as wild young things with the endless beaches and mountains and sun-washed plains of Namaqualand as their playground. That was before the Old Man made the big strike on the Slang River, before there was money for shoes. When Tracey wore dresses made from flour sacks sewn together, and they rode to school each day, all three of them bare-back on a single pony like a row of bedraggled little brown sparrows on a fence.

He remembered how the long sun-drenched weeks while the Old Man was away were spent in laughter and secret games. How they climbed the *kopje* behind the mud-walled shack each evening and looked towards the north across the limitless land, flesh-coloured and purple in the sunset, searching for the wisp of dust in the distance that would mean the Old Man was coming home.

Then the almost painful excitement when the dusty, rackety Ford truck with its mudguards tied on with wire was suddenly there in the yard, and the Old Man was climbing down from the cab, a sweat-stained hat on the back of his head and the dust thick in the stubble of his beard, swinging Tracey squealing above his head. Then turning to Benedict, and lastly to Johnny. Always in that order – Tracey, Benedict, Johnny.

Johnny had never wondered why sometimes he was not first. It was always that way. Tracey, Benedict, Johnny. The same way as he had never wondered why his name was Lance and not van der Byl. Then it had come to an end suddenly, the whole brightly sunlit dream of childhood was gone and lost.

'Johnny, I'm not your real father. Your father and mother died when you were very young.' And Johnny had stared at the Old Man in disbelief.

'Do you understand, Johnny?'

'Yes, Pa.'

Tracey's hand groped for his beneath the table top like a little warm animal. He jerked his own hand away from it.

'I think you'd better not call me that any more, Johnny.' He could remember the exact tone of the Old Man's voice, neutral, matter of fact, as it splintered the fragile crystal of his childhood to fragments. The loneliness had begun.

Johnny accelerated the Jaguar forward and swung into the King's Road. He was surprised that the memory hurt so intensely – time should have mellowed and softened it.

His life from then on had become a ceaseless contest to win the Old Man's approval – he dare not hope for his love.

Soon there were other changes, for a week later the old Ford had come roaring unexpectedly out of the desert in the night, and the barking of the dogs and the Old Man's shouted laughter had brought them, sleepy-eyed, tumbling from their bunks.

The Old Man had lit the Petromax lamp and sat them on the kitchen chairs about the scrubbed deal table. Then with the air of a conjuror he had lain something that looked like a big lump of broken glass on the table.

The three sleepy children had stared at it solemnly, not understanding. The harsh glare of the Petromax was captured within the crystal, captured, repeated, magnified and thrown back at them in fire and blue lightning.

'Twelve carats – ' gloated the Old Man, 'blue-white and perfect, and there is a cartload more where that came from.'

After that there were new clothes and motor cars, the move to Cape Town, the new school and the big house on Wynberg Hill – but always the contest. The contest that did not earn the Old Man's approval as it was designed to do, but earned instead Benedict van der Byl's jealousy and hatred. Without his drive and purpose, Benedict could not hope to match Johnny's achievements in the classroom and on the sports field. He fell far behind the pace that Johnny set – and hated him for it.

The Old Man did not notice for he was seldom with them now. They lived alone in the big house with the thin silent woman who was their housekeeper, and the Old Man came infrequently and for short periods. Always he seemed tired and distracted. Sometimes he brought presents for them from London and Amsterdam and Kimberley, but the presents meant very little to them. They would have liked it better had it stayed the way it was in the desert.

In the void left by the Old Man the hostility and rivalry between Johnny and Benedict flourished to such proportions that Tracey was forced to choose between them. She chose Johnny.

In their loneliness they clung to each other.

The grave little girl and the big gangling boy built

together a castle against the loneliness. It was a bright secure place where the sadness could not reach them – and Benedict was excluded from it.

Johnny swung the Jaguar out of the line of traffic into Old Church Street, down towards the river in Chelsea. He drove automatically and the memories came crowding back.

He tried to recapture and hold the castle of warmth and love that he and Tracey had built so long ago, but instantly his mind leapt to the night on which it had collapsed.

One night in the old house on Wynberg Hill Johnny had come awake to the sound of distant weeping. He had gone barefooted in his pyjamas, following that heart-rending whisper of grief. He was afraid, fourteen years old and afraid in the dark house.

Tracey was weeping into her pillow and he had stooped over her.

'Tracey. What is it? Why are you crying?'

She had jumped up, kneeling on the bed, and flung both arms about his neck.

'Oh, Johnny. I had a dream, a terrible dream. Hold me, please. Don't go away, don't leave me.' Her whisper was still thick and muffled with tears. He had gone into her bed and held her until at last she slept.

Every night after that he had gone to her room. It was innocent and completely childlike, the twelve-year-old girl and the boy who was her brother, in fact if not in name. They held each other in the bed, and whispered and laughed secretly until sleep carried them both away.

Then suddenly the castle was blasted by the bright electric glare of the overhead light. The Old Man was standing in the door of the bedroom, and Benedict was behind him in his pyjamas dancing with excitement and chanting triumphantly.

'I told you, Pa! I told you so!'

The Old Man was shaking with rage, the bush of grey

hair standing erect like the mane of a wounded lion. He had dragged Johnny from the bed, and struck away Tracey's clinging hands.

'You little whore,' he bellowed, holding the terrified boy easily with one hand and leaning forward to strike his daughter in the face with his open hand. Leaving her sobbing, face down on the bed, he dragged Johnny down the passages to the study on the ground floor. He threw him into the room with a violence that sent him staggering against the desk.

The Old Man had gone to the rack and taken out a light Malacca cane. He came to Johnny and, taking a handful of his hair, threw him face down over the desk.

The Old Man had beaten him before, but never like this. Mad with rage the Old Man's blows had been unaimed, some fell across Johnny's back.

Yet in the agony it was deadly important to the boy that he should not cry out. He bit through his lip so the taste of blood was salt and copper in his mouth. He must not hear me cry! And he choked back the moans feeling his pyjama trousers hanging heavy and sodden with blood.

His silence served only as a goad to the Old Man's fury. Flinging the cane aside, he pulled the boy upright and attacked him with his hands. Slamming Johnny's head from side to side with full, open-handed blows that burst in Johnny's skull with blinding flashes of light.

Still Johnny kept on his feet, clinging to the edge of the desk. His lips broken and swollen and his face bloated and darkening with bruises, until at last the Old Man was driven far beyond the borders of sanity. He bunched his fist and drove it into Johnny's face – and with a wonderful sense of relief Johnny felt the pain go out in a warm flood of darkness.

J ohnny heard voices first. A strange voice:

' – As though he's been savaged by a wild beast. I'll have to inform the police.'

Then a voice he recognized. It took him a little time to place it. He tried to open his eyes but they seemed locked tight, his face felt enormous, swollen and hot. He forced the fat lids of his eyes back and recognized Michael Shapiro, the Old Man's secretary. He was talking quietly to the other man.

There was the smell of antiseptic and the doctor's bag lay open on the table beside the bed.

'Listen, Doctor. I know it looks bad – but hadn't you better talk to the boy before you stir up the police?'

They both looked towards the bed.

'He's conscious.' The doctor came to him quickly. 'What happened to you, Johnny? Tell us what happened. Whoever did this to you will be punished – I promise you.'

The words were wrong. Nobody must ever punish the Old Man.

Johnny tried to speak but his lips were stiff and swollen. He tried again.

'I fell,' he said. 'I fell. Nobody! Nobody! I fell down.'

When the doctor had gone Mike Shapiro came and stood over him. His Jewish eyes were dark with pity, and something else – anger perhaps, or admiration. 'I'm taking you to my house, Johnny. You will be all right now.'

He stayed two weeks under the care of Michael Shapiro's wife, Helen. The scabs came away, the bruises faded to a dirty yellow, but his nose stayed crooked with a lump at the bridge. He studied his new nose in the mirror, and liked it. It made him look like a boxer, he thought, or a pirate, but it was many months before the tenderness passed and he could finger it freely.

'Listen, Johnny, you are going to a new school. A fine boarding-school in Grahamstown.' Michael Shapiro tried to sound enthusiastic. Grahamstown was five hundred miles

11

away. 'In the holidays you'll be going to work in Namaqua-land – learning all about diamonds and how to mine them. You'll enjoy that, won't you?'

Johnny had thought about it for a minute, watching Michael's face and reading in it his shame.

'I won't be going home again then?' By home he meant the house on Wynberg Hill. Michael shook his head.

'When will I see—' Johnny hesitated as he tried to find the right words, ' – when will I see them again?'

'I don't know, Johnny,' Michael answered him honestly.

As Michael had promised it was a fine school.

On his first Sunday after the church service, he had followed the other boys back to their classroom for the session of compulsory letter-writing. The others had immediately begun dashing off hasty scribbles to their parents. Johnny sat miserably until the master in charge stopped at his desk.

'Aren't you going to write home, Lance?' he asked kindly. 'I'm sure they'll all want to hear how you are.'

Johnny picked up his pen obediently, and puzzled over the blank writing-pad.

He wrote at last:

Dear Sir,
    I hope you will be pleased to hear that I am now at school. The food is good, but the beds are very hard.
    We go to church every day and play rugby football.
                                Yours faithfully,
                                        Johnny.

From then until he left school and went up to University three years later, he wrote every week to the Old Man. Every letter began with the same salutation and went on, 'I hope you will be pleased to hear—' There was never a reply to any of these letters.

Once each term he received a typewritten letter from

Michael Shapiro setting out the arrangements that had been made for the school holidays. Usually these involved a train journey hundreds of miles across the Karroo to some remote village in the vast dry wasteland, where a light aircraft belonging to Van Der Byl Diamonds was waiting to fly him still deeper into the desert to one of the Company's concession areas. Again, as Michael Shapiro had promised, he learned about diamonds and how to mine them.

When the time to move on to University arrived, it was completely natural that he chose to take a degree in Geology.

During all that time he was an outcast from the van der Byl family. He had seen none of them – not the Old Man, nor Tracey, nor even Benedict.

Then, in one long eventful afternoon, he saw all three of them. It was his final year at University. His degree was a certainty. He had headed the lists at every examination from his first year onwards. He had been elected the senior student of Stellenbosch University, but now there was a further honour almost within his grasp.

In ten days' time the National Selectors would announce the rugby team to meet the New Zealand All Black touring team – and Johnny's place at flank forward was as certain as his degree in Geology.

The sporting press had nicknamed Johnny 'Jag Hond' after that ferocious predator of the African wilds, the Cape hunting dog; an animal of incredible stamina and determination that savages its prey on the run. The nickname had stuck fast, and Johnny was a favourite of the crowds.

In the line-up of the team from Cape Town University was another crowd-pleaser whose place in the National Side to meet the All Blacks seemed equally assured. From his position at full back Benedict van der Byl dominated the field of play with a grace and artistry that were almost god-like. He had grown tall and wide-shouldered, with long powerful legs and dark brooding good looks.

Johnny led the visiting team out on to the smooth green velvet field, and while he jogged and flexed his back and shoulders he looked up at the packed stands seeking assurance that the high priests of rugby football were all there. He saw Doctor Danie Craven sitting with the other selectors in their privileged position below the Press enclosure. While in front of the Doctor, leaning back to exchange a few words with him, sat the Prime Minister.

This meeting between the two universities was one of the high spots of the rugby season, and the *aficionados* travelled thousands of miles to watch it.

The Prime Minister smiled and nodded, then leaned forward to touch the shoulder of the big white-headed figure that sat in the row below him.

Johnny felt an electric tingle run up his spine as the white head lifted and looked directly at him. It was the first time he had seen the Old Man in the seven years since that terrible night.

Johnny lifted an arm in salute, and the Old Man stared at him for long seconds before he turned away to speak with the Prime Minister.

Now the drum majorettes came out in ranks on to the field. White-booted, dressed in Cape Town University colours with short swinging skirts and tall hats, they high-stepped and paraded, lovely young girls flushed with excitement and exertion.

The roar of the crowd drummed with the blood in Johnny's ears, for Tracey van der Byl was leading the first rank. He knew her instantly, despite the passage of years in which she had grown to young womanhood. Her legs and arms were sun-bronzed and her dark hair hung glossily to her shoulders. She cavorted and kicked and stamped shouting the traditional cheers, jiggling her firm young bottom with innocent abandon while the crowds screamed and writhed, beginning already to work themselves into an hysterical frenzy. Johnny watched Tracey. He stood completely still in the thunderous uproar. She was the most beautiful woman he had ever seen.

Then the show was over, the drum majorettes retreating back through the stadium entrance, and the home team trotted on to the field.

The presence of the Old Man and Tracey added intensity to the glare of hatred that Johnny turned on the tall white-clad figure that fell back to take control of the Cape Town back field.

Benedict van der Byl reached his position and turned. From inside his calf-length sock he took a comb and ran it through his dark hair. The crowd bellowed and whistled, loving this little theatrical gesture. Benedict returned the comb to his sock and posed with one hand on his hip, his chin lifted arrogantly as he surveyed the opposition.

Suddenly he intercepted Johnny's glare, and the pose altered as he dropped his eyes and shuffled his feet a little.

The whistle fluted, and play began. It was everything the crowds had hoped for, a match that would long be remembered and gloated over. Massive Panzer offensives by the forwards, long probing raids by the backs with the oval ball flickering from hand to hand, until a bone-jarring tackle smashed the carrier to the turf. Hard and fast and clean play swung from side to side, a hundred times the crowd came up on its feet as one, eyes and mouths wide in screaming unbearable tension, to sink back with a groan as the ball was held by a desperate defence within inches of the try line.

No score and three minutes of play left, Cape Town attacking from a set scrummage, driving through a gap in the defence and then putting the ball in the air with a long raking pass, taken cleanly by the Cape Town wing without a break in his stride. His feet twinkled across the green turf, and again the crowd came up with a gasp.

Johnny hit him low, just above the knee, with his shoulder. The two of them rolled together out of the field of play lifting a puff of white lime from the line and the crowd groaned and sank back.

While they waited to receive the throw, Johnny whispered hoarse orders. His gold and maroon jersey was soaked with sweat, and blood from a grazed hip stained his white shorts.

'Get it back fast. Don't run with it. Give it to Dawie. Kick high and deep, Dawie.'

Johnny leapt high to the flight of the thrown ball, with a bunched fist he punched it back accurately into Dawie's hands, at the same moment twisting his body to block the attackers.

Dawie fell back two paces and kicked. The power of the kick swung his right foot above his head, and the impetus flung him forward to put his forwards 'on side'.

The ball climbed slowly, flying like a dart with no wobble or roll in the air, reaching the zenith of its trajectory high over mid-field, then floating back to earth.

Twenty thousand heads followed its flight, a hush had fallen over the field – and in the unnatural silence Benedict van der Byl was drifting back deep into his own territory, anticipating the drop of the ball with deceptively unhurried strides, yet timing it with the precision of the gifted athlete.

The ball slotted neatly into his arms, and he began moving lazily infield to open his angle for the return kick. Still a tense throbbing mesmeric hush hung over the field, Benedict van der Byl was at the focus of attention.

'Jag Hond!' A single voice in the crowd alerted them, and twenty thousand heads swung downfield.

'Jag Hond!' A roar now. Johnny was well clear of the pack, arms pumping and legs churning as he bore down on Benedict. It was a futile effort, he could not hope to intercept a player of Benedict's calibre from such long range, yet Johnny was burning the last of his physical reserves in that charge. His face was a sweat-shining mask of determination, and clods of torn grass flew from under his savagely driving boots.

Then something happened which was unaccountable, almost past belief. Benedict van der Byl glanced round and saw Johnny. He broke his stride, two clumsy shuffling paces, and tried to pivot away deeper into his own ground. All the assurance had gone from his body, all the skill and grace. He tripped and stumbled, almost fell and the ball popped out of his hands, bouncing awkwardly.

Benedict scrambled after it, groping blindly, looking back over his shoulder. Now on his face was an expression of naked terror. Johnny was very close. Grunting at each stride like a gut-shot lion, massive shoulders already bunching for the strike, his lips drawn back into a murderous parody of a grin.

Benedict van der Byl dropped to his knees and covered his head with both arms, cringing down on to the green turf.

Johnny swept past him without a check, stooping easily in his run to gather the bouncing ball.

When Benedict uncovered his head and, still kneeling, looked up, Johnny stood ten yards away between the goal posts watching him. Then, deliberately, Johnny placed the ball between his feet to complete the formality of the touch-down.

Now, as if by agreement, both Johnny and Benedict looked towards the main grandstand. They saw the Old Man rise from his seat and make his way slowly through the ecstatic crowds towards the exit.

The day after the match, Johnny went back into the desert.

He was down in the bottom of a fifteen-foot prospect trench that had been dug across the grain of the country rock. It was oppressively hot in the confines of the trench and Johnny was stripped to a skimpy pair of khaki shorts, his sun-browned muscles oily with sweat, but he worked steadily at his sampling. He was establishing the contours and profile of an ancient marine terrace that the ages had buried beneath the sand. It was here on the bedrock that he expected to find the thin layer of diamond-bearing gravel.

He heard the Jeep pull up at ground level above him, and the crunch of footsteps. Johnny straightened up and held his aching back muscles.

The Old Man stood at the edge of the trench and looked down at him. He held a folded newspaper in his hand. This was the first time Johnny had seen him at close range in all the years, and he was shocked at the change. The mass of bushy hair was so white, and his features were folded and creased like those of a mastiff, leaving the big hooked nose standing like a hillock from his face. But there was no wasting or deterioration in his body, and his eyes were still that chilling enigmatic blue.

He dropped the newspaper into the trench and Johnny caught it, still staring up at the Old Man.

'Read it!' said the Old Man. The paper was folded to the sports page, and the headline was thick and bold.

JAG HOND IN. VAN DER BYL OUT.

The shock was as delicious as the plunge into a mountain stream. He was in – he would carry the gold and green, and wear the leaping Springbok on his blazer pocket.

He looked up, proud and happy, standing bare-headed in the sun waiting for the Old Man to speak.

'Make up your mind,' said the Old Man softly. 'Do you want to play ball – or work for Van Der Byl Diamonds? You

18

can't do both.' And he walked back to the Jeep and drove away.

Johnny cabled his withdrawal from the team to the Doctor personally. The storm of outraged protest and abuse in the national press, and the hundreds of viperous letters Johnny received accusing him of cowardice and treachery and worse made him thankful for the sanctuary of the desert.

N either Johnny nor Benedict had ever played the game again. Thinking about it, even at this remove of time, Johnny felt the sting of disappointment. He had wanted that green and gold badge of honour so very deeply. Brusquely he pulled the Jaguar off the road and scanned the street map of London and found Stark Street tucked away off the King's Road. He drove on remembering how it had been after the Old Man had taken it from him. The agony of mind had been scarcely endurable.

His companions in the desert were Ovambo tribesmen from the north, and a few of those taciturn white men that the desert produces, as hardy and uncompromising as her vegetation or her mountain ranges.

The deserts of the Namib and the Kalahari are amongst the loneliest places on earth, and the desert nights are long. Not even the day's unremitting physical labour could tire Johnny sufficiently to drug his dreams of a lovely girl in a short white skirt and high boots – or an old white-headed man with a face like a granite cliff.

Out of those long days and longer nights came solid achievements to stand like milestones marking the road of his career. He brought in a new diamond field, small but rich, in country which no one else had believed would yield diamonds. He pegged a uranium lode which Van Der Byl

Diamonds sold for two and a half millions, and there were other fruits from his efforts as valuable if not as spectacular.

At twenty-five, Johnny Lance's name was whispered in the closed and forbidding halls of the diamond industry as one of the bright young comers.

There were approaches – a junior partnership in a firm of consulting geologists, field manager for one of the struggling little companies working marginal ground in the Murderers' Karroo. Johnny turned them down. They were good offers, but he stayed on with the Old Man.

Then the big Company noticed him. A century ago the first payable pipe of 'blue ground' in Southern Africa was discovered on a hard scrabble farm owned by a Boer named De Beer. Old De Beer sold his farm for £6,000, never dreaming that a treasure worth £300,000,000 lay beneath the bleak dry earth. The strike was named De Beers New Rush, and a horde of miners, small businessmen, drifters, chancers, rogues and scoundrels moved in to purchase and work minute claims, each the size of a large room.

From this pretty company of fortune's soldiers two men rose high above the others, until between them they owned most of the claims in De Beers New Rush. When these two, Cecil John Rhodes and Barney Barnato, at last combined their resources, a formidable financial enterprise was born. From such humble beginnings the Company has grown to awesome respectability and dignity. Its wealth is fabled, its influence immeasurable, its income is astronomical. It controls the diamond supply to the world. It controls also mineral concessions over areas of Central and Southern Africa which total hundreds of thousands of square miles, and its reserves of unmined precious and base minerals cannot be calculated. Small diamond companies are allowed to co-exist with the giant until they reach a certain size – then suddenly they become part of it, gobbled up as a tiger shark might swallow any of its pilot fish who become too large and daring. The big Company can afford to buy the best prospects, equipment – and men. It reached out one of its myriad tentacles to draw in Johnny Lance. The price they set on him was twice his present salary, and three times his future prospects.

Johnny turned it down flat. Perhaps the Old Man did not notice, perhaps it was mere coincidence that a week later Johnny was promoted Field Manager of Beach Operation. The nickname that went with the job was 'King Canute'.

Van Der Byl Diamonds had thirty-seven miles of beach concession. The tiny ribbon of shoreline, one hundred and twenty feet above high-water mark, and one hundred and twenty feet below low-water mark. Inland the concession belonged to the big Company. It had purchased the land, a dozen vast ranches, simply to obtain the mineral rights. The sea concessions, territorial up to waters twelve miles off shore, belonged to them also. Granted to them by Government charter twenty years before. But Van Der Byl Diamonds had the Admiralty strip – and it was 'King Canute's' job to work it.

The sea-mist came smoking in like ground pearl dust off the cold waters of the Benguela current. From out of the mist bank the high unhurried swells marched in towards the bright yellow sands and the tall wave-cut cliffs of Namaqualand.

The swells peaked up sharply as they felt the land. Their crests trembled and turned luminous green, began to dissolve in plumes of wind-blown spray, arched over and slid down upon themselves in the roar and rumble of white water.

Johnny stood on the driver's seat of the open Land-Rover. He wore a sheepskin jacket against the chill of the dawn mist, but his head was bare and his dark hair fluttered nervously against his forehead in the wind.

His heavy jaw was thrust forward, and his hands in the pockets of the sheepskin jacket were balled into fists. He scowled aggressively as he measured the height and push of the surf. With his crooked nose he looked like a boxer waiting for the gong.

Suddenly with an awkward angry movement he jerked his left hand from his pocket and looked down at the dial of his wrist watch. Two hours and three minutes to low tide. He pushed his fist back into his pocket, and swivelled quickly to look at his bulldozers.

There were eleven of them, big bright yellow D.8 Caterpillars, lined up along the high-water mark. The operators sat goggled and tense in their high stern seats. They were all watching him anxiously.

Beyond them, standing well back, were the earthloaders. They were ungainly, pregnant-looking machines with swollen bellies, and heavily lugged tyres that stood taller than a man. When the time came they would rush in at thirty miles an hour, drop a steel blade beneath their bellies and scrape up a fifteen-ton load of sand or gravel, race back inland and drop their load, turn and rush back for another gargantuan bite out of the earth.

Johnny was steeling himself, judging the exact moment in which to hurl a quarter of a million pounds' worth of machinery into the Atlantic Ocean, in the hope of recovering a handful of bright pebbles.

The moment came, and Johnny spent half a minute of precious time in scrutinizing his preparations before committing himself to action.

Then 'GO!' he shouted into his loudhailer and windmilled his right arm in the unmistakable command to advance.

'Go!' he shouted again, but his voice was lost. Even the sound of the wild surf was lost in the bull bellow of the diesels. Lowering their massive steel blades, a chorus line of steel monsters, they crawled forward.

Now the golden sand curled before the scooped blades, like butter from the knife. It built up before the monstrous machines, becoming a pile and then a high wall. Thrusting, pulling back, butting, worrying, the bulldozers swept the wall of sand forward. The arms of the operators pumping the handles of the controls like mad barmen drawing a thousand pints of beer, the diesels roaring and muttering and roaring again.

The wall of sand met the first low push of sea water up the beach and smothered it. In seeming astonishment and uncertainty the sea pulled back, swirling and creaming before the advancing dyke of sand.

The bulldozers were performing a complicated but smoothly practised ballet now. Weaving and crossing, blades lifting and falling, backing and advancing, all under the supervision of the master choreographer, Johnny Lance.

The Land-Rover darted back and forward along the edge of the huge pit that was forming, with Johnny roaring orders and instructions through the electric loudhailer.

Gradually a sickle-shaped dyke of sand was thrown out into the sea, while behind it the bulldozer blades cut down, six, ten, fifteen feet through the loose yellow sand.

Then suddenly they hit the oyster line, that thin layer of fossilized oyster shell that so often covers the diamond gravels of South West Africa.

Johnny saw the change in the character of his pit, saw the shell curling from the blades of the bulldozers.

With half a dozen orders and hand signals he had his 'dozers flatten a ramp at each end of his pit, to give the earthloaders access. Then he ordered them away to hold the dyke against the sea.

He glanced at his watch. 'One hour thirteen minutes,' he muttered. 'We're running tight!'

Quickly he checked his pit. Two hundred yards long, fifteen feet deep, the overburden of sand stripped away, the oyster line showing clean and white in the sun, the bulldozers clear of the pit bottom – fighting back the sea.

'Right,' he grunted. 'Let's see what we've got.'

He turned to face the two earthmovers waiting expect-antly above the high-water mark.

'Go in and get it!' he shouted, and gave the windmill arm signal.

Nose to tail the earthloaders roared forward, swinging wide at the head of the pit, then swooping down the ramp and dashing along the bottom. They scooped up a load of shell and gravel without checking their speed and went bellowing up the far ramp, swinging again to race up and deposit their load below the cliff, but above the high-water mark.

Round they went, and round again, chasing their tails, while the bulldozers held back the sea which was now becoming angry – sending its cohorts to skirmish along the dyke, seeking a weak place to attack.

Johnny glanced at his watch again.

'Three minutes to low water,' he spoke aloud, and grinned. 'We're going to make it – I think!'

He lit a cigarette, relaxing a little now. He dropped into the driving seat and swung the Land-Rover up the beach, parking it beyond the mountain of gravel that the earth-loaders were building.

He climbed out and took up a handful of the gravel.

'Lovely!' he whispered. 'Oh sweet! Sweet!'

It was right. All the signs were good. In the single handful he identified a small garnet, and a larger lump of agate.

He scooped another handful.

'Jasper,' he gloated. 'And banded ironstone!'

All these stones were the team-mates of the diamond, you found them together.

The shape was right also, the stones polished round and shiny as marbles, not flattened like coins which would mean they had washed in only one direction. Round stones meant a wave action zone – a diamond trap!

'We've hit a jewel box – I'll take Lysol on that!'

From thirty-seven miles of beach Johnny had picked a two-hundred-yard stretch, and hit it right on the nose. A choice not by luck, but by careful study of the configuration of the coastline, aerial photographs of the wave patterns and bottom contours of the sea, an analysis of the beach sands, and finally by that indefinable 'feel' for ground that a good diamond man has.

Johnny Lance was mightily delighted with himself as he climbed back into the Land-Rover. The earthloaders had scraped the gravel down to bedrock. Their job was finished, and they pulled out of the pit and stood with panting exhausts beside the enormous pile of gravel they had recovered.

'Bottom boys!' roared Johnny, and the patient army of Ovambo tribesmen who had been squatting above the beach came swarming down into the pit. Their job was to sweep and clean the pit bottom, for a high proportion of the diamonds would have worked their way down through the gravel into the crevices and irregularities of the bedrock.

The sea changed its mood, furious at the brutal rape of its beaches it came hissing and tearing at the sand dyke. The tide was making now, and the bulldozers had to redouble their efforts to keep it out.

In the pit the Ovambos worked in a frenzy of activity, sparing only an occasional apprehensive glance for the wall of sand that held the Atlantic at bay.

Now Johnny was tensing up again. If he pulled them out early he would be leaving diamonds down there, if he left them in too late he might drown machinery – and men.

He cut it fine, just a fraction too fine. He pulled the bottom boys out with the sea beginning to break over the dyke, and to seep through under it.

Then he began to pull out his bulldozers, ten of them out – one still coming infinitely slowly, waddling across the wide bottom of the empty pit.

The sea broke through, it broke simultaneously in two places and came boiling into the pit in a waist-high wave.

The bulldozer operator saw it, hesitated one second, then his spirit failed him and he jumped down from his machine; abandoning it to the sea he sprinted ahead of the wave, making for the steep nearest side of the pit.

'Bastard!' swore Johnny as he watched the operator scramble to safety. 'He could have made it.' But his anger was against himself also. His decision to withdraw had been too long delayed, that was £20,000 worth of machinery he had sacrificed to the sea.

He slammed the Land-Rover into gear, and put her to the pit. She went off the edge like a ski jump, falling fifteen feet before she hit the bottom, but her fall was cushioned by the slope of sand and she sprang forward bravely to meet the rush of sea water.

It broke over the bonnet, slewing the vehicle viciously, but Johnny fought her head round and kept her going towards the stranded bulldozer.

The engine of the Land-Rover had been sealed and water-proofed against just such an emergency, and now she ploughed forward throwing a sheet of water to each side. But her forward rush faltered as the green water poured over her.

Now suddenly the entire sand dyke collapsed under the white surf and the Atlantic took control. The tall wave of green water that raced across the pit hit the Land-Rover, upending her, throwing Johnny into the jubilant frothing water, while the Land-Rover rolled over on her back, pointing all four wheels to the sky in surrender.

Johnny went under but came up immediately. Half swimming, half wading, battered by the boisterous sea he struggled on towards the yellow island of steel.

The sea struck him down, and he went under again. Found his feet for a moment, then had them cut from under him once more.

Then suddenly he had reached the bulldozer and was dragging himself up over the tracks to the driver's seat. He was coughing and vomiting sea water, as he reached the controls.

The bulldozer sat immovable, held down by her own twenty-six tons of dead weight on to the hard bedrock of the pit. Although the sea burst over her, and swirled through her tracks, it could not move her.

Through eyes blurred and swimming with salt water and his own tears, Johnny briefly checked the gauges on the instrument panels. She had oil pressure and engine revs, and high above his head the exhaust pipe chugged blue smoke.

Johnny coughed again. Vomit and sea water shot up his throat in a scalding jet, but he pushed the throttle wide and threw in both clutch levers.

Ponderously the great machine ground forward, almost contemptuously shouldering the sea aside, her tracks solidly gripping the bedrock.

Johnny looked about him quickly. The sand ramps at each end of the pit were washed away. The sides were sheer now, and behind him the sea was rushing unimpeded into the pit.

A wave broke over his head, and Johnny shook the water from his hair like a spaniel and looked around with mounting desperation for an avenue of escape.

With a shock of surprise he saw the Old Man. He had thought him to be four hundred miles away in Cape Town, but here he was on the edge of the pit. The white hair shone like a beacon.

Instinctively Johnny swung the bulldozer in his direction, crawling through the turbulent waters towards him.

The Old Man was directing two of the other bulldozers, reversing them as close as he dared to the lip of the bank of sand, while from the service truck parked below the cliff a line of Ovambos came staggering down the beach with the heavy tractor tow chain over their shoulders. They shuffled bow-legged under the tremendous weight of the chain, sinking ankle deep into the sand with each step.

The Old Man roared at them, urging them on, but the words were lost in the thunder of diesel engines and the ranting of the wind and the sea. Now he turned back to Johnny.

'Get her in close,' the Old Man yelled through cupped hands. 'I'll bring the end of the chain down to you!'

Johnny waved an acknowledgement, then grabbed at the controls as the force of the next wave pushed even the giant tractor off its line, and Johnny felt the diesel falter for the first time – the water had found its way in through the seals at last.

Then he was under the high bank of yellow sand that towered twenty feet above him and he scrambled forward over the engine bonnet to meet the Old Man.

The Old Man was poised on the lip of the pit with the end of the chain draped in a loop over both shoulders. He was stooped beneath its weight, and when he stepped forward the sand crumpled away beneath him and he came sliding and slipping down the steep incline, buried waist deep, the great chain snaking after him.

Judging the rush of the sea Johnny jumped down to help him. Together, battered by the sea, they dragged the chain to the bulldozer.

'Fix it on to the blade arm,' grunted the Old Man, and they got a double turn of chain around the thick steel arm.

'Shackle!' Johnny snapped at him, and while the Old Man untied the length of rope which secured the steel shackle around his waist, Johnny looked up at the cliff of sand that hung over them.

'Christ!' he said softly, the sea was attacking it – and now it was soft and trembling above them, ready to collapse and smother them.

The Old Man passed him the huge shackle, and Johnny

began with numbed hands to secure the end of the chain. He must pass the thick case-hardened pin through two links and then screw it closed. It was a Herculean task under these conditions, with the surf bursting over his head, the drag of the sea on the chain, and the cliff of sand threatening to fall on them at any moment. From twenty feet above them Johnny's foreman was watching anxiously, ready to pass the word to the two waiting bulldozers to throw their combined weights on the chain.

The thread of the pin caught, half a dozen turns would secure it, he would have finished the job by the time the word was passed to the 'dozer operators.

'Okay,' he nodded and gasped at the Old Man. 'Pull!'

The Old Man lifted his head and bellowed up the bank, 'Pull!'

The foreman acknowledged with a wave.

'Okay.' And his head disappeared behind the bank as he ran back to the bulldozers, and at that moment the surf swung the chain. A movement of a few inches, but enough to catch Johnny's left index finger between two of the links.

The Old Man saw his face, saw him struggling to free himself.

'What is it?'

Then the water sucked back for a moment, and he saw what had happened. He waded forward to help – but from above them came the throaty roar of the diesels and the chain began running away, snaking and twisting up the bank like a python.

The Old Man reached Johnny and caught him about the shoulders to steady him. They braced themselves in horror, staring at the captive hand.

The chain jerked taut, severing the finger cleanly in a bright burst of scarlet, and Johnny reeled back into the Old Man's arms. The great yellow bulk of the bulldozer was dragged relentlessly down on top of them, threatening to crush them both, but using the next break and push of the sea the Old Man dragged Johnny clear – and they were carried sideways along the bank, tumbled helplessly by the strength of the water out of the bulldozer's path.

Johnny clutched his injured hand to his chest, but it hosed a bright stream of blood that discoloured the water about them. His head went under and salt water shot down his throat into his lungs. He felt himself drowning, the strength oozing out of him.

He surfaced again, and through bleary eyes saw the glistening wet bulldozer half-way up the sand bank. He felt the Old Man's arms about his chest and he went under again relaxing as the darkness closed over his eyes and brain.

When the darkness cleared from his eyes, he was lying on the dry sand of the beach and the first thing he saw was the Old Man's face above him, furrowed and pouched, his silver white hair plastered across his forehead.

'Did we get her out?' Johnny asked thickly.

'Ja,' the Old Man answered. 'We got her out.' And he stood up, walked to the Jeep, and drove away, leaving the foreman to tend to Johnny.

Johnny grinned at the memory, and lifting his left hand off the driving-wheel of the Jaguar he licked the shiny stump of his index finger.

'It was worth a finger,' he murmured aloud, and still searching for road signs he drove on slowly.

He smiled again comfortably, shaking his head with amusement as he remembered his hurt and disappointment when the Old Man had walked away and left him lying on the beach. He had not expected the Old Man to fall on his shoulders sobbing his gratitude and begging forgiveness for all the years of misery and loneliness – but he had expected something more than that.

After a two-hundred-mile round Jeep-journey through the desert night to the nearest hospital where they had trimmed and bound the stump, Johnny was back at the workings the next day in time to watch the first run of gravel from the beach.

In his absence, the gravel had been screened to sieve off all the over-size rock and stone, then it had been puddled through a tank of silicon mud to float off all the material with a specific gravity less than 2.5, then finally what was left had been run through a ball mill – a long steel cylinder containing steel balls the size of baseballs. The cylinder revolved continually and the steel balls crushed to powder all substance softer than 4 on Mohs hardness scale.

Now there was a residue, a thousandth part of the gravel they had won from the sea. In this remainder would be the diamonds – if diamonds there were.

When Johnny arrived back at the shed of galvanized iron and wood on the cliff above the beach that housed his separation plant, he was still half groggy from the anaesthetic and lack of sleep.

His hand throbbed with the persistence of a lighthouse, his eyes were reddened and a thick black stubble covered his jaws.

He went to stand beside the grease table that filled half the shed. He was swaying a little on his feet, as he looked around at the preparations. The massive bin at the head of the table was filled with the concentrated diamond gravels, the plates greased down, and his crew was standing ready.

'Let's go!' Johnny nodded at his foreman, who immediately threw in the lever that set the table shaking like an old man with palsy.

The table was a series of steel plates, each slightly inclined and thickly coated with dirty yellow grease. From the bin at the head of the shuddering table a mixture of gravel and water began to dribble, its consistency and rate of flow carefully regulated by the foreman. It spread over the greased table like spilled treacle, dropping from one plate to the next, and finally into the waste bin at the end of the table.

A diamond is unwettable, immerse it in water, scrub it, – but it comes out dry. A coat of grease on a steel plate is also unwettable, so wet gravel and sea shell will slide over it and keep moving across the agitating, sloping table.

But a diamond when it hits grease sticks like a half-sucked toffee to a woollen blanket.

In the excitement and anxiety of the moment Johnny felt his weariness recede, even the pain in his stump was muted by it. His eyes and whole attention were fastened on that glistening yellow sheet of grease.

The little stuff under a carat in weight, or the industrial black diamond and boart would not be visible on the table; the agitation was too rapid – blurring with speed, and the flow of loose material would disguise them.

So complete was his absorption that it was some seconds before he was aware of a presence beside him. He glanced up quickly.

The Old Man was there, standing with the wide stance and tension-charged attitude that was his own special way.

Johnny was acutely conscious of the Old Man's bulk beside him – and he felt the first flicker of alarm. What if this was a barren run? He needed diamonds now – as he had never needed anything in his life. He scanned the blurring plates of yellow grease, seeking the purchase price that could buy back the Old Man's esteem. The speckled gravel flowed imperturbably across the plates, and Johnny felt a flutter of panic.

Then from across the table the foreman let out a whoop, and pointed.

'Thar she blows!'

Johnny's eyes darted to the head of the table. There beneath the outlet from the bin, half buried in the thick grease by its own weight, anchored solidly while the worthless gravel washed past it, was a diamond.

A big fat five-carat thing, that glowed sulky and yellow, like a wild animal resenting its captivity.

Johnny sighed softly and darted a sideways glance at the Old Man. The Old Man was watching the table without expression, and though he must have been conscious of Johnny's scrutiny, he did not look up. Johnny's eyes were dragged irresistibly back to the table.

By some freakish chance, the next diamond fell from the bin directly on to the one already anchored in the grease.

When diamond strikes diamond it bounces like a golf ball off a tarmac road.

The second diamond, a white beauty the size of a peach pip, clicked loudly as it struck the other then spun head high in the air.

Both Johnny and the foreman laughed involuntarily with delight at the beauty of that twinkling drop of solid sunlight.

Johnny reached across the table with his good hand, and snatched it out of the air. He rubbed it between his fingers – revelling in the soapy feel of it, then turned and offered it to the Old Man.

The Old Man looked at the diamond, nodded in acknowledgement. Then he pulled back the cuff of his coat and checked his wrist watch.

'It's late. I must get back to Cape Town.'

'Won't you stay for the rest of the run, sir?' Johnny realized his tone was too eager. 'We could have a drink together afterwards.' He remembered after he had spoken, that the Old Man abhorred alcohol.

'No.' The Old Man shook his head. 'I have to get back by this evening.' Now he looked steadily into Johnny's eyes. 'You see, Tracey is getting married tomorrow afternoon and I must be there.'

Then he smiled, watching Johnny's face, but nobody could ever guess the meaning of a smile on the Old Man's lips – for it never showed in his eyes.

'Didn't you know?' he asked, still smiling. 'I thought you had received an invitation.' And he went out of the shed to where his Jeep stood in the bright sunshine waiting to take him out to the aircraft landing-strip among the sand dunes.

The pain in his injured hand, and the Old Man's words denied Johnny the sleep he so desperately needed, but it was two o'clock in the morning before he threw back his blankets and lit the lamp beside his camp bed.

'He said I had been invited – and, by God, I'll be there.'

He drove through the night, and the next morning. The first two hundred miles were on desert tracks of sand and stone, then he reached the metalled highway in the dawn and turned south across the great plains and over the mountains. It was noon before he saw the squat blue silhouette of Table Mountain on the skyline dwarfing the city that huddled beneath it.

He checked in at the Vineyard Hotel, and hurried to his room to bath and shave and change into a suit.

The grounds of the old house were crowded with expensive automobiles, and the overflow was parked along both sides of the street outside, but he found a space for the dusty Land-Rover. He walked up through the white gates and across the green lawns.

There was a band playing in the house, and a hubbub of voices and laughter drifted out through the windows of the ballroom.

He went in through the side door. The passages were thronged with guests, and he made his way amongst them seeking a familiar face in the groups of loud-voiced gesticulating men and giggling women. At last he found one.

'Michael.' And Michael Shapiro looked round, recognizing him and letting the conflicting emotions of pleasure, surprise and alarm show clearly on his face.

'Johnny. It's good to see you.'

'Is the ceremony over?'

'Yes, and the speeches also – thank God.' He took Johnny's arm and led him aside. 'Let me get you a glass of champagne.' Michael hailed a waiter and put a crystal glass into Johnny's hand.

'Here's to the bride,' Johnny murmured and drank.

'Does the Old Man know you are here?' Michael came out with the question that was burning his mouth, and when Johnny shook his head, Michael's expression became thoughtful.

'What's he like, Michael, Tracey's husband?'

'Kenny Hartford?' Michael considered the question. 'He's all right, I suppose. Nice-looking boy, plenty of money.'

'What's he do for a crust of bread?'

'His daddy left him the whole loaf – but to fill in the time he does fashion photography.' And Johnny pulled down the corners of his mouth.

Michael frowned. 'He's all right, Johnny. The Old Man picked him carefully.'

'The Old Man?' Johnny's jaw thrust out.

'Of course, you know him – he wouldn't leave an important decision like that to anybody else.'

Johnny finished his champagne in silence, and Michael watched his face anxiously.

'Where is she? Have they left yet?'

'No.' Michael shook his head. 'They're still in the ballroom.'

'I think I'll go and wish luck to the bride.'

'Johnny.' Michael caught hold of his elbow. 'Don't do anything stupid – will you?'

Johnny stood at the head of the marble staircase that led down into the ballroom. The floor was crowded with dancing couples and the music was loud and merry. The bridal party sat at a raised table across the floor.

Benedict van der Byl saw Johnny first. His face flushed and he leaned quickly to whisper to the Old Man, then began to rise from his seat. The Old Man placed a restraining hand on Benedict's shoulder, and smiled across the room at Johnny.

Johnny went down the stairs and made his way through the dancers. Tracey had not seen him. She was talking to the silky-faced young man who sat beside her. He had wavy blond hair.

'Hello, Tracey.' She looked up at Johnny and caught her breath. She was more beautiful than he remembered.

'Hello, Johnny.' Her voice was almost a whisper.

'May I dance with you?' She was pale now, and her eyes went to the Old Man, not to her new husband. The gleaming white bush of hair nodded slightly, and Tracey stood up.

They made one circuit of the dance floor before the band stopped playing. Johnny had planned a hundred different things to say to her, but he was dumb until the music ended and the opportunity was passing. Hurriedly now in the few seconds that were left Johnny told her: 'I hope you will be happy, Tracey. But if you ever need help – ever – I will come, I promise you that.'

'Thank you.' Her voice was husky, and for a moment she looked like the little girl who had cried in the night. Then he took her back to her husband.

The promise had been made five years ago, and now he had come to London to honour it.

Number 23 Stark Street was a neat double-storeyed cottage with a narrow front. He parked outside it. It was dark now and lights burned on both floors. He sat in the parked Jaguar, suddenly reluctant to go further. Somehow he knew that Tracey was here, and he knew it would not be pretty. For a moment he recaptured the image of her as a lovely young woman in a wedding dress of white satin, then he climbed out of the Jaguar and went up the steps to the front door. He reached for the bell before he noticed with surprise that the door was ajar. He pushed it open and walked into a small sitting-room furnished with feminine taste.

The room had been hastily ransacked, one of the curtains was spread on the floor and on it were piled books and ornaments. Pictures had been taken down from the walls and stacked ready for removal.

Johnny picked up one of the books, and opened the cover. On the fly leaf was a handwritten name. 'Tracey van der Byl.' He dropped it back on the pile as he heard footsteps on the stairs from the floor above.

A man came down the stairs. He was dressed in soiled green velvet trousers, sheepskin boots, and shabby frock coat of military cut frogged with tarnished gold braid. He was carrying an armful of women's dresses.

He saw Johnny and stopped nervously, his pink lips opened in vacant surprise but his eyes were beady and bright under the thatch of lank blond hair.

'Hello,' Johnny smiled pleasantly. 'Are you moving out?' And he drifted quietly closer to the man on the stairs and stood looking up at him.

Suddenly from the floor above a low wail echoed down the stairs. It was an eerie sound, without passion or pain, as though steam were escaping from a jet, only just recognizable as human. Johnny went rigid at the sound, and the man on the stairs glanced nervously over his shoulder.

'What have you done to her?' Johnny asked softly, without menace.

'No. Nothing! She's on a trip. A bad trip.' The man's denial was frantic. 'It's her first time on acid.'

'So you're cleaning the place out, are you?' Johnny asked mildly.

'She owes me plenty. She can't pay. She promised – and she can't pay.'

'Oh,' said Johnny. 'That's different. I thought you were hitting the place.' He reached into his overcoat and brought out his wallet, riffling the wad of banknotes. 'I'm a friend of hers. How much does she owe you?'

'Fifty nicker.' The man's eyes sparkled when he saw the wallet. 'I gave her credit.'

Johnny counted off ten fivers, and held them out. The

man dropped the bundle of clothing over the banisters and came eagerly down the last few stairs.

'Did you sell her the stuff – the acid?' Johnny asked, and the man stopped a pace from him, his expression stiffening with suspicion.

'Oh, for God's sake.' Johnny grinned. 'We are not children – I know the score.' He offered the banknotes. 'Did you get the stuff for her?'

The man grinned back at him weakly, and nodded as he reached for the money. Johnny's free hand snapped closed on the thin wrist and he swung him off his feet, forcing his wrist up between his shoulder-blades.

Johnny stuffed the money into his pocket, and marched him up the stairs.

'Let's go and have a look, shall we?'

There was a mattress on the iron bedstead covered with a grey army blanket. Tracey sat cross-legged on the blanket. She wore only a thin cotton slip and her hair hung lank and lustreless to her waist. Her arms crossed over her chest were thin and white as sticks of chalk. Her face also was pale, the skin translucent in the light of the electric bulb. She was rocking gently back and forth and wailing softly, her breath steaming in the icy cold room.

It was her eyes that shocked Johnny the most. They seemed to have expanded to an enormous size, and beneath each was a dark bruised-looking smear. The pupils of the eyes were distended and glittery with the same adamant sheen as uncut diamonds.

The big glittery green eyes fastened on Johnny and the man in the doorway, and the wail rose abruptly to a shriek. The shriek died away, and she bowed forward and buried her face in her hands, covering her eyes.

'Tracey,' said Johnny softly. 'Oh God, Tracey!'

'She'll be all right,' the man whimpered and twisted in his grip. 'It's the first time – she'll be all right.'

'Come.' Johnny dragged him out of the room, and pushed

the door closed with his foot. He held him against the wall, and his face was set and pale, his eyes merciless – but he spoke quietly, patiently as though he was explaining to a child.

'I'm going to hurt you now. I'm going to hurt you very badly. Just as badly as I can without killing you. Not because I enjoy it, but because that girl is a very special person to me. In the future when you think about giving poison to another girl – I want you to remember what I did to you tonight.'

Johnny held him with his left hand against the wall and he used his right hand, punching up under the ribs at an angle to tear the stomach muscles. With three or four blows he was too high, and he felt ribs crack and snap under his fist.

When he stepped back the man sagged slowly face forward, and Johnny caught him cleanly in the mouth snapping his teeth off at the gums, splitting his lips open like the petals of a rose. The man had made a lot of noise. Johnny looked into Tracey's room to make sure she had not been disturbed, but she was still bowed forward, rocking rhythmically on her haunches.

He found the bathroom and dampened his handkerchief to wipe the blood off his hands and the front of his overcoat. He came out into the passage again and stooped over the unconscious body to check the pulse. It was strong and regular, and he felt a lift of relief as he dragged the man's face out of the puddle of his own vomit and blood to prevent him drowning.

He went through to Tracey and, despite her frantic struggles, wrapped her in the greasy army blanket and carried her down to the Jaguar.

She quietened down and lay like a sleeping child in the back seat while he tucked the blanket round her, then he went back into the house and phoned 999, giving the address and hanging up immediately.

He left Tracey in the car outside the Dorchester, while he went in to speak to the reception clerk. Within minutes Tracey was in a wheelchair on her way up to the two-bedroom suite on the second floor. The doctor was there fifteen minutes later.

After the doctor had gone Johnny bathed, and carrying a tumbler of Chivas Regal in one hand he went into Tracey's room and stood by her bed. Whatever the doctor had given her had put her out cleanly. She lay gaunt and pale – yet with a strangely fragile beauty that seemed enhanced by the bruised discoloration of her eye sockets.

He stooped to brush the hair from her cheek, and her breath was light and warm on his hand. He felt such an infinity of tenderness for her then as he had never known for any other person, he was amazed by the strength of it.

He stooped over her and gently brushed her lips with his own. Her lips were dry and flaky white, and their touch was harsh as sandpaper.

Johnny straightened up and went to the armchair across the room. He sank into it wearily, and sipped the whisky, feeling its warmth spread from his belly and untie the knots in his muscles. He watched the pale ruined face on the pillows.

'We are in a hell of a mess, you and I,' he spoke aloud, and felt anger again. For long minutes it was undirected, but slowly it gelled and found an object to focus on.

For the first time in his life he was angry with the Old Man.

'He has brought you to this,' he said to the girl on the bed. 'And me—'

The reaction was swift, his loyalty was a thing grown part of his existence. Always he had trained himself to believe that the Old Man's machinations were just and wise – even if at times the justice and wisdom were hidden from him. Mortal man does not doubt the omnipotence of his gods.

Sickened by his own treachery, he began to examine the Old Man's motives and actions under the bright light of reason.

Why had the Old Man sent Michael Shapiro to fetch him out of the desert?

'He wants you in Cape Town, Johnny. Benedict didn't measure up. The Old Man has given him the London Office, it's a form of exile. He's picked you to take over the Company,' Michael explained. 'Tracey is out of the way. She and her husband are in London also. I guess the Old Man thinks it's safe to have you back in Cape Town now.'

Michael watched Johnny's undisguised joy and went on slowly.

'I'm speaking out of turn, perhaps. Mr van der Byl is a strange man. He's not like other people. I know how you feel about him, I've watched it all, you know – but listen, Johnny, you can go anywhere on your own now. There are a lot of other companies that want you—' But he had seen the expression on Johnny's face, and stopped ' – okay, Johnny. Forget I ever said it. I only spoke because I like you.'

Thinking on it now, there had been substance in Michael's warning. Certainly he was General Manager of Van Der Byl Diamonds, but he was no nearer to the Old Man than he had ever been. He lived under the mountain but the mountain was remote and he had not been able to scale the lowest slopes.

He had found the city as lonely as the desert, and he was ripe for the first attractive woman who set her snares for him.

Ruby Grange was tall and slim with hair the colour they call 'Second Cape' in a diamond, like sunlight through a crystal glass of champagne.

He wondered now at his own naïvety. That he should be so easily misled, and should have rushed so headlong into her web. After the wedding she had revealed herself, exposing the deeply calculating greed, the driving hunger for flattery and material possessions which was her mainspring, and her complete absorption with herself – Johnny had not been able to believe it. For months he fought off the growing certainty until it could be denied no longer, and he looked with chilled dismay on the shallow selfish little creature he had married.

He had withdrawn from her and flung all his energies into the Company.

This, then, was his life and he saw that it was an empty thing, hollowed out by the Old Man's hand.

For the first time his mind skirted the idea that it was a carefully calculated and sadistic revenge for the innocent action of a half-grown boy.

As though it were an escape from thoughts too dreadful to be borne, he fell asleep in the chair and the glass fell from his hand.

Jacobus Isaac van der Byl sat in a leather chair before the X-ray viewer. Fear had blasted the granite of his features, leaving them cracked and sagging, recognizable but subtly alerted below the gleaming white mane.

Fear was in his eyes also, moving below the surface like slimy water creatures in the pale blue pools. With the fear chilling and numbing his limbs he watched the cloudy and swirling images on the screen.

The specialist was talking softly, impersonally, as though he were lecturing one of his classes.

' – enveloping the thymus here, and extending beyond the trachea.'

The point of his gold pencil followed the ghostly outline on the screen. The Old Man swallowed with an effort. It seemed to be swelling in his throat as he listened, and his voice was hoarse and blurred to his own ears.

'You will operate?' he asked, and the specialist paused in his explanation. He glanced at the surgeon across the desk. The exchange was as guilty as that of conspirators.

The Old Man swivelled his chair and faced the surgeon.

'Well?' he demanded harshly.

'No.' The surgeon shook his head apologetically. 'It's too late. If only you had—'

'How long?' The Old Man overrode his explanation.

'Six months, not more.'

'You are certain?'

'Yes.'

The Old Man's chin sank on to his chest and he closed his eyes. There was complete silence in the room, they watched him with professional pity and interest as he reached his own personal acceptance of death.

At last the Old Man opened his eyes and stood up slowly. He tried to smile but his lips would not hold the shape.

'Thank you, gentlemen,' he croaked in this new rough voice. 'Will you excuse me, please. There are many things to arrange now.'

He went down to where the Rolls waited at the entrance. He walked slowly, shuffling his feet and the chauffeur came to him quickly, but the Old Man shrugged away his helping hands and climbed into the back seat of the car.

Michael Shapiro was waiting for him in the study of the big house. He saw the change in him immediately and jumped up from his chair. The Old Man stood in the doorway, his body seemed to have shrunk.

'Six months,' he said. 'They give me six months.' He said it as though he had expected to buy off death, and they had tricked him. He closed his eyes again, and when he opened them there was a glint of cunning in them, even his face had a pinched foxy look to it.

'Where is he? Is he back yet?'

'Yes, the Boeing got in at nine this morning. He's at the

43

office now.' Michael was shocked, it was the first time he had seen the Old Man without the mask.

'And the girl?' He had not called her 'daughter' since the divorce.

'Johnny has her in a private nursing home.'

'Worthless slut,' said the Old Man softly, and Michael stilled the protest before it reached his lips. 'Get your pad. I want you to take something down.' The Old Man chuckled hoarsely. 'We'll see!' he said, making it sound like a threat. 'We'll see!'

Johnny's doctor was waiting at Cape Town airport.

'Take her, Robin. Dry her out, and fatten her up. She's up to her gills with drugs and she probably hasn't eaten for a month.'

Tracey showed her first spark of spirit.

'Where do you think—'

'Into a nursing home.' Johnny anticipated her questions. 'For as long as is necessary.'

'I'm not—'

'Oh, yes, you bloody well are.' He took her arm, and Robin grabbed the other. They walked her, still protesting weakly to the car park.

'Thanks, Robin Old Soldier, give her the full workout.'

'I'll send her back to you like new,' Robin promised and drove away. Johnny took a few moments to look at the massive square silhouette of the mountain – his own private home-coming ceremony. Then he fetched the Mercedes from the airport garage, and hesitated between home or the office, decided he was not up to an interrogation from Ruby and chose the office. He kept a clean shirt and shaving tackle in his private bathroom there.

They descended on him like a tribe of man-eating Amazons as he came in through the glass doors into the lusciously furnished and carpeted reception area of Van Der Byl Diamonds head office.

The two pretty little receptionists began yipping joyously in chorus.

'Oh, Mr Lance, I have a whole sheaf of messages—'

'Oh, Mr Lance, your wife—'

Trying not to run he made it to within ten feet of his own door, when the Old Man's secretary popped out of ambush from behind her frosted-glass panel.

'Mr Lance, where on earth have you been? Mr van der Byl has been asking—'

Which alerted Lettie Pienaar, his own secretary.

'Mr Lance, thank goodness you're back.'

Johnny stopped and held up his hands in an attitude of surrender.

'One at a time, ladies. There is enough to go round – don't panic.'

Which broke the reception team into a quivering jelly of giggles, and sent the Old Man's watchdog back behind her panel sniffing disgustedly.

'Which is the most important, Lettie?' he asked as he went to his desk and flipped through his mail, shrugged out of his coat and began stripping tie and shirt as he headed for his bathroom.

They shouted at each other through the open door of the bathroom, as Johnny shaved quickly and showered, Lettie bringing him up to date on every aspect of Company and domestic business.

'Mrs Lance has phoned regularly. She called me a liar when I told her you were at Cartridge Bay.' Lettie was silent a moment, then as Johnny came out of the bathroom she asked, 'By the way, where have you been?'

'Don't you start that.' Johnny stood over the desk, and began flipping through the accumulated papers. 'Get my wife on the phone, please – no, hold it. Tell her I'll be home at seven.'

Lettie saw she had lost his attention, and she stood and went out. Johnny settled down behind his desk.

Van Der Byl Diamonds was a sick company. Despite Johnny's protests the Old Man had been drawing off its reserves and feeding them into his other ventures – the property-developing company, the clothing factory, Van Der Byl fisheries, the big irrigation scheme on the Orange River – and now the cupboard was almost bare.

The beach concessions were reaching the end of a short but glorious life. They were starting to work break-even ground. The Old Man had sold the Huib Hoch concession to the big Company for a quick profit – but the profit had been just as quickly transferred out of Johnny's control.

There was only one really fat goose left in his pen, and it wasn't laying eggs yet.

Eighteen months earlier Johnny had purchased two offshore diamond grounds from a company which had died in attempting to work them. It had been strangled by its own inefficiency.

Taking diamonds from the sea is about eight times more expensive than working them from a dry opencast. One must dredge the gravel from the wild and unpredictable waters of the Skeleton Coast, load it into dumb barges, tow the barges to a safe base, off-load it and then begin the recovery process – or rather, that was the method the defunct company had attempted.

Johnny had dreamed up, and then ordered a vessel which was completely self-contained. It could lie out at sea, suck up the gravel and process it, spilling the waste gravel back into the sea as rapidly as it was sucked aboard. It was fitted with a sophisticated recovery plant that was completely computerized and contained within the ocean-going hull. It needed only a small crew, and it could work in all weather conditions short of a full tornado.

The *Kingfisher* was lying at Portsmouth dockyards rapidly

nearing completion. Her trials were scheduled for early August.

Financing the building of this vessel had been a nightmare for Johnny. The Old Man had been unhelpful, when he wasn't being downright obstructive. He never discussed the venture without that little smile twitching at his lips. He had restricted Van Der Byl Diamonds' monetary involvement in the project so severely that Johnny had been forced to raise two millions outside the company.

He had found the money, and the Old Man had smiled again.

Kingfisher should have been lying on the grounds three months ago, sucking up diamonds. The whole financial structure of the scheme was based on her completion on schedule, but *Kingfisher* was running six months behind and now the foundations were shivering.

Sitting at his desk Johnny was working out how to shore up the whole edifice and keep it from collapsing before he could get *Kingfisher* working. The creditors were rumbling and creaking, and Johnny had only his own enthusiasm and reputation left to keep them quiet.

Now he must ask them to defer their interest payments for another three months. He picked up the telephone.

'Get me Mr Larsen at Credit Finance,' he said, steeling himself as he did so, jutting out his jaw and thrusting one bunched fist into his jacket pocket.

At five o'clock he stood up from his desk and went to the cabinet. He poured three fingers of whisky and went back to lower himself wearily into his swivel chair. He felt no elation at having won another reprieve, he was too tired.

The unlisted telephone on his desk rang and he picked it up.

'Lance,' he said.

'How was London?' he recognized the voice instantly, feeling no surprise that the Old Man knew about his journey. The Old Man knew everything. Before he could answer the hoarse croak came again, 'Come up to the house – now!' And the receiver clicked dead.

Johnny looked at the whisky in his hand regretfully and set it down untouched. The Old Man would smell it and smile.

Cloud was blowing over the mountain, and the setting sun turned it to the colour of tangerine and peaches. The Old Man stood at the window and watched the cloud cascade down into the valley, dispersing as it fell.

He turned from the window as Johnny entered the study and instantly Johnny was aware that something momentous had taken place in his absence.

He glanced quickly at Michael Shapiro for a cue, but Michael's grey-streaked head was bowed over the papers he held on his lap.

'Good evening.' Johnny addressed the Old Man.

'Sit there.' The Old Man indicated the Spanish leather chair opposite his desk.

'Read it,' the Old Man ordered Michael, and Michael cleared his throat and patted the papers into a neat square before he began.

The Old Man sat with his eyes on Johnny's face. It was a candid, intimate scrutiny, but Johnny felt no discomfort under it. It was almost as though the Old Man's eyes were caressing him.

Mike Shapiro read intelligently, bringing out the meaning of the involved and convoluted legal phrases. The document was the Old Man's Last Will and Testament, and it took twenty minutes for Mike to complete the reading of it. When he had finished there was silence in the room, and the Old Man broke it at last.

'Do you understand?' he asked. There was a gentleness about him that there had never been before. He seemed to have shrunk, the flesh withering on his bones and leaving them dry and light – like the sun-dried bones of a long dead seabird.

'Yes, I understand.' Johnny nodded.

'Explain it to us simply, not in your lawyer's gobbledy-gook, just to be certain,' the Old Man insisted, and Mike began to speak.

'Mr van der Byl's private estate, with the exception of his shares in Van Der Byl Diamond Co. Ltd, after taxes and expenses, is placed in Trust for his two children, Tracey—'

The Old Man interrupted impatiently, swatting Mike's words out of the air as though they were flies.

'Not that. The Company. Tell him about the shares in the Company.'

'Mr van der Byl's shares in the Company are to be divided equally between you and the two van der Byl children, Tracey—'

Again the Old Man interrupted.

'He knows their names, dammit.'

It was the first time ever that either of them had heard him swear. Mike grinned ruefully at Johnny, as though asking for his sympathy, but Johnny was intent on the Old Man, studying his face, feeling the deep satisfying thrill swelling within his chest.

A third share in Van Der Byl Diamonds was no great fortune – nobody knew that better than Johnny.

However, by placing Johnny's name on the list with Tracey and Benedict – he had made him his own. This was what he had worked for all these years. The declaration was public, an acknowledgement to the world.

Johnny Lance had a father at last. He wanted to reach out and touch the Old Man. His chest felt swollen, tight with emotion. Behind his eyelids was a slow soft burning. Johnny blinked.

'This is—' His voice was ragged, and he coughed. 'I just don't know how to tell you—'

The Old Man interrupted him impatiently, silencing him with an imperious gesture, and he croaked at Mike.

'Now read him the codicil to the Will. No, don't read it. Explain it to him.'

Michael's expression changed; he looked down at his papers as he spoke, as though reluctant to meet Johnny's eyes. He cleared his throat unnecessarily and shifted in his seat.

'"By the codicil to the Will, dated the same date, and duly signed by Mr van der Byl the bequest of shares in Van Der Byl Diamond Co. Ltd to JOHN RIGBY LANCE, is made conditional on the issue by the said JOHN RIGBY LANCE of a personal guarantee for the debts of the company, including the present loan account and amounts outstanding to tributary companies for royalties and options."'

'Christ,' said Johnny, stiffening in his chair and turning to stare incredulously at the Old Man. The tightness in his chest was gone. 'What are you trying to do to me?'

The Old Man dismissed Mike Shapiro quietly, without even looking at him. 'I'll call you when I want you.' And when he had gone he repeated Johnny's question.

'What am I trying to do to you?' he asked. 'I am trying to make you responsible for debts totalling about two and a half million Rand.'

'No creditor would come to me for half a million, I would be hard pressed to raise ten thousand on my personal account.' Johnny shook his head irritably, the whole thing was nonsensical.

'There is one creditor who could come to you, and subject you to the full process of law. Not to receive payment in cash – but in personal satisfaction. He would smash you – and delight in doing so.'

Johnny's eyes narrowed disbelievingly. 'Benedict?'

The Old Man nodded. 'For once Benedict will hold the top cards. He won't be able to dislodge you from the management of the company, because Tracey will support you as she always has done – but he will be able to watch every move you make from his seat on the Board of Directors. He will be able to hound you, bring you and the Company down without suffering financial loss himself. And when you fall – you know better than to expect mercy from him. You will be devoured by the ogre you have created.'

'Created?' Johnny's voice was shocked. 'What do you mean?'

'You turned him into what he is now. You broke his heart, made him weak and useless—'

'You are crazy.' Johnny came to his feet. 'I have never done anything to Benedict. It was he who—'

But the Old Man's husky croak brushed aside Johnny's protests. 'He tried to run with you – but could not. He gave up, became small and vicious. Oh, I know about the way he is – how you made him.'

'Please, listen to me. I did not—'

But the Old Man went on remorselessly. 'Tracey also, you have ruined her life. You enslaved her, in your sin—'

'That night!' Johnny shouted at him. 'You never let me explain. We never—'

Now the Old Man's voice was a whiplash.

'Silence!' And Johnny could not defy him, the habit was too deeply engrained. The Old Man was trembling, his eyes glittering with passion. 'Both my children! You have plagued me and my family. My son is a weak-willed drifter, trying to hide his hurt in a hunt for pleasure. I have given him the instruments to destroy you, and when he does so perhaps he will become a man.'

The Old Man's voice was strained now, rusty and pain-racked. He swallowed with an effort, his throat convulsing – but there was no softening of the glitter in his eyes.

51

'My daughter also, torturned by her lust. A lust which you awakened – she also seeks an escape from her guilty passion. Your destruction will be her release.'

'You're wrong,' Johnny cried out, half in protest, half in entreaty. 'Please, let me explain—'

'This is how it will work. I have made you vulnerable, linking you to a crippled and foundering enterprise. This time we will be rid of you.' He stopped to pant quickly, like a running dog. His breathing was strangled, harsh-sounding. 'Benedict will cut you down, and Tracey will have to watch you go. She cannot help you, her inheritance is carefully tied up, she has no control of the capital. Your only hope is the *Kingfisher*. The *Kingfisher* will turn into a vampire and suck your life blood! You asked why I was systematically transferring the assets of Van Der Byl Diamonds to my other companies? Well, now you know the answer.'

Johnny's lips moved. He was very pale. His voice came out small and whispery.

'I could refuse to sign the guarantee.'

The Old Man smiled bleakly, a drawing back of the lips that was without warmth or humour.

'You will sign it.' His voice was wheezy. 'Your pride and conceit will not let you do otherwise. You see, I know you. I've studied you all these years. But if you refuse to sign the guarantee, I will still have smashed you. Your shares will go to Benedict. You will be out. Out! Gone! We will be finished with you at last.' Then his voice dropped, 'But you will sign. I know it.'

Involuntarily Johnny lifted his hands towards the Old Man, a gesture of supplication. 'In all this time. When I stayed with you, when I—' His voice went husky and dried up. 'Did you never feel anything for me – anything at all?'

The Old Man sat up in his chair. He seemed to regain his bulk and he began to smile. He spoke quietly now, he did not have to shout.

'Get out of my nest, Cuckoo. Get out and fly!' he said.

Slowly Johnny's expression changed, the line of his jaw hardened, thrusting out aggressively. His shoulders went back. He pushed his hands into his pockets, balling his fists into bony hammers.

He nodded once in understanding.

'I see.' He nodded again, and then he started to grin. It was an unconvincing grin, that twisted his mouth out of shape and left his eyes dark and haunted.

'All right, you mean old bastard, I'll show you.'

He turned and walked from the room without looking back.

The Old Man's expression lit in deep satisfaction. He chuckled, then his breath caught. He began to cough, and the pain ripped his throat with a violence that left him clinging weakly to the edge of his desk.

He felt the crab of death move within his flesh, sinking its claws more deeply into his throat and lungs – and he was afraid.

He called out in his pain and fear, but there was nobody in the old house to hear him.

*K*ingfisher was launched in August and ran her trials in the North Sea. Benedict was aboard, by the Old Man's express command. With a vessel of such complexity, and of such revolutionary design, it would have been a miracle had she functioned perfectly. August that year was not the month for miracles. At the end of the trials Johnny had compiled a list of twenty-three modifications that were necessary.

'How long?' he asked the representative of the shipyard.

'A month.' The reply was hesitant.

'You mean two,' said Benedict and laughed out loud. Johnny looked at him thoughtfully, he guessed that the Old Man had spoken to him.

'I'll tell you something, Johnny.' Benedict was still laughing. 'I'm glad this cow isn't my dream of paradise.'

Johnny froze. Those words were the Old Man's, repeated parrot fashion. It was all the confirmation that he needed.

Johnny flew back to Cape Town to find his creditors on the verge of mutiny. They wanted to sell out, and take the loss.

Johnny spent two whole precious days on Larsen's wine farm at Stellenbosch calming his fears. When Fifi Larsen, twenty years younger than her husband, squeezed Johnny's thigh under the lunch table he knew it would be all right – for another two months.

During the next hectic, strength-sapping week of argument and negotiation, Johnny made time to see Tracey.

She had been out of the nursing-home for a month now, staying with friends on a small farm near Somerset West.

When Johnny climbed out of the Mercedes, and Tracey came down from the stoop to greet him, he had his first real lift of pleasure in a long time.

'God,' he said. 'You look great.'

She was dressed in a cotton summer dress with open sandals on her feet. Her friends were away for the day, so they walked through the orchards. He studied her openly, noticing how her cheeks and arms had filled out and the colour had come back into them. Her hair was bright and springing with lights in the sun, but there were still the dark smears under her eyes, and she smiled only once when he picked a sprig of peach blossoms for her. She seemed to be afraid of him, and unsure of herself.

At last he faced her and placed his hands on her shoulders. 'All right. What's eating you?'

It came out in a quick staccato rush of words.

'I want to thank you for coming to find me. I want to explain why I was – like that. In that state. I don't want you to believe – well, bad things about me.'

'Tracey, you don't have to explain to me.'

'I want to. I must.' And she told him, not looking at his face, twisting and tearing the blossoms in her hands.

'You see, I didn't understand, I thought all men were like that. Not wanting, I mean not doing it—' She broke off, and started again. 'He was kind, you understand. And there were lots of parties and friends around all the time, every night. Then he wanted to go to London – for his career. There was not enough scope here. Even then I didn't know. Well, I knew he had lots of men friends and that some of them were different – but . . . Then I went to his studio and found them, and they laughed, Kenny and the boy twined together like snakes. "But you must have known," he said. Something just snapped in my head, I felt spoiled, dirty and horrible and I wanted to die. There was nobody to go to and I didn't want anybody – I just wanted to die.' She stopped and stood waiting for him to speak.

'Do you still want to die?' he asked gently, and she looked up startled and shook her shining hair.

'I don't want you to die either.' And suddenly they were both laughing. After that it was good between them and they talked with all the strangeness gone until it was almost dark.

'I must go,' Johnny said.

'Your wife?' she asked, the laughter fading.

'Yes. My wife.'

It was dark when Johnny went in through the front door of the new split-level ranch type in Bishopscourt which was his house but not his home; the telephone was ringing. He picked up the receiver.

'Johnny?'

'Hello Michael.' He recognized the voice.

'Johnny, get up here to the old house right away.'

Michael Shapiro's voice was strained.

'Is it the Old Man?' Johnny asked anxiously.

'No talk – just come, quickly!'

T he curtains were drawn, and a log fire roared on the stone hearth. But the Old Man was cold. The coldness was deep inside him where the flames could not warm it. His hands shook as he picked sheets of paper from the open document box, glanced at them and then dropped them into the fire. They exploded into orange flame, then curled and blackened to ash. At last the box was empty but for a thick wad of multi-coloured envelopes bound together with a ribbon. He loosened the knot, picked out the first envelope, and slipped from it a single sheet of writing-paper.

'Dear Sir,
I hope you will be pleased to hear that I am now at school. The food is good but the beds are very hard—'

He dropped both envelope and letter on the fire and selected another. One at a time he read and then burned them.

'—that I have been selected to play for the first fifteen—'

Sometimes he smiled, once he chuckled.

'—I was top in all subjects except history and religious teaching. I hope to do better next—'

When there was one envelope left he held it a long time in his blue-veined bony hands. Then with an impatient flick of his wrist he threw it on to the fire and reached up to the mantelpiece to pull himself to his feet. As he stood he looked into the gilt-framed mirror above the fireplace.

He stared at his reflection, mildly surprised by the change that the last few weeks had wrought in his appearance. His eyes had lost the sparkle of life, fading to a pale dirty brownish blue – the colour of putrefaction. They bulged from the sockets, in the glassy startled stare which is peculiar to the later stages of terminal cancer.

The watery feeling of limb, and the coldness were not the result of the pain-killing drugs, he knew. Nor was the shuffling feet-dragging gait with which he crossed the thick Bokhara carpet to the stinkwood desk.

He looked down at the oblong leather case with its brass-bound corners, and he coughed, a single flesh-tearing bark. He caught at the desk to steady himself, waiting for the pain to pass before he sprang the catch on the case and laid the lid back.

His hands were quite steady as he took the barrel and butt section of the Purdy Royal twelve-bore shotgun from the case and fitted them together.

He died the way he had lived – alone.

'Good, how I hate black.' Ruby Lance stood in the centre of the bedroom floor, staring at the clothing laid out on the double bed. 'It makes me look so washed out.'

She swung her head from side to side, setting the champagne-coloured cascade of her hair swinging. She turned and moved lazily across the room to the tall mirrors. She smiled at herself, a languid slanting of the eyes, and then she spoke over the shoulder of her own image.

'You say that Benedict van der Byl has arrived from England?'

'Yes,' Johnny nodded. He sat slumped in the chair beside his dressing-room door, pressing his fingers into his eyes.

Ruby came up on her toes, pulling in her stomach and pushing forward her small hard breasts.

'Who else will be there?' she asked, cupping her hands under her breasts and squeezing out the nipples between thumb and forefinger, inspecting them critically. Johnny took his hand from his eyes.

'Did you hear me?' Ruby's voice took on a sharp admonishing note. 'I'm not talking to myself, you know.'

She turned away from the mirror to face him. Standing long and slim and golden as a leopard, even her eyes had the yellow intentness of a leopard's stare. She gave the impression that at any moment she would draw her lips back in a snarl.

'It's a funeral,' he said quietly. 'Not a cocktail party.'

'Well, you can't expect me to die of sorrow. I couldn't stand him.' She crossed to the bed and picked up the pair of peach-coloured panties and rubbed the glossy material against her cheek. Then she stepped into them with two long-legged strides.

'At least I can wear something pretty under the weeds.' She snapped the elastic against her sun-gilt belly, and the almost colourless blonde curls were flattened beneath the sheer silk.

Johnny stood up slowly, and went into his dressing-room. Scornfully she called after him. 'Oh for God's sake, Johnny Lance, stop dragging that long face around as though it's the end of the world. Nobody owes that old devil a thing – he collected all his debts long before they fell due.'

They were a few minutes early, and they stood together beneath the pine-trees outside the entrance to the chapel.

When the pearl-grey Rolls drew up at the gate and brother and sister stepped down and came up the paved path, Ruby could not contain her interest.

'Is that Benedict van der Byl?'

Johnny nodded.

'He's very good-looking.'

But Johnny was looking at Tracey. The change in her appearance since he had last seen her was startling. She walked like a desert girl again, straight and proud. She came directly to Johnny and stopped in front of him. She removed her dark glasses, and he could see she had been weeping, for her eyes were slightly puffy. She wore no make-up, and with the dark scarf framing her face she looked like a nun. The marks that sorrow had left gave her face maturity.

'I did not think this day would ever come,' she said softly.

'No,' Johnny agreed. 'It was as though he would live for ever.'

Tracey moved a step closer to him, she reached out as if to touch Johnny's arm but her fingers stopped within inches of his sleeve. Johnny understood the gesture, it was a sharing of sorrow, an understanding of mutual loss, and an unstated offer of comfort.

'I don't think we have met.' Ruby used her sugar and arsenic tone. 'It is Miss van der Byl, isn't it?'

Tracey turned her head and her expression went flat and neutral. She replaced the dark glasses, masking her eyes.

'Mrs Hartford,' she said. 'How do you do.'

Mike Shapiro stood beside Johnny in the pew. He spoke without moving his lips, just loud enough for Johnny to catch the words.

'Benedict knows the conditions of the Will. You can expect his first move immediately.'

'Thanks, Mike.'

Johnny kept his eyes on the massive black coffin. The candlelight glinted and sparkled on the elaborate silver handles.

As yet he could find no interest for the conflict that lay

ahead. That would come. Now he was too deeply involved in the passing of an era, his life had reached another point of major departure. He knew it would change, had already changed.

He looked across the aisle suddenly, his gaze drawn intuitively.

Benedict van der Byl was watching him, and at that moment the priest asked for the pallbearers.

They went to stand beside the coffin, Benedict and Johnny on opposite sides of the polished black casket among the massed display of arum lilies. They watched each other warily. It seemed to Johnny that the whole scene was significant. The two of them standing over the Old Man's corpse, facing each other, with Tracey looking on anxiously.

Johnny glanced back into the body of the church, looking for Tracey. Instead he found Ruby. She was watching them both, and Johnny knew suddenly that the board had changed more than he realized. A new piece had been added to the game.

He felt Mike Shapiro nudge him, and he stooped forward and grasped the silver handle. Between them they carried the Old Man out into the sunshine.

The handle had cut into his palm with the weight of the coffin. He went on massaging it, even after the coffin had gone down into the pit. The crude mounds of fresh earth were covered with blankets of bright green artificial grass. The mourners began to drift away, but Johnny went on standing there bare-headed. Until Ruby came to touch his arm.

'Come on.' Her voice pitched low, but stinging. 'You're making a fool of yourself.'

Benedict and Tracey were waiting under the pine-trees by the churchyard gate, shaking hands and talking quietly to the departing mourners.

'You are Ruby, of course.' Benedict took her hand, smiling a little, urbane and charming. 'The flattering reports I've had of you hardly do you justice.' And Ruby glowed, seeming like a butterfly to spread her wings to the sun.

'Johnny.' Benedict turned to him, and Johnny was taken off balance by the friendly warmth of his smile and the grip of his hand. 'Michael Shapiro tells me that you have accepted my father's legacy and the conditions attached to it – you have signed the guarantee. It's wonderful news. I don't know what we would have done without you in Van Der Byl Diamonds. You are the only one that can pull the Company though this difficult period. I want you to know I am behind you all the way, Johnny. I intend becoming much more involved with the Company now, giving you all the help you need.'

'I knew I could depend on you, Benedict.' Johnny accepted the challenge as smoothly as it was thrown down. 'I think everything is going to turn out all right.'

'We have a meeting on Monday, then I must return to London on Thursday – but I hope you can have dinner with me before then – you and your lovely wife, of course.'

'Thank you.' Ruby seeing the refusal on Johnny's lips, interrupted quickly. 'We'd enjoy that.'

'You were going to refuse, weren't you?' She sat with her legs curled up sideways under her, watching him from the passenger seat of the Mercedes with the slanting eyes of a Persian cat.

'You're damn right.' Johnny nodded grimly.

'Why?'

'Benedict van der Byl is poison.'

'You say so.'

'Yes, I say so.'

'Could be you're jealous of him.' Ruby lit one of her gold-tipped cigarettes, putting the smoke through her lips.

'Good God!' Johnny gave one harsh snort of laughter, then they were silent awhile, both staring ahead.

'I think he's pretty dreamy.'

'You can have him.' Johnny's tone was disinterested, but her retort was shrill.

'I could too – if I wanted to. Anyway you and that Tracey creature mooning—'

'Cut it out, Ruby.'

'Oh my, I've said the wrong thing. The precious Mrs Hartford—'

'Cut it out, I said.' Johnny's tone was sharp.

'Little Miss Fancy Pants – God! She almost had them down for you in the bloody graveyard—'

'Shut up, damn you.'

'Don't you swear at me.' And she lashed out at him flat-handed, leaning forward across the seat to strike him in the mouth. His lower lip smeared against his teeth, and the taste of blood seeped into his mouth. He took the handkerchief from his breast pocket and held it to his mouth, steering the Mercedes with one hand.

Ruby sat curled in her corner of the seat, puffing quickly at the cigarette. Neither of them spoke again until he drew up in front of the double garage. Then Ruby slipped out of the Mercedes and ran across the lawns to the front door. She slammed it behind her, with a force that rattled the full-length glass panel.

Johnny parked the Mercedes, closed the garage door and followed her slowly into the house. She had kicked off her shoes on the wall-to-wall carpet in the lounge, and run through on to the patio beside the swimming pool. She stood barefooted staring down into the clear water, hugging herself about the shoulders.

'Ruby.' He came up behind her, forcing the anger out of

his voice with an effort, trying to keep it conciliatory.
'Listen to me—'

She spun around to face him, eyes blazing like a cornered
leopard.

'Don't try and gentle talk me, you bastard. What do you
think I am – your damned servant. When did I last get to
do anything I wanted?'

With Ruby he had long ago realized that placation was
the short cut to peace, so he was roused by the implication.

'I've never stopped you from—'

'Good! That's just fine! Then you won't stop me going
away.'

'What do you mean?' He was caught between shock and
a sneaking sense of hope. 'Are you talking about divorce—'

'Divorce? Are you out of your little mind! I know all
about the big bagful of goodies the Old Man left you in his
will. Well, little Ruby is getting her pinkies into that bag –
starting right now.'

'What do you want exactly?' His voice was cold and flat.

'A new wardrobe, and a quick whip around all those nice
places you go to all the time – London, Paris and the rest.
That will do for a start.'

He thought a moment, assessing how far he could stretch
his overdraft; since his marriage his bank statement had
seldom been typed in black. It was worth it, he decided. He
could afford no distraction over the next few months. He
could move faster and think quicker without having Ruby
Lance sitting between his shoulder-blades – much better
she should go.

'All right,' he nodded. 'If that's what you want.'

Her eyes narrowed slightly and her mouth pinched in as
she studied his face.

'That was too easy,' she said. 'You want to get rid of me?
Don't get any ideas, Johnny boy, you put one finger – or
anything else – out of line and I'll chop it off.'

'There is a Mrs Hartford to see you, sir.' Lettie Pienaar's voice whispered through on the intercom, then just audibly she added, 'Lucky you!'

Johnny grinned. 'You're fired for insolence – but send her in before you go.'

He stood up as Tracey came in, and went around his desk to meet her. She wore a no-nonsense grey suit, with her hair scraped back from her face. She should have looked like a school marm – but she didn't.

'You've got your times mixed up, Tracey. The Directors' meeting is at two this afternoon.'

'That's a sweet greeting.' She sat down in an egg-shaped swivel chair, crossing long legs which Johnny dragged his eyes off with an effort. 'I've come looking for a job.'

'A job?' He stared at her blankly.

'Yes, a job. You know – work? Employment?'

'What on earth for?'

'Well, now that you've dragged me back from the bright lights with all the finesse of a caveman – you don't expect me to sit around until I drop dead of boredom. Besides, your tame doctor feels that good healthy employment is essential to the completion of my – ah – cure.'

'I see.' He sank back into his own chair. 'Well – what can you do?'

'Mr Lance.' Tracey widened her eyes suggestively, but made her voice prim. ' – Really!'

'All right,' Johnny chuckled. 'What are your qualifications?'

'You may or may not know that I have a law degree from the University of Cape Town.'

'I didn't.'

'Also, it occurred to me that during the next few months you might need someone around whom you can trust.' She was serious now, and Johnny's smile faded also. 'Like the old days.' She added quietly. They were silent for a few seconds.

'It just so happens that we are looking for a personal assistant in our legal department,' Johnny murmured, and then softly, 'Thanks, Tracey.'

The Board Room of Van Der Byl Diamonds was furnished in soft forest colours, browns and greens. A long luxurious room that reflected the opulence of the days when the Company had been glutted with capital. But now the air was charged with a tension that crackled in the air like static electricity.

The subject of debate was the diamond recovery vessel, *Kingfisher*. The Company's last hope. Her only substantial asset, and Johnny's personal cross.

'This vessel should have been in operation nine months ago. All the estimates were based on that assumption – yet, she is still lying awaiting completion on the slips at Portsmouth.' Benedict was speaking with unconcealed relish. 'In consequence, the interest charges that are accruing put us in a position—'

'The shipyard was out on strike for a total of four months during construction – in addition they were working to rule for—' Johnny's jaw was thrust out, he was ready to fight.

'Ah! I don't think we are particularly interested in the unpredictability of the British workman – the contract should have gone to the Japanese company. Their tender was lower—'

'It would have,' grated Johnny, 'if your father had not insisted—'

'Please, let us not attempt to lay the blame at the door of a dead man.' Benedict's tone was sanctimonious. 'Let us rather try and rectify a grievous situation. When will *Kingfisher* be ready for sea?'

'On the thirteenth of September.'

'It had better be.' Benedict dropped his eyes to his notes.

'Now, this man whom you have engaged to captain the vessel – Sergio Caporetti – let us hear a little about him, please.'

'Fifteen years' experience on offshore oil-drilling vessels in the Red Sea. Three years as Captain of Atlantis Diamonds' offshore dredger operating off the West Coast. He's one of the best, no doubt about it.'

'All right.' Almost reluctantly Benedict accepted this, and consulted his notes. 'Now, we have two sea-concession areas. No. 1 area off Cartridge Bay; No. 2 some twenty miles north of that. Judging by your prospecting results you will elect to work No. 1 area first.'

Johnny nodded, waiting for the next attack to develop. Benedict sat back in his chair.

'Atlantis Diamonds Ltd went broke working our No. 1 area – what makes you think you can succeed where they failed?'

'We've been over this before,' Johnny snapped.

'I wasn't there, remember? Humour me, please. Go over it again.'

Quickly Johnny explained that Atlantis Diamonds' costs had been inflated by their method of operation. Their dredgers were not self-propelled but had to be towed by tugs. The gravel they recovered had been stored, taken into Cartridge Bay in bulk, transhipped ashore to be processed at a land-based plant. *Kingfisher* was a self-propelled and self-contained vessel. She would suck up the gravel, process it through the most sophisticated system of cyclone and X-ray equipment and dump the waste overboard.

'Our costs will be one quarter those of Atlantis Diamonds,' he finished.

'And our loan account is a mere two millions,' Benedict murmured dryly. Then he looked towards Mike Shapiro at the bottom of the table. 'Mr Secretary, please note the following motion – "That this Company proceed to sell the vessel *Kingfisher* presently building at Portsmouth. That it then sells all diamond concessions at the most advantageous terms negotiable, and goes into voluntary liquidation forthwith." Have you got that?'

It was a direct frontal attack. Clearly if the motion succeeded the Company was worthless. They could not recover the price of the *Kingfisher* on a forced sale. There would be a shortfall – and Johnny had signed the guarantee. It was a straight test that Benedict was making. A setting of the lines of battle. Tracey held the balance between Johnny and Benedict. He was forcing her to declare herself.

Benedict watched her while the motion was put to the vote. He leaned forward in the padded leather chair, a slightly amused smile on the full red lips. Beautifully groomed and tailored, with the grace that wealth and position give to a man and which cannot be counterfeited. But the clean athletic lines of his body were fractionally blurred by indulgence, and there was a little too much flesh along the line of his jaw that gave him the petulant look of a spoilt child.

Tracey voted with Johnny Lance, not hesitating a second before lifting her hand. Returning Benedict's smile levelly, and watching her brother's smile alter subtly – become wolfish, for Benedict did not like to lose.

'Very well, my darling sister. Now we know how we stand at least.' He turned easily to Johnny. 'I presume you wish me to continue with my duties in London.'

For years now Benedict had handled the London sales of the Company's stones. It was an unexacting task, which the Old Man had judged within his capabilities.

'Thank you, Benedict,' Johnny nodded. 'Now, I have a proposal to put to the meeting – "That the Directors of this Company, as a gesture of solidarity, agree to waive their rights to Directors' fees until such time as the Company's financial position is on a more sound footing."'

It was a puny counter-attack, but the best he could mount at the moment.

Take-off was in the first light from Youngsfield, and Johnny swung the twin-engined Beechcraft on to a northerly heading, leaving the blue massif of Table Mountain on the left hand.

Tracey wore an anorak over her rose-coloured shirt, and the bottoms of her denim pants were tucked into soft leather boots, her dark hair caught at the nape of her neck with a leather thong.

She sat very still, looking ahead through the aircraft's windshield at the dawn-touched contours of the land ahead. At the bleak lilac and purple mountains and the great lion-coloured plains spreading down to meet the mists that hung over the cold Atlantic.

In her stillness Johnny sensed her excitement and found it infectious.

The sun exploded over the horizon, washing golden and bright over the plains, and tipping the mountains with flame.

'Namaqualand.' Johnny pointed ahead.

She laughed with excitement, like a child at Christmas, turning in the seat to face him.

'Do you remember—' She began, then stopped in confusion.

'Yes,' said Johnny. 'I remember.'

They landed before noon on a rough airstrip bulldozed out of the wilderness. There was a Land-Rover waiting to take them down to the beach to inspect the progress of the workings.

There was little remaining along the thirty-seven-mile Admiralty strip worth working. It was a clean-up and shut-down operation.

When the reigning 'King Canute' handed over the parcel of diamonds that made up the month's recovery, he was apologetic.

'You took out all the plums, Johnny. It's not like the old days.'

Johnny prodded the pathetic pile of small, low-grade stones with his forefinger.

'No, it's not,' he agreed. 'But every little bit helps.'

They climbed back into the Beechcraft and flew on northwards.

Now they passed over areas where the desert had been scratched and torn over wide areas.

The tractors had left centipede tracks in the soft earth.

'Ours?' asked Tracey.

'I wish they were. We'd have no worries then. No, all this belongs to the big Company.'

Johnny checked his watch, automatically comparing the progress of the flight to his estimates. Then he lifted the microphone from the R/T set.

'Alexandra Bay Control. This is Zulu Sugar Peter Tango Baker.'

He knew that they had him on the radar plot, and were watching him – not because they were worried about his safety, but because he was now over the Proclaimed Diamond Area of South West Africa – that vast jealously guarded tract of nothingness.

The radio crackled back at him instantly, demanding his permit number, his flight plan, querying his intentions and his destination.

Having convinced Control of his innocence, and received their permission to continue his flight, he switched off his R/T set, and grimaced at Tracey.

He felt ruffled by this small brush with Olympus. He knew that most of it was professional jealousy. He smarted under the knowledge that he was working ground that the big Company would despise as not sufficiently lucrative to bother about.

Sometimes Johnny dreamed about discovering a fault in a land title, or an error in a survey that had been casually performed seventy years previously before the value of this parched denuded earth had been realized. He imagined himself being able to claim the mineral rights to a few square miles plumb in the middle of the big Company's richest field. He shivered voluptuously at the thought, and Tracey looked at him enquiringly.

He shook his head, then his line of thought took him on to a further destination.

He banked the aircraft, crossing the coastline with its creamy lines of surf running in on the freezing white sands of the beach.

'What?' She was expectant, receptive to the new tone in his voice.

'Thunderbolt and Suicide,' he said, and she made a small grimace of incomprehension.

'There.' He pointed ahead, and through the light smoke of the sea mist she saw them show bare – white and shiny, like a pair of albino whales.

'Islands?' she asked. 'What's so special about them?'

'Their shape,' he answered. 'See how they lie like the mouth of a funnel, with a small opening between them.'

She nodded. The two islands were almost identical twins, two narrow wedges of smooth granite, each about three miles long, lying in a chevron pattern to each other – but not quite meeting at the peak. The mighty Atlantic swells bore up from the south and ran into the mouth of the funnel. Finding themselves trapped in this granite corral, the swells reared up wildly and hurled themselves on the cliffs in massive bomb-bursts of spray before streaming out in white foam through the narrow opening between the two islands.

'I can see how Thunderbolt gets its name.' Tracey eyed the wild booming surf with awe. 'But how about Suicide?'

'The old guano collectors must have called it that, after they tried landing on it.'

'Guano,' Tracey nodded. 'That accounts for the colour.'

Johnny put the Beechcraft into a shallow dive, hurtling in low over the green water. Ahead of them the seabirds rose in alarm, streaming in a long black smear into the sky, the cormorants and gannets whose excreta through the ages had painted the rocks that glaring white.

As they flashed through the gap below the level of the cliffs, Tracey exclaimed, 'There's some sort of tower there – look! In the back of the island.'

'Yes,' Johnny agreed. 'It's an old wooden gantry they used for loading the guano into the longboats.'

He pulled the Beechcraft up in a climbing turn, gaining height to look down on the two islands.

'Do you see where the surf comes through the gap? Now look beneath the surface, can you see the reefs under the water?'

They lay like long dark shadows through the green water, at right angles to the drift of white foam.

'Well, you are looking at the most beautifully designed natural diamond trap in the world.'

'Explain,' Tracey invited.

'Down there,' he pointed south, 'are the big rivers. Some of them dried up a million years ago, but not before they had spat the diamonds they carried into the sea. The tide and the wind has been working them up towards the north for all these ages. Throwing some of them back on the beach but carrying others up this way.'

He levelled the Beechcraft out and resumed their interrupted flight northwards.

'Then suddenly they run up against Thunderbolt and Suicide. They are concentrated and squeezed through the gap, then they are confronted by a series of sharp reefs across their path. They cannot cross them – they just settle down in the gullies and wait for someone to come and suck them out.'

He sighed like a man crossed in love.

'My God, Tracey. The smell of those diamonds reeks in my nostrils. I can almost see the shine of them through a hundred and sixty feet of water.'

He shook himself as though waking from a dream.

'I've been in the game all my life, Tracey. I've got the "feel", the same as a water-diviner has. I tell you with absolute certainty there are millions of carats of diamonds lying in the crotch of Thunderbolt and Suicide.'

'What's the snag?' Tracey asked.

'The concession was granted twenty years ago to the big Company.'

'By whom?'

'The Government of South West Africa.'

'Why aren't they mining it?'

'They will – sometime in the next twenty years. They aren't in any hurry.'

They lapsed into silence, staring ahead, though once Johnny clucked his tongue irritably and shook his head – still thinking about Thunderbolt and Suicide.

To distract him Tracey asked, 'Where do they come from in the first place – the diamonds?'

'Volcanic pipes,' Johnny answered. 'There are more than a hundred known pipes in Southern Africa. Not all yield stones, but then some do. New Rush – Finsch – Dutoitspan – Bulfontein – Premier – Mwadui. Great oval-shaped treasure chests, filled with the legendary "Blue Ground" – the mother lode of the diamond.'

'There are no pipes here – surely?' Tracey turned towards him in his seat.

'No,' Johnny agreed. 'We are after the alluvial stones. Some of those ancient pipes exploded with the force of a hydrogen bomb, spraying diamonds over hundreds of square miles. Others were sub-marine pipes that discharged their treasure into the restless sea. Others of the more passive volcanic pipes were simply eroded away by wind and water and the diamonds were exposed.'

'Then they were washed down to the sea?' she guessed.

Johnny nodded. 'That's right. Over millions of years they

were moved infinitely slowly by landslides, floods, rivers and rainwater. Where all the other pebbles and stones were abraded and worn away to nothingness – the diamonds, four hundred times harder than any other natural substance on earth, were unmarked. So at last they reached the sea and mingled with the others from the sub-marine pipes, to be laid down by wave action on the beaches, or finally to come up against a place like Thunderbolt and Suicide.'

Tracey opened her mouth to ask another question, but Johnny interrupted.

'Here we are. There is Cartridge Bay.' And he pushed the nose of the aircraft down slightly. It was more a lagoon than a bay. Separated from the sea by a narrow sandspit, it spread away into the treeless waste, an enormous extent of quiet shallow water in tranquil contrast to the unchecked surf that burst on the sandspit. There was a deep water entrance through the sandspit, and a channel meandered across the lagoon to where a cluster of lonely whitewashed buildings sprang up on the edge of the desert.

Johnny banked steeply towards the buildings, and below them flocks of black and white pelicans and pink flamingoes rose in panic from the shallows.

Johnny landed and taxied across to the waiting Land-Rover with the white lightning insignia of Van Der Byl Diamonds painted on its side.

Lugging the cool box that contained their lunch, Johnny led Tracey to the vehicle and introduced her to his foreman. Then they climbed in and went bumping down to the buildings on the lagoon. Johnny received from his foreman a report on progress of the work. The buildings had been abandoned by the defunct Atlantis Diamond Company. Johnny was renovating them to serve as a base for the *Kingfisher*; a rest and recreation centre for the crew, a radio centre, a refuelling depot and a workshop to handle running maintenance and repairs. In addition he was putting a jetty out into the lagoon for the converted seventy-foot pilchard trawler that would be *Kingfisher*'s service boat – acting as tender and ferry.

They ran an extensive inspection of the base. Johnny was pleased with the interest Tracey showed, and he enjoyed answering her questions for his own enthusiasm was high. It was nearly two o'clock before they had finished.

'How are the watchtowers coming?' Johnny asked.

'All up, ready and waiting.'

And suddenly Johnny had a two-edged inspiration.

'Might as well go and have a look.' He made it casual.

'Okay, I'll fetch the Land-Rover,' the foreman agreed.

'I know the way.' Johnny put him off. 'You go and get your lunch.'

'It's no trouble—' the foreman began, caught Johnny's frown, cut himself short, then glanced at Tracey. 'Yeah! Sure! Fine! Okay – here are the keys.' He handed Johnny the Land-Rover keys, and disappeared into his own quarters.

Johnny checked the grub box, and they climbed into the open Land-Rover.

'Where are we going?' Tracey asked.

'Inspect the watchtowers along the sandspit.'

'Watchtowers?'

'We've put up a line of fifty-foot wooden towers along the beach. From them we will take continual bearings on *Kingfisher* when she is working offshore. By radio we will be able at any time to give her the exact position over the bottom to within a few feet, as a check to the computer.'

'My, you are clever.' Tracey fluttered her eyelashes at him in mock admiration.

'Silly wench,' said Johnny, and let out the clutch. He swung down past the radio shack on to the hard wet sand at the edge of the lagoon; accelerating he hit second then third and they went away around the curve of the lagoon, headed towards the great yellow wind-carved dunes that lined the coast.

Tracey stood up on her seat, clutching the edge of the windscreen, and the wind snatched at her hair. She pulled the retaining thong from it, and shook it out into a shiny black flag that snapped and snaked behind her.

'Look! Look!' she cried as the flocks of startled flamingoes lurched into flight, streaming white and pink and black over the glossy silver water.

Johnny laughed with her, and swung the Land-Rover towards the dunes.

'Hold on!' he shouted, and she clung to the windscreen, shrieking in delicious terror as they flew up the steep side of a dune, spinning a cloud of sand from the rear wheels and then dropped over the crest in a stomach-churning swoop. They crossed the sandspit and hit the beach, racing along it, playing tag with the waves that shot up the sand.

Five miles up the beach Johnny parked above the high-water mark and they ate cold chicken and drank a bottle of chilled white wine sitting side by side in the sand, leaning against the seat cushions from the Land-Rover. Then they went down to the edge of the sea to wash the chicken grease from their fingers.

'Yipes! It's cold.' Tracey scooped a double handful of sea water. Then she looked at Johnny and her expression became devilish.

He backed away, but not quickly enough. The icy water hit him in the chest, and he gasped.

'War!' It was their childhood cry.

Tracey whirled and went off long-legged along the beach, with Johnny pounding after her. She sensed him gaining on her, and shouted.

'It was a mistake! I didn't mean it! I'm sorry!'

At the last moment as he reached out to grip her shoulder, she jinked and ran knee-deep into the sea. Turning at bay to face him, she kicked a spray of water at him, shouting defiance and laughter.

'All right, come on then!'

Braving the flying spray, he reached her and picked her up kicking and struggling and waded out waist deep.

'No, no – please. Johnny. I give in – I'll do anything.'

At that moment a freak wave, bigger and stronger than the others, knocked Johnny's legs out from under him. They went under, and were rolled up the beach, to stagger out, completely soaked, clinging together, helpless with laughter.

They stood beside the Land-Rover trying to wring the water out of their clothing.

'Oh, you beast!' sobbed Tracey through her laughter. Her hair was a sodden mass, and drops of sea water clung in her eyelashes like dew.

Johnny took her in his arms and kissed her, and they stopped laughing.

She went loose against his chest, her eyes tightly closed and her lips, salty with sea water, opened against his.

The radio telephone in the Land-Rover beside them began to bleat fretfully, flashing its little red warning light.

They drew apart slowly, reluctantly, and stared at each other with dazed, bemused eyes.

Johnny reached the Land-Rover, unhooked the microphone and lifted it to his lips.

'Yes?' his voice cracked. He cleared his throat and repeated. 'Yes?'

The foreman's voice was distorted and scratchy through the speaker.

'Mr Lance, I'm sorry to have—' he was clearly about to finish ' – interrupted you.' But he stopped abruptly, and began again. 'It's just that I think you should know we've had a gale warning. Northerly gale building up quickly. If you want to get back to Cape Town you had better get airborne before it hits us – otherwise you could be shut in for days.'

'Thanks. We'll be back right away.' He hung up, and

Tracey smiled shakily. Her voice was also husky and unnatural-sounding.

'And a damn good thing too!'

Tracey's hair was still damp, and the borrowed polo-neck jersey swamped her. The grey trousers were also borrowed, rolled up to show her bare feet.

She sat very quietly and thoughtfully in the passenger seat of the Beechcraft. Far below them a small fishing vessel lay with a white cloud of seabirds hovering over it, and she watched it with exaggerated attention. There was a heavy feeling of restraint between them now, they could no longer meet each other's eyes.

'Pilchard trawler.' Johnny noticed her gaze.

'Yes,' said Tracey, and they were silent again.

'Nothing happened.' Johnny spoke again gruffly.

'No,' she agreed. 'Nothing happened.' Then shyly she reached out and took his hand. Lightly she rubbed the stump of his missing finger.

'Still friends?' she asked.

'Still friends.' He grinned at her with relief, and they flew on towards Cape Town.

Hugo Kramer watched the aircraft through his binoculars, balancing easily against the roll and pitch of the bridge.

'Police patrol?' asked the man at the helm beside him.

'No,' Hugo replied without lowering the glasses. 'Red and white twin Beechcraft. Registration ZS – PTB. Private aircraft, probably one of the diamond companies.'

He lowered the glasses, and crossed to the wing of the bridge. 'Anyway, we are well outside territorial waters.'

The drone of the aircraft engine faded away, and Hugo transferred his attention to the frantic activity on the deck below him.

The trawler, *Wild Goose*, lay heeled over under the weight of fish that filled her purse seine-net; at least a hundred tons of seething silver pilchards bulging the net out alongside the trawler into a round bag fifty feet across. While above it a shrieking canopy of seabirds swirled and wheeled and dived, frantic with greed.

Three of the crew on a scoop-net which hung from the overhead derrick were dipping the fish out of the net, swinging a ton of fish at each scoop over the side, and dropping them like a silver cloudburst into the trawler's hold. The donkey engine on the winch clattered harshly in time to their movements.

Hugo watched with satisfaction. He had a good crew, and although the fishing was only a cover for the *Wild Goose* – yet Hugo took pride in his teutonic thoroughness which dictated that the cover should be as solid as possible. In any case, all profits from fishing were for his personal account. It was part of the agreement with the Ring.

He packed the binoculars carefully into their leather case, and hung them behind the chartroom door. Then he clambered swiftly down the steel ladder to deck level, moving with catlike grace despite the heavy rubber hip boots he wore.

'I'll take her here for a while,' he told the man at the winch controls. He spoke in Afrikaans, but his accent was shaded with the German of South West Africa.

Wide-shouldered under the blue fisherman's jersey, he worked with smooth economic movements. His hands on the winch control were rough and reddened by wind and sun, for his skin was too fair to weather. The skin of his face was also red, and half-boiled, peeling so there were pinky raw places on his cheeks and black scabs on his lips.

The hair that hung out under his cap was white as

bleached sisal, and his eyelashes were thick and colourless, giving him a mild near-sighted look. His eyes were the palest of cornflower blue, yet without being weak and watery as those of most albinos; they were slitted now, as he judged the roll and dip of the boat – engaging the clutch to meet the movement, or pulling on the drum brake.

'Skipper!' A shout from the bridge above him.

'Ja.' Hugo did not allow his attention to waver as he replied, 'What is it?'

'Gale warning! There is a northerly buster building up.'

And Hugo grinned, pulled on the brake and shut the throttle.

'All right, clean up. Cut the purse rope, let the fish go free.'

He turned and swarmed up the ladder to the bridge, and went to his chart table.

'It will take us three hours to get in position,' he muttered aloud, leaning over the chart, then he barged out on to the wing of the bridge again to chase up his crew.

They had cut the purse rope on the net, allowing the net to fall open like a woman's skirt, and the fish were pouring out, a dark spreading stain through the gap. Two men had the pressure hose on, washing loose fish from the deck into the sea, others were slamming the hatch-covers closed.

Within forty minutes *Wild Goose* was running south under full throttle to take up her waiting station.

The diamond coast of South West Africa lies in the belt of the Trades. The prevailing wind is the south-easter, but periodically the wind system is completely reversed and a gale comes out of the north, off the land.

It is a Scirocco-type wind like the 'Khamsin' of the Libyan desert, or the 'Simoom' of Tripoli.

It was the same searing dry wind out of the desert, filling the sky with brooding dust and sand clouds, smothering everything beneath a hellish pall like the smoke from a great battlefield.

The dust clouds were part of the design, the Ring had taken account of them when they planned the system – for the north wind lifted into the sky such a quantity of mica dust that the radar screens of the diamond security police were cluttered and confused, throwing up phantom echoes and making it impossible to pick up the presence of a small airborne object.

Turn Back Point was three miles inland, and sixty miles north of the Orange River. The name was given by the first travellers, and expressed their views on continuing a journey northwards. Those old travellers had not known that they stood in the centre of an elevated marine terrace, an ancient beach now lifted above the level of the sea, and that it was the richest prospect of an area so diamond-rich that it was to be ring-fenced, patrolled by Jeep and dog and aircraft, guarded by gun and radar, a laager so secure that a man leaving it would have to submit to X-ray, and take nothing out with him but the clothes he wore.

At Turn Back Point was one of the four big separation plants where all the gravel from the big Company's workings from miles around was processed. The settlement was comparatively large, with plant, workshops and stores, and accommodation for five hundred men and their families. Yet not all the Company's efforts to make it attractive and liveable could alter the fact that Turn Back Point was a hell-hole in a savage and forbidding desert.

Now with the north wind blowing, what had been unpleasant before was almost unbearable. The buildings were tightly sealed, even the joints around the windows and doors were plugged with cloth or paper – and yet the red dust seeped in to powder the furniture, the desks, the bed linen, even the interior of the refrigerators, with a thin gritty film. It settled in the hair, was sugary between the teeth, clogged the nostrils – and with it came that searing heat that seemed to dry the moisture from the eyeballs.

Outside the dust was a red glittering fog which reduced visibility to a dozen yards. Men who were forced out into that choking dry soup wore dust goggles to protect their eyes, and the mica dust covered their clothing with a shiny coating that glittered even in that dun light.

Beyond the settlement a man moved now through the fog, carrying a small cylindrical object. He leaned forward into the wind, moving slowly away into the desert. He reached a shallow depression and went down into it. Setting his burden on the sand, he rested a moment. Then he knelt over the cylinder. He appeared monstrous under his leather jacket and cap, his face covered by goggles and a scarf.

The fibre-glass cylinder was painted with yellow fluorescent paint. At one end was a transparent plastic bubble which housed an electric globe, at the other end was a folded envelope of rubberized nylon material attached to the cylinder by a stainless steel coupling, and linked to the coupling was a small steel bottle of hydrogen gas. The whole assembly was eighteen inches long, and three inches in diameter. It weighed a few ounces more than fifteen pounds.

Within the cylinder were two separate compartments. The larger contained a highly sophisticated piece of transistorized electronic equipment which would transmit a homing signal, light or extinguish its lamp on long-distance radio signal command, and also at command it would control the inflow of hydrogen gas into the nylon balloon through the connecting coupling.

The smaller compartment held simply a sealed plastic container into which were packed twenty-seven diamonds. The smallest of these stones weighed fourteen carats, the largest a formidable fifty-six carats. Each of these stones had been selected by experts for colour, brilliance, and perfection. These were all first-water diamonds, and once they were cut they would fetch in the open market between seven hundred thousand and a million pounds – depending on the skill of the cutting.

There were four members of the Ring at Turn Back Point. Two of them were long service and trusted diamond sorters employed behind the guarded walls of the processing plant. They worked together, to check each other, for the Company operated a system of employee double check – which was completely useless when there was collusion. These men selected the finest stones and got them out of the plant.

The third member of the Ring was a diesel mechanic in the Company workshops. It was his job to receive and assemble the equipment which arrived concealed in a marked drum of tractor grease. He also packed the stones into the cylinder and passed it on to the man who was now kneeling out in the desert, preparing to launch the cylinder into the swirling dust fog.

His final check completed, the man stood up and went to the lip of the depression and peered out into the dust storm. At last he seemed satisfied, and hurried back to the yellow cylinder. With an incisive twist of the bevelled release ring he opened the valve on the bottle of hydrogen gas. There was a snakelike hiss, and the nylon balloon began to inflate. The folds of material crackled as they filled. The balloon lifted, eager to be gone, but the man restrained it with difficulty until the balloon was smooth and tight. He let go, and the balloon with its dangling cylinder leapt into the sky, and almost instantly was gone into the dust clouds.

The man stood with his face lifted to the dark furnace-red sky. His goggles glinted blindly, but his attitude was one of triumph, and when he turned away he walked lightly with the step of a man freshly released from danger.

'One more package,' he promised himself. 'Just one more,

and I'll pull out. Buy that farm on the Olifants River, do a bit of fishing, take a shooting trip every year—'

He was still dreaming when he reached the parked Land-Rover and climbed into the driver's seat. He started the engine, switched on the headlights, and drove slowly down the track towards the settlement.

The sign on the rear of the departing Land-Rover was in white paint so that it showed clearly through the haze of red dust.

'SECURITY PATROL,' it read.

*W*ild *Goose* lay on station, with her diesels throbbing softly, ticking over to hold her head into the wind. Even twenty miles out at sea the wind was searing hot and the occasional splatter of spray on Hugo's face was refreshing.

He stood in the corner of the bridge where he could watch the sea and the helmsman, but he was anxious. *Wild Goose* had been lying on station for fifteen hours now, during ten of which the norther had howled dismally through her rigging.

He was always anxious at the beginning of a pick-up. There was so much that could have gone wrong, anything from a police sweep to a tiny electrical fault in the equipment.

'What time is it, Hansie?' he shouted and the helmsman glanced up at the chronometer above his head.

'Three minutes after six, skipper.'

'Dark in half an hour,' Hugo grunted disgustedly, slitted those pale-lashed eyes into the wind once more, then shrugged and ambled back into the bridge house.

He stopped at the console beside his chart table. Even to an experienced eye the machine was an ordinary 'Fish-Finder', an adaptation of the old wartime anti-submarine device, the ASDIC, to the more prosaic business of plotting the depth and position of the pilchard shoals beneath the surface.

However, this model had undergone a costly and specialized conversion. The Ring had flown an expert out from Japan to do the work.

Now that the set hummed softly, its control panel lit soft green by the internal light, but the sound was neutral, and the circular glass screen was blank.

'You want some coffee, Hansie?' Hugo asked the old coloured man at the wheel. His crew were handpicked, loyal and trusted. They had to be – one loud mouth could blow a multi-million pound business.

'*Ja dankie*, skipper.' The old man creased his weather-battered face in appreciation, and Hugo shouted down the companionway to the galley.

'Cooky, how's it for a pot of coffee?'

But the reply was lost, for at that moment the console came to life dramatically. A row of lights blinked on above the control panel, the muted hum changed to a rapid beep-beep signal, and the screen glowed ghostly green.

'She's up!' Hugo shouted his relief, and ran to the set. His first mate rushed through from his cabin behind the bridge, tucking his shirt into unbuttoned trousers, his face puckered with sleep.

'About bloody time,' he blurted, groggily.

'Take over from Hansie,' Hugo told him, and he settled into the padded seat in front of the ASDIC set.

'Right, bring her round two points to port and open her up.'

The *Wild Goose* swung her head into the sea, and her motion changed from easy swoop and glide to a crabbing butting lunge, and the spray burst over the glass of the bridge.

Sitting before the console Hugo was tracking the flight of the balloon and keeping *Wild Goose* on an interception course.

Driven by the forty-knot norther the balloon crossed the coastline, climbing swiftly to three thousand feet. Hugo manipulated the knob on the console which sent the balloon a command to release gas and maintain altitude. Her response was recorded immediately on the screen.

'Good,' Hugo whispered. 'Good girl.' Then louder. 'Bring her round a bit, Oscar – the balloon is drifting to the south.'

For twenty minutes more they butted through the swells.

'Okay,' Hugo broke the silence. 'I'm going to ditch her.' He twisted the knob clockwise slowly, expelling all the gas from the nylon balloon.

'Ja. That's it. She's down.' He looked out of the window above the set. The dust-laden clouds had brought the night on prematurely. It was dark outside, with a low black ceiling through which no star showed.

Hugo turned his attention back to the set.

'That's it, Oscar. You're right on course. Hold her there.'

Then he glanced across at old Hansie and another younger crewman. They were sitting patiently on the bench against the far bulkhead. Both of them were clad in full oilskins, shiny yellow plastic from head to ankle, with gumboots below that.

'Okay, Hansie,' Hugo nodded. 'You can get up in the bows. We are only a mile or so away now.'

They climbed down on to the wave-swept deck, and Hugo watched them scuttling forward between each green burst of water and crouching in the bows. Both of them ducking each time another swell poured over the top of them, their yellow plastic suits showing clearly in the murky deck lights.

'I'm going to switch her on now,' Hugo warned the helm. 'We should have her on visual.'

'Right.' Oscar peered ahead, and Hugo flicked a switch on the panel, commanding the balloon to turn on her guide light.

Almost immediately there was a shout from Oscar.

'There she is. Dead ahead!'

Hugo jumped up and ran forward. It took a few seconds for his eyes to adjust, then he made out the tiny red firefly of light ahead of them in the vast blackness of sea and sky. It showed for a second then was gone in the trough of the next wave.

'I'll take her.' Hugo replaced Oscar at the wheel. 'You get on the spotlight.'

The beam of the spotlight was a solid white shaft through the darkness. The fluorescent yellow paint of the cylinder glowed in the circle of the spot.

Hugo lay *Wild Goose* upwind of the cylinder, and then allowed her to drift down gently on it. Hansie and his assistant were ready with the twenty-foot boat-hook.

Delicately Hugo manoeuvred down over the bobbing yellow cylinder, and grunted with satisfaction as the boat-hook slipped through the recovery ring and the cylinder was hauled in over the bows.

He watched while the two dripping oilskin-clad figures clambered back up the ladder into the wheelhouse, and laid the cylinder on the chart table.

'Good! Good!' Hugo slapped their backs heartily. 'Now, go and get dry – both of you!' They climbed down the companionway, and Hugo handed the wheel over to Oscar.

'Home!' he instructed him. 'As quick as you like.' And he carried the cylinder through into his cabin.

Sitting at the fold-down table in his cabin, Hugo unscrewed the lower section of the cylinder and took out the plastic container. He opened it and spilled the contents out on the table top.

He whistled softly, and picked up the biggest stone. Although he was no expert he knew instinctively that it was a brilliant of exceptional quality. Even the roughness of its exterior could not mask the fire in its depths.

To him it was worthless, there was nowhere he could market a stone like that. There was no temptation to take it out of the Ring – all it would mean for him was fifteen years at hard labour.

The Ring was based on this mutual reliance, no one part of it could function without all the others – yet each part was self-contained and watertight. Only one man knew all its parts, and nobody knew who that one man was.

From the drawer beside him Hugo took out his tools and set them on the table. He lit the spirit stove and set the pot of paraffin wax in the gimbal above it to heat.

Then he poured the diamonds into a shiny metal can. It was the type of ordinary commercial can used for packing and preserving foodstuffs.

Balancing against the ship's motion, he lifted the pot from the stove, and poured the steaming liquid wax over the diamonds, filling the can to rim level.

The wax cooled and solidified quickly, turning opaque and white. The stones were now incorporated in a cake of wax that would prevent them rattling, and would give the sealed can authentic weight.

Hugo lit a cigarette and crossed the cabin to look out into the wheelhouse. The helmsman winked at him and Hugo smiled.

He went back to the table, the can was cool enough to handle. He placed the circular lid over it, and moved to the portable Jenny bolted to a chest of drawers. Carefully he clinched the lid into place, his eyes squinting at the smoke from the cigarette that dangled from his lips.

Satisfied at last he set the sealed can on the table, while he went to where his jacket hung on the door. From the inside pocket he pulled out a manilla envelope, then from the envelope he drew a printed, colour-screened label. He came back to the bench and meticulously pasted the label around the can. On the label was a highly glamorized artist's conception of a leaping pilchard, making it look like a Scottish salmon.

'Pilchards in Tomato Sauce.' Hugo read the label aloud,

as he leaned back to admire his work. 'A product of South West Africa.' He smiled with satisfaction and began packing his equipment away.

'How much?' The foreman of the fish pump called across the narrowing gap between *Wild Goose* and the jetty.

'About fifty tons,' Hugo shouted back. 'Then the norther chased us home.'

'*Ja*. None of the boats stayed out.' The foreman watched his gang secure the mooring ropes, and swing the hose of the vacuum pump over *Wild Goose*'s hold to begin pumping out her pilchards.

'Take over, Oscar.' Hugo picked up his jacket and cap. 'I'll be back tomorrow.' He jumped down on to the jetty and strode down towards the canning factory with its awesome stink of pilchard oil. His jacket was slung over his shoulder, one finger hooked through the tag.

He went down an alley between the boiler rooms and the fish-drying plant, across a wide yard where the bags of fish meal were piled to the height of a double-storey building. He turned in through the double doors of the cavernous warehouse filled to roof height with cardboard cartons, each stencilled with the words:

1 gross cans.	Pilchards in tomato sauce.
Consign to:	Vee Dee Bee Agencies Ltd.
	32, Bermondsey Street,
	London, S.E.1.

He went into the cubicle that served the warehouse storeman as an office.

'Hello, Hugo. Good trip?' The storeman was Hugo's brother-in-law.

'Fifty ton.' Hugo hung his coat casually on the hook behind the door. 'I've got to take a leak,' he said, and went to the latrine across the floor of the warehouse.

He came back, and drank a cup of tea with his brother-in-law. Then he stood and said, 'Jeannie will be waiting.'

'Give her my love.'

'She don't need yours. She's going to get plenty of mine!' Hugo winked, and took his coat from the hook. It was lighter now, the can was gone from the pocket.

He went through the main gates of the harbour, exchanging a casual greeting with the customs officer, and went to the battered early model convertible in the car park.

He kissed the girl at the driving-wheel, threw his coat on the back seat and climbed in over the door.

'You drive,' he told her, grinning. 'I want both hands free.'

She squeaked and pulled his hand out of her skirts.

'Can't you wait till we get home?'

'I've been at sea for five days and I'm hungry as hell.'

'You're a caution, you are.' She laughed at him and started the car.

This was Sergio Caporetti, the man Johnny had chosen to captain *Kingfisher*. He was a round man, the same shape as a snowman. He filled the doorway of Johnny's office, and his great belly bulging into the room ahead of him. His face was round also, like a baby's – but the beautiful dark Italian eyes fringed with thick lashes like a girl's.

'Come in, Sergio,' Johnny greeted him. 'Nice to see you.'

The Italian crossed the room deceptively quickly, and Johnny's hand was completely engulfed by the enormous hairy paw.

'So, at last we are ready,' Sergio grunted. 'Three months

I sit on bum – do nothing. Look at me – ' He slapped his belly with a sound like a pistol shot. ' – fat! No good.'

'Well, not quite ready.' Johnny qualified the statement. He was flying Sergio and his crew over to England well ahead of time. He wanted the big Italian to have plenty of opportunity to study and get to know the revolutionary new equipment with which *Kingfisher* was fitted. Then when the vessel was ready for sea, Sergio would sail her out to Africa.

'Sit down, Sergio. Let's go over the crew list—'

When Sergio left an hour later, Johnny went as far as the lift with him.

'If you have any problems phone me, Sergio.'

'*Si.*' Sergio shook hands. 'Don't worry – Caporetti is in charge. All is well.'

On his way back Johnny stopped at the reception desk.

'Is Mrs Hartford in today?' he asked one of the little receptionists, and both of them replied in chorus like Tweedledum and Tweedledee.

'No, Mr Lance.'

'Has she phoned to say where she is?'

'No, Mr Lance.'

Tracey had disappeared. Five days now there had been no sign of her, her new office was deserted and unused. Johnny was worried and angry. He was worried that she had gone on another binge, and he was angry because he missed her.

He was scowling ferociously as he went back into his office.

'Goodness me.' Lettie Pienaar stood beside his desk with a batch of mail in her hand. 'We do look happy. Here's something to cheer you.'

She handed him a postcard with a colour picture of the Eiffel Tower. It was the first word from Ruby since she had left. Johnny read it quickly.

'Paris – ' he said, ' – is fun, it seems.' He tossed the card on to the desk and plunged back into the day's work.

He worked late, stopped at a steakhouse to eat, then drove back to the silent house in Bishopscourt.

The crunch of tyres on the gravel drive and headlights flashing across the bedroom wall woke him. He sat up in bed as the front-doorbell began a series of urgent peals and he switched on the bedside light. Two o'clock – Christ!

He pulled a dressing-gown over his nudity and tottered down the passage, switching on lights as he went. The doorbell kept ringing.

He turned the front door key. The door flew open and Tracey came in like a strong wind, clutching a briefcase to her chest.

'Where the hell have you been?' Johnny was suddenly fully awake, angry and relieved.

'Johnny! Johnny!' She was dancing with excitement, incoherent, her cheeks flaming and eyes shining. 'I've got them – at least, it, both of them.'

'Where have you been?' Johnny was not to be so easily sidetracked, and with an obvious effort Tracey brought her excitement under control, but she was still smiling and gave the impression of humming like an electric motor.

'Come.' She took his hand and dragged him into the lounge. 'Get yourself a large whisky and sit down,' she ordered, imperious as a queen.

'I don't want a whisky, and I don't—'

'You'll need one,' she interrupted, and went to the open liquor cabinet, poured a massive whisky into a crystal glass, squirted soda into it, and brought it back to Johnny.

'Tracey, what the hell is going on?'

'Please, Johnny. It's so wonderful, don't spoil it for me. Just sit there, please!'

Johnny sank reluctantly into the chair, and Tracey

slipped the catch on her briefcase and drew out a sheaf of documents. She stood in the centre of the floor, and took up the pose of a Victorian actress.

'This – ' she explained, ' – is a translation from the original German of a proclamation by Governor in Council dated 3rd May 1899 and issued at Windhoek. I will leave out the preamble and go straight to the meat.'

She cleared her throat and began reading:

'In consideration of the sum of 10,000 marks which is hereby paid and received, the rights to mine, win, recover, collect or carry away all metals, whether base or precious, stones whether base, semi-precious or precious, minerals, guano, vegetation and other substances organic or in-organic for a period of Nine Hundred and Ninety-Nine years is granted to Messrs Farben, Hendryck and Mosenthal S.A., Guano Merchants of 14 Bergenstrasse, Windhoek, in respect of a circular area ten kilometres in radius whose centre shall be a point situated at the highest elevation of the island lying on latitude 23° 15' South and longitude 15° 12' East.'

Tracey paused and looked at Johnny. He was frozen, stony-faced, staring at her with all his attention. She went on quickly, gabbling it out.

'All the old German mineral concessions and rights were ratified by the Union Parliament when the Union of South Africa took over the mandate after the Great War.'

He nodded, unable to speak. Tracey's smile kept breaking out.

'That concession still has all the force of law behind it. The grant of any subsequent rights is invalid, and although the original grant was mainly for the recovery of guano – yet it covers precious stones also.'

Again Johnny nodded, and Tracey put the document at the bottom of the sheaf of papers in her hand.

'The concession Company, Farben, Hendryck and

Mosenthal S.A., is still in existence. The Company's only remaining asset, apart from any long-forgotten concessions, is an old building at 14 Bergenstrasse, Windhoek.'

Tracey seemed to change the subject suddenly.

'You asked me where I have been, Johnny. Well I've been to Windhoek, and over most of the worst roads in South West Africa.

'The Farben, Hendryck and Mosenthal Company is owned by the brothers Hendryck, a couple of Karakul fur farmers. They are a pair of horrible old men, and when I saw them slitting the throats of those poor little Persian lambs just to prevent the fur uncurling, well—' Tracey paused, and gulped. 'Well, I didn't explain to them about the concession. I just offered to buy the Company, and they asked twenty thousand and I said "sign", and they signed and I left them chuckling with glee. They thought they'd been terribly clever. There! It's all yours!'

Tracey handed the Agreement to Johnny and while he read it she went on.

'I made the Agreement in the name of Van Der Byl Diamonds, I signed it as a Director – I hope you don't mind.'

'Christ!' Johnny took a long deep swallow of whisky, then set the glass down and stood up.

'Mind?' he repeated. 'You bring me the concession to Thunderbolt and Suicide – and ask me if I mind.'

He reached for her and eagerly she went to him.

'Tracey, you're wonderful.' They hugged each other ecstatically, and Johnny swung her off her feet. Without either of them planning it they were suddenly lying, still in each other's arms, on the couch. Then they were kissing, and the laughter dwindled into small murmurs and incoherent sounds.

Tracey pulled away from him at last, and slipped off the couch. She stood in the centre of the floor. Her breathing was ragged. Her hair was a dark tangle.

'Whoa! That's enough.'

'Tracey.' He started up from the couch, wild for her, but she held him at the full stretch of her arms, her hands flat on his chest, backing away in front of him.

'No, Johnny, no!' She shook her head urgently. 'Listen to me.'

He stopped. The wild look faded from his eyes.

'Look, Johnny, God knows I'm no saint, but – well, I don't want us to – well, not on a couch in some other woman's house. That's not how I want it to be.'

Benedict eased the big honey-coloured Bentley out of the traffic stream that clogged Bermondsey Street and turned into the gates of the warehouse. He parked beside the loading bay and climbed out.

As he pulled off his gloves, he glanced along the bank. Mountains of goods were stacked ready for distribution. Cases of Cape wine and spirits, canned fruit in brown cartons, canned fish, forty-gallon drums of fish oil, bundles of raw hides stiff as boards, and cases of indefinable goods – all of it the produce of Southern Africa.

Vee Dee Bee Agencies had grown out of all recognition in the ten years since Benedict had launched it.

Benedict climbed the steps to the bank three at a time, and strode down between the towering stacks of goods that reached up into the murk of the high ceiling. He walked with the assurance of a man on his own ground, the skirts of his overcoat swirling about his knees, broad-shouldered and tall. The storemen and porters greeted him deferentially as he passed, and when he entered the main office there was a stirring and whispering among the ranks of typists as though a wind had blown through a forest.

The Managing Director hurried out of his office to greet Benedict and usher him in.

'How are you, Mr van der Byl? There's tea coming now.'
And he stood behind Benedict to take his coat.

The meeting lasted half an hour, Benedict reading
through the weekly sales and cost reports, querying an item
here, remarking on a figure with pleasure or displeasure as it
deserved. Many people watching him work would have been
startled. This was not the indolent playboy they thought
they knew, this was a hard-eyed businessman coldly and
unemotionally milking the maximum profit from his
enterprise.

There would have been others who wondered where
Benedict had found the capital to finance a business of this
magnitude, especially if they had known that he owned the
premises, and that Vee Dee Bee Agencies was by no means
his only stake in the world of business. He had not received
money from his father – the Old Man had not believed
Benedict capable of successfully negotiating the purchase of
a pound of butter.

The meeting ended, and Benedict stood up and shrugged
on his overcoat, while his Managing Director went to the
grey steel safe in the corner, tumbled the combination and
swung the heavy door open.

'The shipment arrived yesterday,' he explained as he
reached into the safe and brought out the can. 'On the SS
Loch Elsinore from Walvis Bay.'

He handed the can to Benedict, who examined it briefly,
smiling a little at the painting of the leaping fish and the
lettering 'Pilchards in Tomato Sauce'.

'Thank you.' He slipped the can into his briefcase, and
the Managing Director walked with him back to the
Bentley.

B enedict left the Bentley in a garage in Broadwick Street, and walked through the jostle of Soho until he reached the grimy brick building behind the square. He pressed the bell opposite the card that read Aaron Cohen, Manufacturing Jeweller, and when the door opened he climbed the stairs to the top and fourth floor. Again he rang, and after a while an eye peeped at him through the peephole – but the door opened almost immediately.

'Hello, Mr van der Byl. Come in! Come in!' The young doorman welcomed him in and locked the door behind him. 'Papa is expecting you!' he went on as they both looked up at the eye of the closed-circuit TV camera above the wrought-iron grille that barred the passage.

Whoever was viewing the screen was satisfied, for there was an electrical buzz and the grille swung open. The doorman led Benedict down the passage.

'You know the way. Papa is in his office.'

Benedict was in a shabby little reception room, with a threadbare carpet and a pair of chairs that looked like Ministry of Works rejects. He turned to the right-hand door and went through it into a long room that clearly occupied most of the top floor of the building.

Along one side of the room ran a narrow bench, to which were bolted twenty small lathes. Each machine ran off a belt from a central drive below the bench. The man tending the machines wore a white dust jacket, and he grinned at Benedict. 'Hello, Mr van der Byl, Papa is expecting you.' But Benedict delayed a moment to watch the operation of the saws. In the jaws of each lathe was set a diamond, and spinning against the diamond was a circular blade of phosphor bronze. As Benedict watched, the man turned back to the task of spreading a fine paste of olive oil and diamond dust on to the cutting edge of each blade – for it was not the bronze that cut. Only a diamond will cut a diamond.

'Some nice stones, Larry,' Benedict remarked, and Larry Cohen nodded.

'All of them between four and five carats.'

Benedict leaned close and examined one of the diamonds. The line of the cut was marked with Indian ink on the stone. Benedict knew what heart-searching and discussion, what examination and drawing upon the rich storehouses of experience had preceded the positioning of that ink line. It might take two days to saw through each diamond, so Benedict left the bench and moved on.

In a row down the other side of the room sat the other Cohen brothers. Eight of them. Old Aaron was a great breeder of boys. They ranged in age from nearly forty to nineteen years and there were a couple who were still in school and hadn't yet come into the business.

'How do you like this one, Mr van der Byl?' Michael Cohen looked up as Benedict approached. Michael was shaping a fine diamond, cutting it into a round using a lesser stone as a blade. A small tray beneath the lathe caught the dust from the two stones. This dust would be used later for sawing and polishing.

'A beauty,' said Benedict. These men were of the brotherhood, working with diamonds all their lives and loving them as other men loved women or horses and fine paintings.

He moved on down the room, greeting each of the brothers, stopping to watch for a minute the loving care with which the elder boys, master craftsmen each of them, were cutting the precisely angled facets that make up the perfect round brilliant. The fifty-eight facets – table, stars, pavilions and the others which endow a cut stone with its mystic 'life' and 'fire'.

Leaving them crouched over their wheels, so similar to those of a potter, he went through the door at the end of the room.

'Benedict, my friend.' Aaron Cohen came from his desk

to embrace him. He was a tall thin man in his late sixties with a thick silver-grey mane of hair, round-shouldered from years of crouching over a diamond wheel. 'I did not know you were in London, they told me you were in Cape Town. Yesterday was Ruby's birthday. If we had known—'

Benedict took the envelope from his pocket and shook twenty-seven diamonds on to the blotter of the desk.

'What do you think of those, Papa?'

'*Shu! Shu!*' Papa patted his own cheeks with delight, and he reached instinctively for the biggest stone.

'I should live to see such a stone!' He screwed a jeweller's *loupe* into his eye, turning to catch the natural light from the high windows, and scrutinized the diamond through the eyepiece.

'Ah, yes. There is a feather*, but small. V.V.S.I.† But we will cut through it. Yes, we will take two gems from this stone. Two perfect diamonds of ten or twelve carats each, and perhaps five smaller ones.' More than half a diamond's bulk is lost in the cutting.

'Yes! Yes! From this stone we will sell a hundred thousand pounds' worth of polished diamonds!'

Aaron crossed to the door. 'Boys! Come see! I will show you a prince among diamonds.' And his sons crowded into the office. Michael took it first and gave his opinion. 'A good stone, yes. But not of the same water as the stone we had in the last batch. You remember that octahedron crystal—'

'What you talking!' his father interrupted. 'You wouldn't know a diamond from a piece of gorgonzola cheese already!'

'He is right, Papa.' Larry joined in the discussion. 'The other stone was better.'

'So the Big Lover argues with his father! Little shiksas with skirts up around their tochis you know all about.

* Semi-transparent veinlike flaw.
† Very very slight imperfection.

98

Dancing the Watsui and the Cha-Cha. Yes! But diamonds you know from nothing.' This declaration precipitated a full-scale, family argument in which each of the brothers joined with gusto.

'Shuddup! Shuddup! Back to work all of you! Out! Out!' Aaron broke up the meeting, driving his sons from the office and slamming the door behind them.

'*Shu!*' He looked to heaven. 'What a business! Now we can weigh the stones.'

When they had weighed and tallied the stones, and Aaron had locked them into the safe, Benedict told him:

'I am thinking of breaking up the Ring.'

Aaron froze and looked across the desk at Benedict. Between them there was always the pretence that their relationship was legitimate. They never spoke about the Ring, or where the unregistered stones came from, or how the finished gems were sent to Switzerland.

'Why?' Aaron asked carefully.

'I am a rich man now. With my father's money, and what I have made from the Ring and invested. A very rich man. I no longer need to take the risks.'

'Such problems I wish I had. But perhaps you are wise – I would not think to argue with you.'

'There will be one or two more packages. Then it will be finished.'

Aaron nodded. 'I understand,' he said. 'Like all good things it must end.'

It was a little after noon when Benedict parked the Bentley outside the mews flat off Belgrave Square. He went to shower immediately he was home. In all the years he had lived here he had never grown accustomed to London's grime-laden atmosphere, and he bathed or showered at least three times a day.

He sang in the shower, and then enveloped in a huge bath towel he left a string of damp footprints through to the lounge where he mixed a Martini, and screwed up his eyes at the first stinging taste of the drink.

The phone rang.

'Van der Byl,' he said into the mouthpiece, and then his expression changed as he listened. Quickly he put down the glass and used both hands to hold the telephone receiver.

'What on earth are you doing here?' His tone of astonishment was not faked.

'What a wonderful surprise. When can I see you? How about right now – for lunch? That's great! No, nothing I can't put off – this is a pretty special occasion, you know. Where are you staying? The Lancaster. Fine. Look, give me forty-five minutes, and I'll meet you in the Looking-Glass Room on the top floor. Yes, ten past one. God, what a delightful – I've said that already. See you in three-quarters of an hour.'

He replaced the receiver, swallowed the remains of his Martini and headed for his bedroom suite. This would make a good day into a truly remarkable one, he thought, as he quickly selected a silk shirt. He looked at his reflection in the mirror and grinned.

'The ball has really started bouncing your way, Benedict,' he whispered.

She was not at the bar, nor in the Looking-Glass Room. Benedict crossed to the tall picture windows for a glimpse of one of London's finest views across Hyde Park and the Serpentine. It was a smoky blue day, and the pale sun added bronze to the autumn shades of gold and red in the park.

He turned from the windows, and she was crossing the room towards him. His stomach swooped with delight for she also was pale gold with the coppery sheen of sun on her long legs and bare arms. The grace of her carriage was as he remembered it, the precise lifting and laying down of narrow feet on the thick pile of the carpet.

He stood quite still, letting her come to him. Heads turned all across the room, for she was a splendid golden creature. Benedict knew suddenly and clearly that he wanted this woman for himself.

'Hello, Benedict,' she said, and he stepped forward to take her hand in both of his.

'Ruby Lance!' He squeezed her long fingers gently. 'It's so good to see you again.'

The use of her surname was the clue to the strength of his reaction. She belonged to the one man in the world that Benedict most envied and hated. For this reason she was infinitely desirable.

'Let us celebrate with a little drink. I think the occasion deserves at the very least a champagne cocktail.'

She sat with those long slim legs neatly crossed, leaning back in her chair, holding the stemmed glass with tapering fingers. Her hair hung straight to her shoulders, like some rare silken tapestry in white gold, and her eyes watched him with a catlike candour, a calm feline intentness that seemed to look into his soul.

'I should not have bothered you,' she said. 'But I know so few people here.'

'How long can you stay?' He brushed aside the disclaimer. 'I must cancel my other arrangements.'

'A week.' She made it sound like an offer that was subject to negotiation.

'Oh, no!' His voice was mock distressed. 'You can do better than that – we won't be able to do half what I had planned in so short a time. You can stay longer, surely?'

'Perhaps,' she agreed, and lifted the glass an inch. 'It's good to see you.'

'And you.' Benedict agreed with emphasis. They sipped the sparkling wine watching each other's eyes.

Where others must wait weeks and months Benedict went in immediately as though it were his right. A smile and a murmured word, and theatre tickets were his or the doors of fashionable restaurants opened magically.

That first night he took her to the National Theatre, then for dinner at Le Coeur de France where a very famous movie actor stopped at their table.

'Hello, Benedict. We are all going on to the yacht later for a bit of a party. Join us, won't you?' And those legendary eyes turned to Ruby. 'And bring your beautiful friend with you.'

They ate breakfast under the awning on the after-deck of the yacht, eggs and bacon and Veuve Clicquot champagne, and watched the hubbub of dawn traffic on the wondrously smelly old Thames. Ruby was the only girl in the party without a fur to cheat the chill of the river dawn. Benedict made a mental note of the fact.

On the way home she sat with those long legs curled under her in the seat of the Bentley, still sleek and golden despite the night's exertions, but with the lightest touch of blue beneath her eyes.

'I can't remember having enjoyed an evening so much, Benedict.' She patted a tiny pink-lipped yawn. 'You're a wonderful companion.'

'Tonight again?' he asked.

'Yes, please,' she murmured.

She sensed an urgency in him, when she came down into the lobby of the Lancaster that evening. He came quickly to meet her as she stepped out of the lift, and the quiet assurance with which he kissed her cheek and took her arm surprised her.

They were silent as he snaked the Bentley through the

evening traffic. Ruby realized that at the tips of her long tapered fingers, within touching distance, was a fortune such as she had never before allowed herself to dream about. She was deadly afraid. A wrong move, even a wrong word might drive that fortune beyond her grasp for ever. She would never have a chance like this again, and she was afraid to move, almost paralysed with fear. The decision she knew she would have to make very soon would be fateful. Must she encounter his advance with withdrawal, or must she meet it as frankly as it was made.

She was so deeply involved with her thoughts that when the Bentley came to a standstill she looked up with surprise. They were parked in a mews outside an expensive-looking flat.

Benedict came round and opened her door, and led her without protest into the flat.

She looked about her curiously, recognizing some of the art works on display in the entrance hall. Benedict took her through into the long lounge and settled her solicitously into the tapestry-covered chair which dominated the room like a throne, and suddenly her fear was gone. She felt queenlike in her control. She knew with certainty that this would all be hers.

Benedict stood in the centre of the room, almost a petitioner in his attitude, and he began to speak. She listened quietly, her expression showing no hint of the triumphant surge of her spirits, and when he stopped to wait for her reply she did not hesitate.

'Yes,' she said.

'I will be with you when you tell him,' Benedict promised.

'It won't be necessary,' Ruby assured him. 'I can handle Johnny Lance.'

'No.' Swiftly Benedict crossed to her chair and took her hands, drawing her to her feet. 'I must be there with you. Promise me that.'

103

Then it became suddenly evident to Ruby that the strength of her position was unassailable. Benedict needed her not for any physical reasons – but merely because she belonged to Johnny Lance.

Looking steadily into Benedict's eyes she determined to test her intuition.

'He does not have to know about you,' she said. 'I could arrange a divorce with him.'

'He *must* know about me. That's what I want, don't you see?'

'Yes, I see.' She was secure.

'It is agreed?' He could barely conceal his anxiety.

'Yes,' she nodded. 'It's agreed.' And they smiled at each other – each completely satisfied.

'Come.' He led her almost reverently into his bedroom, and Ruby stopped in the doorway with a little cry of delight.

The double bed was a mountain of glowing fur in a score of shades ranging from soft pinkish cream, through beige and oyster, pale smoky blue to midnight and jet glossy black.

'Choose one!' he ordered her. 'To seal our bargain.'

She moved like a sleepwalker towards the bed, but as she reached the centre of the Khedive carpet Benedict called out softly.

'Wait.'

She stopped obediently and he came up behind her. She felt his hands on the back of her neck, and she lowered her chin, shaking her hair forward so that he could unhook the clasp and draw down the fastening of her dress.

She stepped out of the dress as it dropped around her ankles, then waited passively as he carefully removed her brassiere.

'Now,' he said. 'Try them on.'

In her stockings and high-heeled shoes she went to the bed, subtly emphasizing the lilt of her movements, and took up the first fur.

Benedict was sprawled in the wing-back chair across the room as she glanced back at him. His face was gloating and flushed, so that his features seemed swollen and coarsened as he stared at her. She understood now that this was a form of ritual in which they were engaged. Like a victorious Roman general, Benedict was conducting his own personal triumph, reviewing the spoils and the plunder. It had no basis in sexual or physical desire, but was rather a service of worship to Benedict himself. She was the priestess of this rite.

Yet, knowing this, Ruby felt no resentment. Rather, she found herself excited by the cold perversity of the pageant. As she paraded and postured, turned and swirled and flared the skirts of a wild mink, she was very conscious of his eyes upon her body. She knew it was perfect, and his scrutiny stirred her physically for the first time in her life. She felt her blood quicken and pound, felt her heart flutter within its cage of ribs like a captive bird, and her loins tighten like a clenching first. For her also the ritual was narcissistic – satisfying her own deep emotional need.

As she discarded each of the coats she dropped it in the centre of the floor, until there was a knee-high pile of precious fur.

At last she faced him, hugging the soft creamy cloud tightly about her body. Then she opened her arms, and the coat also, standing on tip-toe to tighten and highlight the hard muscle in her legs and flanks.

'This one,' she whispered, and he came out of the chair, picked her up in his arms and laid her, still wrapped in mink, on the great pile of furs.

Ruby woke in the double bed to a feeling of excitement and enormous well-being such as she had not experienced since she was a schoolgirl on the first morning of a holiday.

The morning was far advanced, pale sunshine in a square shaft poured through the open window like a stage effect.

Benedict in a yellow silk dressing-gown stood beside the bed watching her with an unfathomable expression which changed immediately he realized that she was awake.

'My man has collected your luggage from the Lancaster. Your toilet things are in the bathroom, your clothing in the dressing-room.'

He sat down carefully on the edge of the bed, and leaned forward to kiss her forehead and then each cheek.

'We will breakfast when you are ready.' He sat back and watched her eyes; clearly he was waiting for her to say something important. Immediately she was on guard, wary of making a mistake, seeking a clue in his expression.

'Last night,' he asked. 'Was it as good for you, as it was for me?'

Understanding washed over her in a warm wave. He wanted assurance, a comparison between himself and Johnny Lance.

'I have never in my life – ' She placed the emphasis carefully. ' – experienced anything like it.'

He nodded, relieved, pleased – and stood up.

'After breakfast we will go to town.'

This morning, Edmund, Benedict's man, chauffeured the Bentley. When they alighted at the north end of Bond Street and walked arm in arm along the pavement, Edmund tailed them at a dignified crawl, steadfastly ignoring the abuse of other drivers.

The morning was cool enough for Ruby to wear her new cream mink, and the looks of admiration and envy she drew from the other strollers delighted Benedict. He wanted to impress her, he wanted to flaunt his wealth.

'The wife of a diamond man must have diamonds.' He spoke on impulse as they came up to an expensive-looking jewellers. Ruby squeezed his arm and turned to look into the window.

'Good Lord,' Benedict laughed. 'Not here!' And Ruby looked at him with surprise.

Mockingly Benedict began reading the signs in the window.

'"Paradise Jewellers. A large selection of blue-white gems. Certificate of flawlessness with every diamond. Perfect flawless stones at bargain prices as advertised on T.V. and in the national Press. Small deposit secures your ring now. A diamond is forever – show her you really care."'

'But they are such a well-known firm. They have branches all over the world – even in South Africa!' Ruby protested, and bridled a little as Benedict smiled patronizingly.

'Let me explain about diamonds. They are bought for two reasons by two different types of people. Firstly by rich men as investments that will not erode and can only increase in value. These men buy notable stones on the advice of experts, the best of the gem diamond production goes to them. So when Richard Burton buys Liz a £300,000 diamond he is not being extravagant – on the contrary he is being ultra-conservative and thrifty with his money.'

'That's the kind of meanness I like,' Ruby laughed, and Benedict smiled at her honesty.

'You may find me as thrifty,' he promised.

'Go on,' she said, 'tell me more about diamonds.'

'Well, there is another type who buys diamonds. Usually just one in his life, luckily for him – and he very seldom tries to resell it again or he would get a nasty shock. This type is Joe Everybody – who wants to get married. He usually goes to somebody like Paradise Jewellers.' Benedict poked a derisive finger at the sign in the window. 'Because he has seen it on telly and he can get a ring on the instalment plan. In many cases the deposit covers the dealer for the cost of the stone – the rest goes on advertising, finance charges and, of course, profit.'

'How do you know Paradise Jewellers are that type?' Ruby's attention was wide-eyed and girlish.

'You recognize them firstly by the big advertising splurge, then by their language.' Again he studied the notices in the window. '"A large selection of blue-white gems" – of every thousand stones of jewellery quality produced only one is fine enough in colour to be termed blue-white. It is unlikely they have a large selection. "Gem" is a special term reserved for a diamond which is in every way superb. "Flawless stones at bargain prices" – the lack of flaws in a diamond is only one of many factors governing its value. As for bargain prices – there ain't no such animal. Prices are maintained at the lowest level by fierce competition among expert and canny dealers, and there are no "sales" or special prices for anyone.'

'But where should a person buy a diamond?' Ruby was impressed and dismayed despite herself.

'Not here.' Benedict chuckled. 'Come, I will show you.' And before she could protest he had taken her arm and swept her into the shop, to be greeted with enthusiasm by the manager who must have noticed Ruby's mink and the attendant Bentley, which was causing a small traffic jam outside the shop.

'Good morning, madam and sir. May I be of service to you?'

'Yes,' Benedict turned to Ruby, as they settled down in the manager's office with a tray of diamond rings in front of them. 'You cannot examine a diamond properly in its setting.'

He selected the biggest diamond, took from his pocket a

gold-plated penknife fitted with a special tool and prised open the claws of the setting to a chorus of horrified squeals from the staff.

'I will make good any damage,' he snapped, and they subsided as Benedict took the loose stone and laid it on the velvet-covered tray.

'Firstly, size. This stone is about one carat.' He looked for confirmation to the manager who nodded. 'Let us say the value of this stone is £500. Ten similar stones will be worth £5,000, right? However, a ten-carat stone may be worth as much as £75,000. So the price per carat rises sharply as the total weight of the stone increases. If I were investing I would not touch a stone under three carats.'

The staff were listening now with as much attention as Ruby.

'Next, colour,' said Benedict, and glanced at the manager. 'A sheet of clean white paper, please.'

The manager scratched in his drawer and laid a sheet of paper in front of Benedict who placed the stone upon it, bottom upwards.

'We compare the colour it "draws" from white paper in good natural light.' He looked up at the manager. 'Switch off the fluorescent lights, and open those curtains, please.'

The manager obeyed with alacrity.

'This is a matter of experience. The colour is judged by a standard. We forget about the fancy rare colours like blue and red and green, and take our top standard as blue-white. A stone so white as to appear slightly blue, after which the distinctions drop to "fine white", and "white". Then stones which "draw" a yellowish tinge which we call "Cape" – in different shades, then finally stones which "draw" a brown colour – which will reduce the value of a stone by up to eighty per cent.'

Benedict fished in his fob pocket and pulled out a guinea case which he opened.

'Every expert carries a special diamond which he uses as

a gauge for colour by which to judge all other stones. This is mine.'

The staff exchanged apprehensive looks as Benedict placed a small diamond beside the other. He studied them a moment then replaced his gauge in the case.

'Second Silver Cape, I'd say,' he grunted, and the staff looked suitably abashed. 'Now we consider the stone's perfection.' He looked at the manager. 'Please lend me your *loupe.*'

'*Loupe?*' The manager was mystified.

'Yes, your jeweller's glass.'

'I—' the manager was deeply embarrassed.

'You sell diamonds – yet you do not own a *loupe.*' Benedict shook his head in disapproval. 'No matter, I have my own.'

Benedict took the glass from his inner pocket and placed it in his eye.

'Imperfections can be almost negligible – a "natural" at the girdle, or a bubble or pinpoint of carbon in the stone, on the other hand they can be gross "cracks", "clouds", "ice", or "feathers" which will ruin the value of the stone. But this one is flawless – so when the certificate of flawlessness is issued there will be no misrepresentation.' Benedict closed the glass and tucked it back into his pocket. 'However, in order to produce a flawless stone, the cut has been squeezed.'

He held up the stone between thumb and forefinger.

'The cut or "make" of a stone is the fourth and final decider of its value. The "make" should conform closely to the "ideal". This stone has been cut to exclude a flaw, and in consequence it is badly proportioned – heavy and out of round. I would prefer to see a graceful stone which includes a slight imperfection rather than a grotesque little cripple like this.'

He put the diamond down on the desk.

'The asking price by Paradise Jewellers for this stone is

£500 – which would be fair and correct for a gem. However, the colour is poor and although it is flawless it is of ungainly make. Its true value would be about – ah, let's see – £185 approximately.'

There was another chorus of protest from the assembled staff, led by the manager.

'I assure you, sir, that all our stones have been most carefully appraised.'

'How long have you been with Paradise Jewellers?' Benedict demanded brusquely. 'Four months, isn't it?'

The manager gaped at him.

'Before that you were a salesman in the showroom of a large firm of embalmers and undertakers.'

'I, well – I mean.' The manager fluttered his hands weakly. 'How did you know that?'

'I like to know about all my employees.'

'Employees?' The manager looked stunned.

'That's correct. My name is Benedict van der Byl. I own Paradise Jewellers.'

Ruby clapped her hands and cooed her applause.

'What a bundle of surprises you are!' she exclaimed.

Benedict smiled in acknowledgement and inclined his head.

'Now,' he said, as he rose and helped Ruby to her feet. 'We will go and buy some real diamonds.'

Aaron Cohen sold them two fine white twin marquise-cut brilliants, and Ruby chose the mounting for a pair of white-gold earrings from a leather-bound catalogue.

Benedict gave Aaron his cheque for twenty thousand pounds, then turned to Ruby.

'Now,' he said. 'We'll have lunch at the Celeste Grill-room. The food is bloody awful – but the decor is stupendous. We had best phone and reserve a table – it isn't really necessary but they get terribly hurt if you don't.'

As they settled back in the lush upholstery of the Bentley, Benedict instructed the chauffeur.

'Go past Trafalgar Square, Edmund. I want to pick up the newspapers from South Africa House.'

Edmund double-parked outside the Ambassador's entrance, and the doorman recognized the car and hurried inside to fetch the bundle of newspapers.

As they pulled away around the square towards Haymarket, Benedict selected a copy of the *Cape Argus*.

'Let's see what's happened at home.' He glanced at the front page, and stiffened perceptibly.

'What is it?' Ruby leaned towards him anxiously, but he ignored her. His eyes were darting across the page like the shuttle of a loom. She saw the colour fade from his face, leaving it white and intent. He finished reading, and pushed the paper towards her. She spread the page.

'VAN DER BYL DIAMONDS WIN VALUABLE CONCESSION.
APPEAL COURT SUPPORTS KAISER'S MINERAL GRANT.
LANCE GETS THUNDERBOLT AND SUICIDE.
Bloemfontein, Thursday.

'In an urgent application by the Central Diamond Mines Ltd, to prevent Van Der Byl Diamonds Ltd prospecting and mining a concession area off the South West African Coast, Mr Justice Tromp today dismissed the application with costs stating in his judgment: "The original concession granted by German Imperial Decree in 1899, and subsequently ratified by Act of the Union Parliament in Act 24 of the 1920 must hold good in law, and will take precedent over any subsequent grant or concession purporting to have been made by the Minister of Mines to any other party."

'The area in dispute covers 100 square kilometres surrounding two small islands lying some fifteen miles south of Cartridge Bay and five miles offshore. The islands are known as Thunderbolt Island and Suicide Island, and at the turn of the century were the site of considerable exploitation by a German guano company. Mr John Rigby Lance, the General Manager of Van Der Byl Diamond Co. Ltd, acquired the rights to the concession when he took over the inoperative guano company.

'In Cape Town today Mr Lance stated: "It's the opportunity I have waited for all my life. All indications are that Thunderbolt and Suicide will prove to be one of the richest marine diamond fields in the world."

'Van Der Byl Diamond Co. had a diamond-dredging vessel nearing completion in the United Kingdom, and Mr Lance stated that he hoped to begin recovery operations off Thunderbolt and Suicide Islands before the end of the year.'

R uby lowered the paper and looked at Benedict. What she saw was an intense physical shock.

Benedict had crumpled down in the seat. Gone was all the assurance and *savoir faire*. His face was deathly pale, but now his lips trembled and with disgust she saw that his eyes were swimming with tears. He hunched forward over his hands, shaking his head gently and hopelessly.

'The bastard,' he whispered, and his voice was soggy and muffled. 'He does it every time. I thought that I had him at last but – Oh God, I hate him.'

He looked at her, his face soft with self-pity. 'He does it every time. Often I've thought I had him, but he just—'

She was mystified by his reaction.

'Aren't you pleased? Van Der Byl Diamonds will make millions—'

'No! No!' he cut in savagely, and then the years of hatred and frustration and humiliation began pouring out. Ruby listened quietly, slowly beginning to understand it all, marvelling at the accumulation of pain and hatred that he exposed for her. He remembered conversations from twenty years ago. Small childhood episodes, innocent remarks that had festered and rankled for a decade.

'You don't want him to succeed, is that it?' she asked.

'I want to crush him, break him, humiliate him.'

For ten seconds Ruby was silent.

'Well, what are we going to do about it?' she asked flatly.

'Nothing, I suppose.' Benedict's tone irritated her. 'He always comes out on top, you just can't—'

'Nonsense,' Ruby snapped. She was angry now. 'Let's go over it carefully, and see how we can stop him. He is only human, and you have shown me enough to prove you are a brilliant and successful businessman.'

Benedict's expression changed, becoming trusting and animated. He turned to her almost eagerly: he blinked his eyes. 'Do you really believe that?'

The bunk was too narrow, Sergio Caporetti decided, much too narrow. He would have one of the carpenters alter it today.

He lay on his back, wedged in firmly, with the blanket-covered mound of his belly blocking his view southwards. He lay and assessed his physical condition. It was surprisingly good. There was but a small blurred pain behind his eyes and the taste of stale cigars and rank wine in the back of his throat was bearable. The leaden feeling in his lower limbs alarmed him until he realized that he was still wearing his heavy fisherman's boots. He remembered one of the girls complaining about that.

He hoisted himself on one elbow, and looked at the girls. One on each side of him, jamming him solidly into the bunk with magnificent hillocks of pink flesh. Big strong girls both of them, he had chosen them with care, neither of them an ounce under twelve stone. Sergio sighed happily – it had been a wonderful weekend. The girls were snoring, in such harmony that it might have been a rehearsed stage act. He listened to them with mild admiration for a few minutes, then crawled over the outside girl and stood in the centre of the cabin, clad only in his heavy boots. He yawned extravagantly, scratching the thick black wiry curls that covered his chest and belly, and cocked an eye at the bulkhead clock. Four o'clock on a Monday morning, but it had been a truly memorable weekend.

The table was hidden under a forest of empty wine bottles, and dirty plates. There was a congealed mass of cold spaghetti bolognaise in a dish and he picked it up. As he clumped out of the cabin on to *Kingfisher*'s bridge he was scooping up spaghetti with his fingers and cramming it into his mouth.

He stood at the rail of the bridge, a naked hairy figure in tall black boots clutching a dish of spaghetti to his chest, and looked around the dockyard.

Kingfisher was in stocks undergoing the modifications that Johnny Lance had ordered. She was standing high above the level she would attain when she was launched. Although she was a vessel of a mere 3,000-ton displacement, she appeared black and monstrous in the floodlights that illuminated the ship-builders' yard. It was obvious from her unusual silhouette that she was designed for a special purpose. Her superstructure was situated well aft like that of an oil tanker, while her foredeck was crowded by the huge gantry which would control the dredge, and by the massive storage tanks for the compressed air.

At this hour of the morning the shipyard was deserted, and wisps and tendrils of sea mist drifted about *Kingfisher*'s bulk.

Standing fifty feet above the dry dock, still wolfing cold spaghetti, Sergio urinated over the rail – deriving a simple honest pleasure from the long arching stream and the tinkle of liquid striking the concrete far below.

He clumped back into his cabin, and looked down fondly

on his two sleeping Valkyries while he finished the last of the spaghetti. Then he wiped his fingers carefully on his chest hair and called to them gently.

'Come, my kittens, my little doves, the time for play she has passed – the time for work she commences.'

With Latin gallantry he bundled them into a taxi at the dockyard gates, pressing on to each of them a lusty kiss, a banknote, a bottle of Chianti, protestations of deep affection, and the promise of another party next Friday night.

He picked his way back through the dockyard jungle of machinery and buildings, lighting a long black cigar and inhaling smoke pleasurably until he came in sight of *Kingfisher* and halted with surprise and annoyance. There was a big honey-coloured Bentley parked near the gangway that led up to *Kingfisher*'s deck. He resented visits from the Company bosses, especially this one, and especially at this ridiculous hour on a Monday morning.

T he hose spiralled down into greenness, and they followed it down holding hands. Tracey was still a little nervous. This was not like the Mediterranean, a warm blue friendly embrace of waters to welcome the diver – it was the wild Atlantic, coldly menacing, green and untamed. It frightened her, and Johnny's hand gave her comfort.

Their Draeger demand valves repeated their breathing in a singing metallic wheeze, and icy leaks and rivulets kept finding their way into the cuffs and neck of Tracey's rubber suit.

Sixty feet below the surface Johnny paused, and peered into the glass window of her mask. He grinned at her, his mouth distorted by the bulky mouthpiece, and she gave him a thumbs-up sign. They both looked upwards. The surface was silvered like an imperfect mirror, and the black cigar shape of the boat was lapped in strange light. The hose and anchor chain pierced the silver ceiling and hung down into the shady green depths.

Johnny pointed downwards, and she nodded. They put their heads down, pointed their flippers to the surface, and still hand in hand they paddled steadily towards the sea bed.

Tracey was aware of a crackling hissing sound now, and from out of the greeny blackness below them scudded clouds of silver bubbles twisting and writhing towards the surface. She strained her eyes downwards, following the line of the hose, and slowly out of the murk materialized the black rubber-clad forms of the two men working at the end of the hose; they appeared weird and mystical like black priests performing a satanical mass.

She and Johnny reached the sea bed and hung just above it, a little way off from the two men on the hose. Johnny indicated the depth gauge that he wore like a wrist watch. It showed a depth of 120 feet. Then he turned and by a hand signal showed her the direction of the reefs.

They were in a valley between these long peaked underwater ridges of black rocks, the same reefs that Tracey had seen from the air. There was a distinct pull of water as the current drifted at right angles to the direction of the reefs.

Johnny squeezed her hand, and then pulled her down. They lay on their bellies on the floor of the sea, and Johnny scooped a handful of the white sand, washed it quickly so that the smaller particles were carried away in a cloud on the current, then he showed her the coarse gravel which remained. Again he grinned, and she returned his smile.

Still leading her by the hand, he swam slowly towards the two men working on the hose, and stopped to watch them.

Attached to the end of the hose was a rigid steel pipe two inches in diameter, and twenty feet long – although now only half of its length was visible above the sand bottom. The two divers were forcing it down through sand and gravel to reach bedrock. The hose itself was attached to a compressor on the deck of the boat which was generating a vacuum in the hose and sucking up the sand and gravel as the steel pipe was forced downwards.

They were prospecting the Thunderbolt and Suicide field. Taking these two-inch samples at 500-foot intervals to ascertain the depth of water, the thickness of the overburden, and the content of the gravel beds. They were also mapping and plotting the reefs, so that by the time *Kingfisher* arrived they would have a fairly clear picture of the topography and aspect of the field. They would know where to begin dredging, and roughly what to expect when they did.

So far the results had endorsed Johnny's most optimistic expectations. There was a good thick catchment of gravel in all the gullies between the reefs. As he had expected, the heavier gravels had been laid down in the gullies closest to the gap between Thunderbolt and Suicide, and the smaller and lighter gravels had been carried further. In some of the gullies the gravel beds were fifteen feet deep, and the types of stone present were all highly promising. He had isolated garnet, jasper, ironstone, beryl chips and titanium dust.

However, the conclusive and definite proof had also come up through that two-inch hose out of the depths. They had already pulled the first diamonds from the Thunderbolt and Suicide fields. When you considered the odds against finding a stone in a two-inch sample at 500-foot centres and that payable gravel contained one part diamond in fifty million, it was exciting and encouraging that they had already recovered four diamonds. Small stones, to be sure, not one of them more than half a carat, but diamonds for all that, and some of them of excellent quality.

One of the men on the hose turned and gave Johnny a flat-handed cut-out sign. The pipe was on bedrock. Johnny nodded and jerked a thumb upwards, and drawing Tracey with him, started for the surface.

They climbed the ladder over the survey boat's counter, moving clumsily under the weight of the air bottles strapped to their backs, but there were willing hands to help them aboard and strip off the heavy equipment, and unzip the clinging rubber suits.

Tracey accepted a towel gratefully from one of the crew, and while she tilted her head to dry her sodden mane of hair, she looked across half a mile of green sea to the two white whale-backed islands with their attendant clouds of seabirds. The wave bursts on the cliffs sounded like distant artillery, or far thunder.

'God, this is a wild and exciting place.' Her voice bubbled with excitement as she scrubbed at her hair. 'It makes one come alive.'

Johnny understood her feelings, it was the forbidding restless sea and the harsh land that promised danger and adventure. He was about to reply, but the two hose men came aboard at that moment, the taller of them spitting out his mouthpiece and letting it fall to his chest.

'We'll move up to the next point, if it's okay by you, Mr Lance?' The man pulled off his mask and hood, exposing white-blond hair and a sun-broiled face.

'Fine, Hugo,' Johnny agreed, and watched approvingly as Hugo Kramer gave the orders to get the anchor and the hose up before taking *Wild Goose* seawards to her next prospecting point. Johnny had been reluctant to charter *Wild Goose* as the prospecting vessel and as the service boat for *Kingfisher*. He did not know Hugo Kramer, and Benedict van der Byl's insistence on the man had made him suspicious.

However, it was natural that they should use a skipper from the van der Byl fleet and Johnny was now prepared to admit he had been wrong. Kramer was an intelligent and willing worker, resourceful and trustworthy, a fine seaman who handled *Wild Goose* with all the skill it would need to bring her alongside *Kingfisher* in a heavy sea. His unfortunate physical appearance Johnny hardly noticed any more, although the original shock of that pink face, white hair and those blind-looking eyes had been considerable.

Tracey was not so charitable. The man made her uneasy. There was a wild-animal ferocity about him, a barely controlled violence. The way he looked at her sometimes made her skin prickle. He did it now; turning back from issuing his orders he ran his eyes over her body. In the black silk costume her good round breasts showed at their best, and Hugo Kramer looked at them with those white-fringed bland eyes. Instinctively she covered them with the towel, and it seemed as though his lips twitched with amusement as he turned to Johnny.

'They tell me this dredger of yours is something special, Mr Lance?'

'She is, Hugo. Not like the other half-baked barges and bastardized conversions that have been tried by other companies. She's the first diamond recovery vessel designed expressly for the job.'

'What's different about her?'

'Nearly everything. Her hose is operated off a gantry on the foredeck, it goes out through a well pierced through her hull.'

'What kind of hose?'

'Eighteen-inch armoured woven steel with rubber liner. We can get it down to a hundred fathoms, and it has a compensating section in it to stop it plunging with the wave action of the hull.'

'Eighteen inches is pretty big. How will you build up vacuum?'

'That's the point, Hugo. We don't suck – we blow! We evacuate water from the hose by purging it with compressed air, the inrush of water into the opening of the hose sucks in the gravel.'

'Hey, that's neat. So the deeper you work the more effective it will be!'

'Right.'

'What about the actual recovery? Are you going to have the usual screening, ball mill, and grease table arrangement?'

'That's what killed the other companies – trying to separate by the old methods. No. We've got a cyclone to start with.'

'Cyclone?'

'You know a cream separator?'

'Yeah.'

'Same principle. Just spin the gravel in a circular tank and float off everything with a specific gravity of less than 2.5. Take what is left, dry it, spread it on a conveyor belt and run it under an X-ray machine which pinpoints every single diamond. As you know, diamonds fluoresce under X-rays and they show up crisply. The X-ray machine reports the diamond to the central computer. . . ' Johnny's voice and whole attitude was charged with enthusiasm which was impossible for his listeners to resist. Tracey was carried along with him, watching his eyes and his mouth as he talked, smiling when he smiled, her lips following his faithfully.

'This is the cyclone room,' Benedict van der Byl explained as, with a hand on her elbow, he helped Ruby Lance down off the last rung of the ladder. 'I explained to you how it worked.'

'Yes.' Ruby nodded, and looked around the room with interest. The roughly riveted and grey painted plating of *Kingfisher*'s hull formed a square metal box, in the centre of which stood the cyclone. It was also painted battleship grey, a ten-foot-high cone-shaped circular tower.

'The gravel is blown in through here.' Benedict indicated the eighteen-inch pipe which entered the cyclone room through the forward bulkhead, then connected to the bottom of the cyclone. 'Up it goes.' Benedict flung his hand upwards. 'And round it goes.' He made a stirring motion. 'The heavy stuff is thrown off and led away through that.' A smaller pipe emerged from the shoulder of the cyclone and disappeared through the farther bulkhead. 'While the lighter stuff shoots out through the top and is sprayed overboard again.'

'I understand. Now, where is the weak spot?' Ruby asked.

'Come.' Benedict led her across the room, picking their way among the litter left by the workmen who still swarmed through *Kingfisher*. They reached a steel door in the bulkhead.

'Watch your head.' They ducked into a long passageway with doors at both ends. On their right hand was an enclosed tunnel that ran the length of the room.

'This is the conveyor room,' Benedict explained. 'The concentrated gravels fall through a hot air draught from an electric furnace to dry them. They are gathered on a conveyor belt, concealed in that tunnel, and carried through into the X-ray room.'

'This is where you will fit it?' Ruby asked.

'Yes. In the conveyor tunnel. It will mean moving that inspection hatch back twelve feet to give us the space.'

Ruby nodded. 'The man who will do the work – can you trust him?'

'Yes. He has worked for me before.' Benedict did not add that the same man had designed the electronic equipment for the balloons used by the Ring, and had flown out from Japan to convert the ASDIC equipment on *Wild Goose*.

'All right.' Ruby seemed satisfied. More and more she was becoming the driving force in the alliance, bolstering

Benedict's resolution when he showed timidity or when he tried to evade the actions which must, in time, lead to a confrontation with Johnny Lance.

'Let's see the X-ray room.'

It was a tiny cupboard-like compartment. The floor, roof and all four walls were clad with thick sheet lead. Suspended from the roof was the X-ray machine, and under it a circular table the surface of which was covered with a honeycomb-patterned stainless steel sheet.

'The concentrated gravel spills on to the table, and the table revolves under the X-ray machine which fluoresces each diamond and the computer picks it up and reports its size and exact position on the table. The computer then commands one of those – ' Benedict pointed to a forest of hard plastic tubes, each attached to a metal arm, ' – to swing out over the table exactly above the diamond and suck it up. The computer selects the correct diameter of tube for the size of the diamond – and, after the tube has obeyed the computer, the table passes under a second X-ray machine which confirms that the diamond has been col-lected. If, by chance, the tube fails to suck up the stone, then the computer automatically sends the table on another circuit. If, however, the diamond is safely gathered then the waste material is scraped from the table and it swings round to pick up more gravel from the cyclone room – and repeat the whole process. The system is 100 per cent effective. Every single diamond is recovered by it. Even stones as small as sugar grains.'

'Where is the computer?' Ruby asked.

'There.' Benedict pointed through the small leaded glass window which overlooked the X-ray table. Beyond it was another small compartment. Ruby flattened her nose against the glass, and peered in. The computer occupied most of the room, a huge glossy enamelled cabinet not unlike a refrigerator despite the switches and dials. Benedict peered in beside her.

'The computer runs the entire operation. It controls the flow of compressed air into the dredger pipe, it regulates the cyclone, runs the X-ray machine and the table, it weighs and counts the diamonds recovered before depositing them in a safe, and it even navigates the *Kingfisher* and reports to the bridge her exact position over the sea bed, it checks the lubrication and temperature of the engines and power plant and on request will make a complete and immediate report of the whole or any part of the operation.'

Ruby was still peering into the computer room.

'What happens to the diamonds once they have been picked off the revolving table?' she asked.

'They are sucked through an electronic scale which weighs each stone, then they are carried through into the computer room and deposited in that safe.' Benedict pointed out the steel door set in the bulkhead. 'The safe has a time and combination lock. So the system works without a diamond being touched by human hand.'

'Let's go and talk to the Italian peasant,' suggested Ruby, and as she turned from the window Benedict slipped his arm about her shoulders and hugged her possessively.

'Not now,' snapped Ruby irritably, shrugging off his arm, and she led the way out of the X-ray compartment, passing the locked door of the computer control room opposite the door to the conveyor room. She was impressed with the ingenuity of the system – but the fact that it had been constructed by Johnny Lance made her angry.

Her loyalties had changed completely, going to the highest bidder.

Sergio Caporetti felt a small twinge of pity when he looked at Ruby Lance. So thin, and with a backside like a boy. She would be little comfort to a man on a cold night. Sergio worked the cheroot from one corner of his mouth to other, anointing the stub with saliva in the process. Also she was cold-blooded, he decided. Sergio had a very sensitive intuition when it came to judging the temperature of a woman's passion. Cold like a snake, he decided, his pity giving way to revulsion. He repressed a small shudder as he watched her settle on to the day couch in his cabin, and cross her long golden legs precisely. Just like a snake, she would eat a man as though he were a little hopping frog. Sergio had admiration for Johnny Lance, but – he decided – not even he would be safe with a woman like this.

'You like my ship?' he asked, an attempt at friendliness. 'She is *very* fine ship.'

Sergio actually used a more forceful adjective than *very*, one that suggested *Kingfisher* was capable of procreation, and Ruby's lips curled with disgust. She ignored the question and lit a cigarette, swinging one leg impatiently, and turned her head to stare through the porthole.

Sergio was hurt by the rebuff, but he had no time to brood on it for Benedict van der Byl came to stand in the centre of the cabin with his hands clasped lightly behind his back.

'Mr Caporetti—' he asked quietly. 'How much do you like money?'

Sergio grinned, and pushed the grubby maritime cap to the back of his head. 'I like it pretty good, I like it better than mother – and I love my mother like my life,' he said.

'Would you like to become a rich man?' Benedict asked, and Sergio sighed wistfully.

'*Si!*' he nodded. 'But it is the impossible thing. There is too much *vino*, too much lovely girls, and the cards they are cruel like – ' Sergio paused to find a suitable simile and glanced at Ruby, ' – like a thin woman. No. Money she does not stay long, she comes and she goes.'

'What would you do for £25,000?' Benedict asked.

'For twenty-five thousand – ' Sergio's eyes were dark liquid and lovely as those of a dying gazelle or a woman in love, ' – there is nothing I will not do.'

*K*ingfisher sailed for Africa on the 4th of October. As the representative of the owners, Benedict van der Byl drove down from London to bid her *bon voyage*, and he spent an hour behind locked doors with Sergio Caporetti before the departure of the vessel.

Kingfisher made good time southwards on her first leg of the voyage, but the unscheduled delay of ten days at the island of Las Palmas infuriated Johnny. His urgently cabled enquiries from Cape Town elicited the reply that there were teething troubles in *Kingfisher*'s engine room which were being attended to in the Las Palmas dockyards. The voyage would be resumed as soon as the repairs had been effected.

The Japanese gentleman who welcomed *Kingfisher* to Las Palmas was named Kaminikoto. This was too much for Sergio's tongue, so he called him 'Kammy'.

Sergio's crew was sent ashore with the excuse that the work on *Kingfisher* was dangerous. They were installed in the best tourist hotel and liberally supplied with intoxicating liquor. Sergio did not see them for the next ten days that he and Kammy were busy on the modifications to *Kingfisher*'s computer, and recovery equipment.

During those ten days Sergio and Kammy discovered that despite physical appearances they were brothers.

Kammy had mysterious packing-cases brought on board and they worked like furies from dawn until after dark each day. Then they relaxed.

Kammy was half Sergio's size with a face like a mischievous monkey. At all times he wore a Homburg hat. On the one occasion that Sergio saw him in his bath without his headgear he discovered that Kammy was as bald as St Peter's dome.

Kammy's abundant tastes in women were identical to Sergio's. This made the hiring of partners an easy matter, for what suited the one suited the other. Sergio took south with him fond memories of the little Japanese clad only in his Homburg hat, uttering bird-like cries of encouragement and excitement, while perched like a jockey on top of a percheron mare.

When at last Sergio shepherded his debauched crew back aboard *Kingfisher* the only obvious sign of their labours was that the inspection hatch on the conveyor tunnel had been moved back twelve feet.

'It is my best work,' Kammy told Sergio. Already he was sad at the prospect of parting. They were brothers. 'I signed my name. You will remember me when you see it.'

'You good guy, Kammy. The best!' Sergio embraced him, lifting him off his feet and kissing him heartily on each cheek while Kammy clutched desperately at his Homburg.

They left him standing on the wharf, a forlorn and solitary figure, while *Kingfisher* butted out into the Atlantic and swung away southwards.

Ruefully Johnny Lance glanced over at the mountain of empty champagne bottles beyond the barbecue pits. The bill for this little party would be in the thousands, but it was not an extravagance. The guest list included all Van Der Byl Diamond Company's major creditors and their wives. Johnny Lance was showing them all what they were getting for their money. To appear prosperous was almost as reassuring to a creditor as being prosperous. He was going to stuff them full of food and champagne, show them over the *Kingfisher* and fly them back home, hoping sincerely that they would be sufficiently impressed to stop badgering him for a while – and let him get on with the business of taking the Company out into the clear.

Tracey caught his eye. Her humorous roll of the eyes was a plea for sympathy, for she was surrounded by a pack of middle-aged bankers and financiers whom champagne had made susceptible to her charms. Johnny winked at her in reply, then glanced around guiltily to find Ruby, and was relieved that she was in deep conversation with Benedict van der Byl in a far corner of the marquee.

He made his way out of the crowd to the edge of the dune, and lit a cigarette while he looked back across Cartridge Bay.

The chartered Dakotas that had flown the guests and caterers up from Cape Town were standing on the airstrip beyond the buildings.

The marquee was situated on the crest of a sand dune overlooking the narrow entrance to the bay. The dune had been bulldozed to accommodate the tent, the laden tables, and the barbecue pits around which white-clad servants were busy, and the spitted carcasses of three sheep and a young ox were already browning crisply and emitting a cloud of fragrant steam.

Tracey watched Johnny standing out on the edge of the dune. He looked tired, she thought. The strain of the last few months had worn him down. Looking back on it now she realized that every few days had thrust a crisis upon him. The terrible worry of the court case that had won them Thunderbolt and Suicide had barely ended before Johnny had faced the delays in the construction of *Kingfisher*, the bullying of creditors, the sniping of Benedict and a hundred other worries and frustrations.

He was like a prize-fighter coming out to the bell of the last round, she thought tenderly, as she studied the profile of his face now staring out to sea. His stance was still aggressive, the big jaw pushed out and the hand with the missing finger that held the cigarette balled into a fist, but there were blue shadows under his eyes and lines of tension at the corners of his mouth.

Suddenly, there was an alertness in Johnny's attitude, he shaded his eyes with a hand before turning back towards the marquee.

'All right, everyone!' he called, stilling the babble of their voices. 'Here she comes.'

Immediately the uproar was redoubled and the whole party trooped out into the sunlight, their excitement and the shrillness of their voices enhanced by the Pommery they had been walloping back since mid-morning.

'Look! There she is!'

'Where? Where?'

'I can't see her.'

'Just to the left of that cloud on the horizon.'

'Oh yes! Look! Look!'

Tracey took a second glass of champagne from one of the waiters, and carried it across to Johnny.

'Thanks.' He smiled at her with the ease that now existed between them.

'It's taken her long enough to get here.' Tracey picked out the faraway speck on the green ocean that was *Kingfisher*. 'When will she begin working?'

'Tomorrow.'

'How long will it be before we know – well, if it has come off?'

'A week.' Johnny turned to her. 'A week to be certain, but we'll know in a day or two how it's shaping up.'

They were silent then, staring out at the gradually approaching speck. The crowd lost interest quickly and drifted back to the liquor, and the fragrant steaming platters of golden-brown meat that were coming from the barbecue pits.

Tracey broke the long friendly silence at last. She spoke hesitantly, as though reluctant to bring up a painful subject.

'How long has Ruby been back now – ten days?'

'About that,' Johnny agreed, glancing at her quickly. 'I haven't seen much of her,' he admitted. 'But she seems to be a lot more relaxed – and at least she's kept off my back.'

'She and Benedict seem to have become very pally.' Tracey glanced across to where the other couple were now included in a boisterous circle of revellers.

'She bumped into him in London,' Johnny agreed, sounding offhand. 'She tells me they had lunch a couple of times.'

She waited for him to continue, to express some suspicion or reservation, but he seemed to have no further interest in the subject; instead he began running over the day's further arrangements with her.

'I'm relying on you to take charge of the wives when we go aboard. Keep an eye on Mrs Larsen particularly – she's up to her gills in bubbly.'

For the next two hours that it took *Kingfisher* to make her approach and enter the channel of Cartridge Bay, Johnny hardly took his eyes from her unusual silhouette. She was not a pretty vessel but the white lightning insignia of Van Der Byl Diamonds on her funnel gave her a special beauty in his eyes. As she passed below them and entered the bay, Larsen proposed a toast to her successful career, then they all descended the dune and climbed into the waiting Land-Rovers and drove round the bay to meet her. By the time they arrived *Kingfisher* had made fast alongside the jetty, and Captain Sergio Caporetti was waiting to welcome them aboard.

He stood at the head of the gangway, and sensible to the importance of the moment he was decked in his finest and best; a double-breasted suit with a cream and lilac pinstripe set off the tomato-red silk tie, but his two-tone black and white crocodile skin shoes drew attention to his large feet and his gait was that of an emperor penguin. A liberal application of a hair pomade with a penetrating smell of violets had flattened his black hair into a shiny slick, bisected by the ruler-straight line of white scalp which was his parting. However, the aroma of the pomade was at odds with the particularly stinky cheroot of a brand which Sergio reserved for weddings, funerals and other special occasions.

His beautiful gazelle eyes became passionate and dark as they lit on Fifi Larsen. Mrs Larsen's tight-fitting slacks moved as though they were full of live rabbits and her pink sweater was straining its seams. Her eyes were sparkling with champagne and she giggled without apparent reason, flushing under Sergio's scrutiny.

The tour of *Kingfisher* began, Sergio Caporetti taking up an escort position directly behind Mrs Larsen. They had hardly descended the first ladder when Mrs Larsen let out a small squeak and shot about eighteen inches into the air, before coming back to earth with all her plentiful woman-hood aquiver.

'My dear Fifi, whatever is wrong?' Her husband was all solicitude, while behind her Sergio Caporetti wore an expression of cherubic innocence. Johnny felt dizzy with alarm, for he had seen Sergio's great hairy paw settling comfortably on to those majestic buttocks. Mrs Fifi Larsen had been thoroughly goosed.

In relieved disbelief Johnny heard her reply, which was preceded by another giggle.

'I seem to have twisted my ankle. Perhaps there is somewhere I could sit down.'

Johnny looked around frantically for Tracey to get Mrs Larsen out of Sergio's clutching range, but before he could signal her, Fifi was limping away on Sergio Caporetti's arm, bravely declining all offers of help.

'Please don't let me spoil your fun. I'll just sit in the Captain's cabin for a few minutes.'

Quickly Johnny moved up beside the silver-haired Larsen

and resolved to stay close beside him. Even if he could not prevent Fifi visiting Sergio's quarters, he was going to make good and sure that the husband didn't join the party.

'This is the explosives locker.' Johnny took Larsen's arm and led him away. 'We keep a store of plastic explosives for underwater blasting—'

Larsen's concern at his wife's injury dissolved and he became immersed in the tour of *Kingfisher*. Johnny followed the line of production for him from the moment the gravel was sucked in through the dredge.

As they left the cyclone room Johnny preceded him, holding the steel door open for Larsen.

'From the cyclone the concentrates pass through here into—' He stopped with surprise as they entered the narrow compartment beyond the cyclone.

'What's wrong, Lance?' Larsen demanded.

'No. It's nothing,' Johnny assured him. After the surprise of finding that the inspection plate in the conveyor tunnel had been moved he realized that it was as well from a security angle. Probably the marine architects had ordered the modification. 'The concentrates are carried through into the next compartment to the X-ray room. This way, please.'

As Johnny led the way to the next door he resolved to check with the architects. Larsen asked a question and he replied and the conveyor tunnel was forgotten. They went through into the X-ray room.

'He noticed it.' Benedict puffed quickly and nervously at the cigarette cupped in his hand. 'He doesn't miss a thing. The bastard.'

'He noticed it, yes. But he accepted it.' Ruby was definite. 'I know him. I was watching him. He was disturbed for a second then he rationalized it. I could almost see his mind work. He accepted it.'

They stood together on the exposed angle of *Kingfisher*'s bridge. Suddenly Ruby laughed.

'Don't look so worried,' she warned him merrily. 'We are being watched by your sister again. She's down on the foredeck. Come.'

Still smiling she led him around the angle of the bridge house, and out of sight she was immediately deadly serious again.

'That sister of yours is getting suspicious. We must keep away from each other until you tell Johnny.'

Benedict nodded.

'When are you going to tell him?' she demanded.

'Soon.'

'How soon?' Ruby would not be able to rest until it was out in the open, until Benedict had committed himself, yet she must not push him too hard.

'As soon as *Kingfisher* runs the Company under. I will pick the moment that he is beaten financially, then I will tell him. I want it to be the *coup de grâce*.'

'When will it be, Benedict darling? I am so anxious to be with you – without all this subterfuge.'

Benedict opened his mouth to reply and froze like that, his expression changing slowly into that of a man who doubts the evidence of his own eyes. He was staring over Ruby's shoulder.

Ruby turned quickly. The curtain across the Captain's porthole behind her was open a chink. She looked in upon a spectacle of such whole-hearted rubicund magnitude that it should have occurred only to Olympus between Jupiter and Juno.

In the cabin Fifi Larsen was receiving treatment for her sprained ankle.

'Well, you've got your toy now. Let's hope for all our sakes you can do something with it,' Benedict smiled pleasantly as he came across to where Johnny stood with Larsen under the great gallows-shaped gantry on the foredeck of *Kingfisher* that would raise and lower the dredging head.

'Toy, Mr van der Byl?' Larsen's white eyebrows bristled. 'Surely you have no doubts? I mean, now that you've got this Thunderbolt and Suicide concession?'

'Oh, I wouldn't say doubts, Mr Larsen. Reservations perhaps, but not really doubts. Mr Lance has been the champion of this venture. His enthusiasm has carried it – in the face of all opposition. Even that of my late father.' Benedict turned to Larsen smoothly.

'Your father opposed the scheme? I didn't know that!' Larsen was perturbed.

'Not opposed it, Mr Larsen.' Benedict smiled reassuringly. 'Not really opposed it. But you will notice that he was prepared to risk your money – not his own. That will give you some idea of how he felt.'

There was a chilled silence, before Larsen turned to Johnny.

'Well, Lance, thank you for an interesting day. Very interesting. I'll be watching your progress with attention – close attention.' And he turned away and strode to where a subdued and demure Fifi was waiting with a group of the other wives.

'Thanks.' Johnny gave Benedict a bleak grin.

'Don't mention it.' Benedict smiled that charming boyish smile.

'At the end of this week I'll take that little speech of yours, roll it into a ball and ram it down your throat,' Johnny promised him softly, and Benedict's expression changed. His eyes slitted and his grin showed his teeth and tightened the soft line of his jaw.

134

'You're pretty slick with your mouth, Lance.'

They glared at each other, the antagonism so apparent, as elemental as a pair of rutting stags, that they were suddenly the centre of all attention. The guests stared curiously, aware of the drama but not understanding it.

Ruby started forward quickly to intervene, taking Johnny's elbow, her voice sugary.

'Oh, Benedict, do you mind if I talk to Johnny a moment? I have to know if he's returning to Cape Town with me this evening.'

She led him away, and the tension dissolved. The disappointed guests began drifting to the gangplank and filing down on to the jetty.

In the confusion of embarkation aboard the two Dakotas, Johnny managed to exchange a last word with Tracey.

'You'll stay here until you know?' she asked. He nodded.

'Good luck, Johnny. I'll pray for you,' she whispered, then followed Ruby Lance up into the fuselage of the Dakota.

Johnny watched the two big aircraft taxi down to the end of the strip, turn in succession and roar away into the purple and red sky of evening.

After they had gone it was very still, and the silence of the desert was complete. Johnny sat in the open Land-Rover and smoked a cigarette while the night came down around him.

He was uneasy, aware of a deep-down tickle of apprehension and foreboding which he could not pin down.

The last glow of sunset faded from the western sky, and the desert stars were bright and hard and close to the earth, silvering the dome of space with the splendour that the city-dweller would never guess at.

Still Johnny hunched in the seat of the open Land-Rover trying to explore the source of his uneasiness, but with so little success that at last he must attribute it to the strain and fatigue of the last few months, his involvement with Tracey, his steadily worsening relationship with Ruby – and the latest clash with Benedict.

He flicked the stub of his cigarette away, watching morosely the explosion of red sparks as it struck the earth, then he started the Land-Rover and drove slowly down towards the jetty.

Kingfisher's lights were smeared in paths of yellow and silver across the still waters of the bay. Every porthole was lit brightly, giving her the festive air of a cruise ship.

Johnny left the Land-Rover at the head of the jetty, and walked out to her. The muted throb of her engines cheered him a little, the knowledge that the vessel was preparing for the morrow.

On deck he paused beside the gigantic compressed air tanks, each the size of a steam locomotive, and checked the pressure gauges. The needles were moving perceptibly around the dials, and his mood lightened a little.

He went up the ladder to the bridge, and into the chart-room where Sergio and Hugo were drinking coffee.

'Not my fault, Mr Lance,' Sergio began defensively. 'I am a gentleman – I cannot refuse a lady.'

'You'll dig your own grave with that spade of yours one day,' Johnny warned him grimly, as he went to the chart table and hung over it.

'Now let's get cracking.' Johnny's sense of dread lifted completely as he looked down at the large-scale Admiralty chart. The twin humps of Thunderbolt and Suicide were clearly marked. 'Hugo, have you got the prospecting schedules?'

'There, on the table.' Hugo and Sergio came to stand on each side of Johnny while he opened the bound file of typewritten sheets.

'The soundings we made differ from the Admiralty chart. We'll put in our figures, before we plot the dredging pattern.'

The three of them settled over the chart with dividers

and parallels to begin marking in the path that *Kingfisher* would follow through the maze of reefs and gullies.

It was long after midnight before Johnny made his way wearily to the guest cabin below the bridge. He kicked off his shoes, lay on the bunk to rest a moment before undressing and fell into a deathlike sleep of exhaustion.

He was awakened by one of the crew with a mug of coffee and he pulled on a windbreaker before hurrying on to the bridge.

Kingfisher was just passing out through the channel of Cartridge Bay into the open sea, and Sergio grinned at him from where he stood beside the helm.

Dawn was only a lemon-coloured promise over the desert behind them, and the sea was black as washed anthracite, kicked into a chop by the small morning wind. They stood on the darkened bridge and sipped steaming coffee, cupping their hands around the enamel mugs.

Then they turned and ran south, parallel to the desert which was now touched with hot orange and violet. The seabirds were up, a flight of malgas turned to glowing darts of fire by the early sun as they winged swiftly across the bows.

With a dramatic suddenness the sun came up over the horizon, and highlighted the chalk-white cliffs of Thunderbolt and Suicide far ahead so that they shone like beacons on the cold green sea. The curtains of spray that burst on the islands flashed and faded as they shot into the sky and fell again.

Wild Goose was waiting for them lying under the lee of the islands, but she came out to meet them, staggering and plunging theatrically over the short uneasy sea that hooked around the islands or boiled through the gap between them.

The radio telephone began crackling and squawking as the sighting reports from Johnny's watchtowers on the shore started coming in, cross-referencing to give *Kingfisher* her position over the ground. There were short exchanges between Sergio and Hugo on *Wild Goose* as they came together, and the little trawler worked in close, ready to give assistance with the laying of the cables if she were needed.

But standing in the angle of the bridge, Sergio Caporetti had the situation under his control. The grubby marine cap pushed to the back of his head and a long black cheroot stuck in the side of his mouth, he stood balanced on the balls of his feet, his eyes darting from judging the set of the sea surf to the repeater of the computer which was feeding him his soundings and position – yet attentive to the R/T reports from shore and from *Wild Goose*.

Johnny was contented with his choice of man as he watched Sergio at work. *Kingfisher* crept slowly up into the lee of Suicide Island, half a mile from the pearly white cliffs, then she hung there a moment before Sergio punched one of the buttons on her control panel.

From forward there was the harsh metallic roar of an anchor cable running out, and as *Kingfisher* backed away leaving a yellow-painted buoy the size of a barrage balloon bobbing under the cliffs of Suicide so one of the massive deck winches began automatically paying out its six-inch steel cable.

Kingfisher backed and crept forward, drifted down on the current or butted up against it while she went through the laborious but delicate operation of laying her four anchors at each point of the compass. Chained above each anchor floated the huge yellow buoys, and from each buoy the steel cables led to the winches on *Kingfisher*'s deck. On instructions from the computer the winches on each quarter would pay out or reel in the cable to hold *Kingfisher* steady over the ground while she worked.

It was mid-afternoon before *Kingfisher* was ready, pinned down like an insect to a board, and the computer reported that she was directly over the gully that Johnny had selected as the starting point. She had twenty-five fathoms of water under her – and then the thick bank of gravel.

'All is ready.' Sergio turned to Johnny, who had stood by quietly all this time – not interfering in the task of positioning. 'You will begin the programme now?'

'Yes.' Johnny stirred himself.

'I would like to watch,' Sergio suggested, and Johnny nodded.

'All right, come.' Sergio handed over the bridge to the helmsman and they went down to the armoured door of the computer room.

Johnny opened the lock. There were only two keys to this compartment. Johnny had one and Benedict van der Byl had the other. He had insisted on having the duplicate, and Johnny had reluctantly agreed not knowing that the key would be used in Las Palmas.

The heavy steel door swung back, and Johnny stepped over the coaming and seated himself before the console of the computer. Covered in cellophane and suspended on a clip above the keyboard of the computer were the cards containing the various programme codes.

Johnny selected the sheet headed: PRIMARY OPERATION: DREDGING AND RECOVERY, and began feeding the code into the computer, punching it on the keyboard.

'Beta, stroke, oh, oh, seven, alpha.'

And within the enamelled console, a change of sound heralded the beginning of the new programme, the hum of her reels and the click of the selectors, while on her control panel the lights blinked and flashed.

Now the computer's screen began to answer the instruction, spelling out her response like a typewriter.

'New programme.'
'Primary Operation. Dredging and Recovery.'
'Phase One.'

'Initiate safety procedure:—
a) Report air pressure . . . 1
b) Report air pressure . . . 2'

Johnny leaned back in the padded stool and watched the exhaustive check that the computer now made of *Kingfisher*'s equipment, typing out the results on the screen.

'What she do now?' Sergio asked curiously, as though he had never spent ten days in this compartment assisting his Japanese friend. Johnny explained the procedure briefly.

'How come you know this so good?' Sergio enquired.

'I spent a month at the Computer Company's head office in America last year while they designed this machine.'

'You the only one in the Company who can work it?'

'Mr Benedict van der Byl has done the course as well as I.' Johnny told him, then he leaned forward again. 'Now she is set.'

The screen on the computer reported itself satisfied.

'Phase One Completed.
Initiate Phase Two.
Lowering and siting of dredge head.'

Johnny stood up. 'Okay, let's get upstairs.'

He locked the door of the computer room and followed Sergio up to the bridge.

Johnny went to stand beside the repeater screen on the bridge, which was relaying the computer's signals exactly as they were printed on the main screen in the compartment below. He could see out through the windows of the wheelhouse, and he watched the automatic response of the heavy equipment on the foredeck.

The gantry swung forward, and the steel arms picked the dredge head from its chocks, and lifted it with the armoured suction hose dangling behind it. Then the gantry swung back, and with a jerky mechanical movement lowered the head through the square opening in the deck. This well pierced the hull, and through it the hose began to snake – a monstrous black python sliding into its hole. The huge reels that held the hose revolved smoothly, as the dredge was lowered to the sea bed.

'Head on bottom.'

The computer screen reported, and the hose reels stopped abruptly.

'Phase Two Completed.
Initiate Phase Three.
Cyclone Revolutions 300.
Vent dredge pump.'

There was a rising high-pitched whine now, like the approach of a jet aircraft. The sound reached a peak, and steadied – and immediately another sound overlaid it. The dull roar of high-pressure air through water, a sound of such power and excitement that Johnny felt the hair on his forearms prickle erect. He stood still as a statue, his expression rapt and his lips set in a small secret smile. That sound was the culmination of two years of planning and endeavour, the sweet reward of the driving dedication that had made a dream into reality.

Suddenly he wished that Tracey was with him to share this moment, and then he knew instinctively that she had deliberately left him alone to savour his moment of triumph.

He grinned then, as he watched the thick black hose engorge and pulse with internal life, like a great artery – pumping, pumping, pumping.

In his imagination Johnny could see the rich porridgy mixture of sea water and mud and gravel that shot up the hose into the spinning cyclone, he could imagine the steel head on the sea bed below the hull surging rhythmically to stir the sand and pound loose any gravel that pressure had welded into a conglomerate.

From the waste pipe over *Kingfisher's* stern poured a solid steam of dirty yellow water mixed with the sand and gravel that had been rejected and spun out of the cyclone. It stained the green sea with a cloudy fecal discharge, like the effluent from a sewage outlet.

For three days and two nights *Kingfisher's* pumps roared, and she inched forward along the marine gully like a fussy housewife vacuuming every speck of dust from her floor. As the third evening spread its dark cloak over her, Johnny Lance sat on the padded seat in front of the computer console. He sat forward on the stool with his elbows on his knees and his face in his hands for a full hour. He sat like that in the attitude of despair.

When he lifted his head, his face was haggard and the lines of defeat were clearly cut into his features with the cold chisel of failure.

From the meagre recovery of small diamonds that *Kingfisher* had made in the last three days it was clear beyond reasonable doubt that despite all the indications the Thunderbolt and Suicide field would not support the running costs of the vessel, let alone cover the overheads, or the interest charges and capital repayments on the loan account.

Van Der Byl Diamond Company was finished – and Johnny Lance was financially ruined beyond any possibility of ever finding redemption.

It remained only for the jackals to assemble and squabble over the carcass.

Sergio Caporetti leaned over the railing of the bridge, blowing long streamers of blue cheroot smoke from mouth and nostrils to help foul a morning which was already thick and grey with sea-fret. The islands of Thunderbolt and Suicide were blanketed by the mist, but the surf broke against their hidden cliffs like distant artillery and the seabirds' voices were plaintive and small lost souls in the void.

Wild Goose came bustling up out of the mist, swinging in under *Kingfisher*'s side to hover there under power with two of her crew fending off.

Hugo Kramer stuck his white blond head out of the wheelhouse window, and shouted up at the deck.

'Okay, boss. Come on!'

Sergio watched the tall figure on *Kingfisher*'s deck rouse and look around like a man waking from sleep. Johnny Lance lifted his head and looked up at the bridge, and Sergio noticed that he was unshaven, a new beard darkened his jaw and emphasized its prominence. He looked as though he had not slept, and he hunched into the windbreaker with the collar turned up against the mist. He did not smile, but lifted one hand in farewell salute to Sergio – who noticed incongruously that the index finger was missing from the hand. Somehow, that pathetic little detail struck Sergio. He was sorry, truly sorry. But there is always a loser in every game, and twenty-five thousand pounds is a lot of money.

'Good luck, Johnny.'

'Thanks, Sergio.' Johnny went to the rail lugging his briefcase and swung over it; he dropped swiftly down the steel rungs set in *Kingfisher*'s hull and jumped the narrow gap of surging water to *Wild Goose*'s deck.

The trawler's engine bellowed, and she pulled away, rounding on to a course for Cartridge Bay. Johnny Lance stood on her open deck looking back at *Kingfisher*.

'He's a good guy.' Sergio shook his head with regret.

'He's a boss,' the helmsman grunted. 'No boss is any good.'

'Hey, you! I am also a boss,' Sergio challenged him.

'Like I said.' The helmsman suppressed a grin.

'I kiss your mother,' Sergio insulted him with dignity, then changed the subject. 'I go below now, take over.'

Sergio opened the door to the control room with the duplicate key. He closed the door behind him, seated himself at the console and took from his pocket a sheet of paper headed: KAMINIKOTO SECONDARY RECOVERY PROGRAMME.

Ten minutes later he came out of the control room and locked the door.

'Kammy, I love you,' he chuckled as he closed off the watertight doors that isolated this deck from the one above. He wound the locking bars into position to ensure that he was not interrupted by one of his own crew.

From the tool cupboard on the bulkhead he selected a pair of set spanners and went through into the conveyor room. It took him twenty minutes to unscrew the heavy, deeply threaded bolts that secured the hatch. It had been designed to resist easy entry – a deterrent to casual investigation, but at last Sergio could lift the steel plate off its seating.

He eyed the small square opening with distaste, and reflexively sucked in his pendulous belly. The hatch had not been designed to afford passage to a man of his dimensions.

He took off his cap and jacket and hung them on the cock of one of the pipes, then he ground out his cheroot under his heel and brushed back the hair from his forehead with both hands, checked that his flashlight was in his pocket, and committed himself to the hatch.

He wriggled and kicked, and grunted and built up a heavy sweat for five minutes before he had squeezed through into the conveyor belt tunnel. He squatted on his haunches, panting heavily and flashed his torch along the tunnel. Above his head the conveyor belt carrying the gravel ran smoothly, but the residual heat from the driers made it unbearably hot. He began to crawl rapidly to the end of the tunnel.

From the inside it was impossible to tell, without measuring, that the conveyor belt tunnel was shorter by twelve feet than the external length.

The end of the tunnel was false, and beyond it was a secret cubicle only just large enough to house Kaminikoto's equipment through which all the gravel passed on its journey to the X-ray room.

The Japanese genius for miniaturization was demonstrated by the equipment in this secret cubicle. It was an almost exact copy of the sorting equipment in the main X-ray compartment – except that it had been scaled down to one tenth of the size without affecting its efficiency; in addition, this miniature plant could discriminate in the diamonds it selected. It would not allow a stone over four carats to pass through, and it screened out fixed percentages of the smaller stones – allowing only a proportion of the smaller and less valuable diamonds to proceed through into the main X-ray room.

It was an amazing piece of electronic engineering, but Sergio was unimpressed as he lay on his side in the cramped hot tunnel and began laboriously to unscrew another smaller plate in the false bulkhead.

At last it was open, and he reached through the opening; after a few seconds of fiddling and groping and heavy breathing he brought out a stainless steel cup with a capacity of about two pints. There were clamps on the cup to hold it in position below the chute under Kaminikoto's machine.

The metal cup was heavy, and Sergio placed it carefully on the deck beside him before propping himself on an elbow and shining the flashlight into the cup and took something out of it, stared at it a moment then dropped it back.

'By the blood of all the martyrs!' he gasped with shock, and then immediately contrite for his blasphemy he crossed himself awkwardly with the hand holding the flashlight. Then again he shone the torch into the cup, and shook his head in disbelief. Quickly he pulled a canvas drawstring bag from his pocket, and lying on his side he carefully poured the contents of the cup into the bag, drew the string tight and stuffed it back into his pocket where it made a big hard bulge on his hip like a paper sack of rock-candy. He clamped the stainless steel cup back into position, screwed the coverplate over the opening, and backed away down the tunnel on hands and knees.

He very badly needed a cheroot.

Four hours later Hugo Kramer shinned up the ladder on to *Kingfisher*'s deck while his helmsman took the trawler down to leeward to wait for him.

Sergio shouted down from the bridge.

'Johnny he has gone?'

'*Ja!*' Hugo shouted back. 'He should almost be in Cape Town by now. That Beechcraft is a fast plane.'

'Good.'

'How did it go with you?' Hugo countered.

'Come up – I'll show you.'

Sergio led him into his cabin behind the bridge and locked the door carefully. Then he went to each of the portholes and drew the curtains across them, before crossing to his desk and switching on the reading lamp.

'Sit down.' Sergio indicated the chair opposite the desk. 'You want a drink, or something?'

'Come on,' Hugo grated impatiently. 'Stop mucking around, let's have a look.'

'Ah!' Sergio looked at him sadly. 'You Germans, you are always too much hurry. You cannot rest, enjoy life—'

'Cut the crap!' Hugo's pale eyes were on his face, and Sergio was suddenly aware that this man was dangerous, like a tiger-shark. Coldly dangerous, without malice or passion. Sergio was surprised he had not noticed it before. I must be careful with this one, he thought, and he unlocked the drawer of his desk and took out the canvas bag.

He loosened the drawstring and poured the diamonds on to the blotter. The smallest was the size of a match head – perhaps point one of a carat, and the poorest quality was black and granular-looking, ugly little industrial stones, for Kammy had been careful not to take out only the best and so distort the *Kingfisher*'s recovery as to arouse suspicion. There were hundreds of these tiny crystals and chips which would fetch a few pounds in the industrial market; but there were other stones in the full range of quality and shapes and sizes – as big as green peas, or as marbles, and a few bigger than that. Some of them were perfect octahedron crystals, others water-worn, chipped or amorphous in shape.

They formed a dully glittering pile in the centre of the blotter, in all perhaps five hundred diamonds, yet all of these were dwarfed by one single stone that lay in the centre of the pile, rising out of it the way Mount Everest rises from her foothills.

There are freak diamonds so large or unusual that they become legend. Diamonds who have their own names and whose histories are recorded and invested with romance. The great 'paragons' – stones of the first water whose cut and finished weight exceed one hundred metric carats.

Africa has produced many of them: the *Jonker Diamond*, a 726-carat rough cut to a brilliant of 125 carats that hangs about the throat of the Queen of Nepal; The *Jubilee Diamond*, a superb 245-carat cushion of unearthly fire fashioned out of 650-carat rough – then the biggest of them all, a monstrous rough stone of 3,106 carats, the *Cullinan* which yielded not one, but two paragons. The

Great Star of Africa at 530 carats and *The Cullinan II* at 317 carats. Both these stones grace the Crown Jewels of England.

Now on Sergio Caporetti's desk lay a rough stone which would add yet another paragon to the list.

'Have you weighed it?' asked Hugo, and Sergio nodded.

'How much?'

'Three hundred and twenty carats,' Sergio said softly.

'Jesus!' whispered Hugo, and Sergio crossed himself quickly to dissociate from the use of names.

Reverently Hugo Kramer leaned forward and picked up the big diamond. It filled the palm of his hand, the cleavage plane that formed its base was smooth and clean as an axe-stroke. There were bigger diamonds in history, but this diamond had a special feature which would set it in a niche of its own and endow it with peculiar value.

Its colour was the serene blue of a high summer sky.

This stone could pay half the total bill for *Kingfisher*'s construction – if it were ever used for that purpose.

Hugo replaced the blue diamond on the desk and lit a cigarette without taking his eyes from it.

'This field – it is bigger – richer, far richer than we had guessed.'

Sergio nodded.

'In three days we have taken diamonds that I hoped to see once in five years,' Hugo went on as he began picking out the larger diamonds from the pile and laying them in a line across the desktop in approximate order of size, while Sergio opened his desk drawer and took out a box of his special occasion cheroots.

'We must tell the boss,' Hugo decided. He began arranging the diamonds in a neat circle about the big blue, thinking deeply. 'He must know how rich it is before he talks to Lance. He must make arrangements. He will know what to do – he's a clever one.'

'What about these?' Sergio indicated the treasure on the desk. 'Are you going to take them off?'

Hugo hesitated. 'No,' he decided. 'We could never get rid of this big Blue through the usual channel, it is too big, too distinctive. We will keep it aboard. When the boss takes over the Company again – then we will just declare it all nice and legal. No trouble.' He stood up. 'Look after them. I must hurry if I am to get a message to Cape Town in time.'

'The Company bears my father's name, Mr Larsen. It's as simple as that.' Benedict's voice was husky with emotion, and he looked down at his hands. 'I have a duty to my father's memory.'

'My boy, well—' Larsen came to lay his hand on Benedict's arm. 'Well, I just don't know what to say. Honour is a rare and precious thing these days.' With his free hand he was groping almost frantically for the bell on the desk behind him. He must get this signed up solid before the youngster changed his mind.

'I tried to warn you, Mr Larsen. My father and I never had any faith in this marine recovery scheme. Lance pushed it through—'

'Yes, quite so,' Larsen agreed, and turned to his assistant who came into the office at the trot in response to the bell. 'Ah, Simon. The Van Der Byl Diamond loan. Will you have an agreement made out immediately – Mr van der Byl will take over the capital amounts, and the outstanding interest as well.' By rolling his eyes Larsen tried to convey to his assistant the deadly urgency of the situation. The young man understood and fifteen minutes later laid the Agreement on Larsen's desk. Larsen unscrewed the cap of his pen and handed it to Benedict.

Larsen and three of his young men ushered Benedict out through the glass doors of the bank and across the pavement to where the Rolls stood in the reserved parking bay in Adderley Street.

Benedict settled into the back seat, acknowledged the bank official's farewells, and tapped on the chauffeur's window. As they pulled away, Ruby Lance slipped her hand through his arm and squeezed it.

'Did you get it?' she asked.

Benedict grinned happily. 'I frightened five years' growth out of old Larsen. He almost broke his neck in the hurry to give it to me.'

'Now you've got it all.' Ruby snuggled a little closer to him on the soft leather upholstery. Benedict nodded, and checked his watch.

'The meeting is set for fifteen minutes' time. I'll go up the front way, but I want you to go up in the private lift from the basement garage, and wait in my office. We will be in the Board Room. I will ring you at the right moment.'

The Rolls picked its way slowly down around the Heerengracht and double-parked outside the building. The chauffeur came to open the door, but before he alighted Benedict smiled into Ruby's face.

'This will be one of the high moments of my life,' he said softly. 'This time I've got the bastard cold.'

'I'll be waiting for you,' Ruby said, and he climbed out of the Rolls. He waited until it had turned into the entrance ramp of the basement garage, then he crossed the pavement into the main lobby of the skyscraper. He strode to the elevator with long eager strides, and his mouth kept pulling into a small excited smile.

The Board Room was set high, and the picture windows looked up at the great squat mountain, whose sheer cliffs dropped directly to the wooded slopes up which the first buildings of the city straggled.

Johnny Lance stood at the head of the table. He had lost weight in the last few days, so that his shoulders appeared bony and gaunt under the white silk shirt. He had discarded his jacket, and pulled the knot of his tie down an inch. The bones of his cheeks and jaw made harsh angles that were accentuated and not softened by the deep shades of fatigue that darkened his eyes. His hands were thrust deep into his pockets, and he spoke without reference to the sheaf of paper that lay on the table before him.

'Our working costs are as close as dammit to a hundred pounds an hour; right Mike?' And Michael Shapiro nodded. 'Well, we worked the Suicide main gully for sixty-six hours, and we recovered a princely 200 carats of the lousiest pile of junk I've ever seen. If we get a thousand quid for the lot we'll be doing well. This for an expenditure of six and a half thousand.'

Johnny paused, and looked around the table. Michael Shapiro was doodling on his note pad with fierce concentration, Tracey van der Byl was pale, her eyes never left Johnny's face and her expression ached with pity and helpless compassion; Benedict van der Byl was looking out of the window at the mountain, he was slumped comfortably in his chair, smiling a little and listening politely.

'The Suicide main gully is one of the five most likely parts of the entire concession. It's no good, so the rest of the field may be useless. We have the two other concessions, the original fields, to try. However, it will take three or four days to get *Kingfisher* moved up the coast.' Johnny paused, and Benedict swivelled his chair, still with the small smile on his lips.

'The interest payments fall due on the 30th – three days'

time. Where are you going to find one hundred and fifty thousand Rand?'

'Yes,' Johnny nodded. 'I think I can persuade Larsen to extend for a few weeks; he will bloody well have to if he wants to protect his—'

'Hold on,' Benedict murmured. 'Larsen has got nothing to do with it.'

Johnny was silent, watching him warily. 'Explain,' he invited.

'I've taken over the loan from Larsen,' Benedict told him. 'I'm not interested in extending.'

'Larsen wouldn't have negotiated without warning me.' Johnny was stricken, his disclaimer was wrung from him in pain.

'Shapiro?' Benedict turned to Michael Shapiro for confirmation.

'Sorry, Johnny. It's true. I've seen the documents.'

'Thanks, Michael.' Johnny's voice was bitter with accusations. 'Thanks for letting me know.'

'He showed me a few minutes before the meeting, Johnny. I swear I didn't know.' Michael's expression was distressed.

'Right.' Benedict straightened up in his chair, his voice was brisk. 'Let's get down to first principles. You've ruined my father's Company, Lance – but, thank God, I may be able to retrieve the situation. Call it sentiment or what you like, but I want your shares and yours.' He turned to Tracey and nodded at her.

'No,' said Tracey sharply.

'Right.' Benedict smiled at her. 'Then I'm going to hammer Johnny Lance for his full obligations. That way I get the Company anyway, but I'll make damn sure he remains an unrehabilitated bankrupt for the rest of his life.'

Tracey lifted her hand to her throat, and turned her eyes to Johnny. Waiting for him to set a lead. There was a long stark silence, then Johnny Lance dropped his eyes.

'I've still got three days.' His voice was gruff and tired.

'Three days you have.' Benedict grinned coldly. 'And you're welcome to them.'

Johnny picked up his papers and put them under one arm; he took his jacket off the back of the chair and swung it over his shoulder.

'Wait,' ordered Benedict.

'What for?' Johnny's grin was twisted. 'You've had your fun.'

Benedict lifted the receiver of the telephone on the table and dialled swiftly.

'Come through, please, darling.' He spoke into the mouthpiece and smiled at Johnny as he hung up. Then as the door opened he went to meet Ruby Lance, and kissed her on the mouth. The two of them stood, arm in arm, and looked at Johnny.

'The Company is not the only thing I've taken from you,' Benedict said softly.

'I want a divorce.' Ruby looked steadily into Johnny's face. 'Benedict and I are going to get married.'

They were all watching Johnny, and they saw him flinch. He looked from one face to the other, then his mouth tightened and his forehead furrowed.

Tracey saw his anger mounting, and her eyes flicked to Benedict's face. He was leaning forward expectantly, his lips quivering with expectation, his eyes alight with triumph. Tracey wanted to scream out a warning to Johnny, stop him falling into the trap that Benedict had set so carefully.

Johnny took a pace forward, coming up on to the balls of his feet. He was about to make his defeat total and ineradicable. Then Benedict spoiled it for himself, he goaded once more.

'Game, set and match, Johnny Lance,' he crowed.

The effort of will that Johnny made to recover his reason was not shown on his face, he made the step forward seem natural and he continued towards the door.

'The house is in your name, of course, Ruby, so would you please send my things down to the Tulbagh Hotel,' he asked quietly.

He stopped in front of the couple and spoke to Ruby.

'You'll want to protect your reputation, of course, so I'll not sue for adultery. We'll call it desertion.'

'You're eating your guts out,' jeered Benedict. 'Lance can't keep his woman. Van der Byl took her away from him. Go on, sue for adultery – let the world hear it.'

'As you wish,' Johnny agreed.

And he walked out of the Board Room to the elevators.

Johnny flopped on to the bed fully dressed, and rubbed his closed eyes with his fingertips. He felt confused and off-balance, the edge of his mind which usually slashed quickly and incisively through a problem was dulled. This problem was so multiplied and tangled that he felt like a man in a thicket of African ebony trying to cut his way out with a blunt machete.

Without opening his eyes he groped for the telephone, and the girl on the hotel switchboard downstairs answered. He gave her a number in Kimberley.

'Person to person, Mr Ralph Ellison.'

'Fifteen minutes' delay, Mr Lance,' the girl told him.

'Okay,' Johnny replied. 'Ask room service to send me up a Chivas Regal and soda.' He suddenly needed liquor, something to dull the pain. 'Make that a double, honey – no, make it two doubles.'

He had drained both glasses by the time his Kimberley call came through.

'Ralph?' Johnny spoke into the receiver.

'Johnny, how nice of you to call.' There was an echo like distant laughter beneath those cool ambassadorial tones in Ralph Ellison's voice and Johnny knew instantly that the word was out. Damn it, he was slow – of course Benedict would have blocked him.

'Are you still interested in a deal on the Thunderbolt and Suicide Concession?' Johnny loosed a despairing long-range shot.

'Of course, you know we are always interested,' Ralph replied.

'The price is two million.' Johnny lost interest and lay back on the bed, closing his eyes again. He knew Ralph was having his revenge – you didn't take this boy to court and win without sowing yourself a minefield to retreat over.

'Two million,' Ralph murmured. 'Now that's a little high – for a field that's yielding 200 carats of small industrial diamonds per 10,000 loads, that's definitely on the high side. Of course we wouldn't want that battleship of yours either – we are not starting our own navy.' Ralph chuckled juicily. 'We could talk around fifty to a hundred grand – no more than that, Johnny.'

'Okay, Ralph.' Johnny spoke wearily. 'Thanks all the same. We'll have a drink together sometime.'

'Any time, Johnny,' Ralph agreed. 'Any time at all. You call me.'

Johnny dropped the receiver back on its hook and looked at the ceiling. He had heard that a gunshot wound was numb at first – he felt numb now. All that energy had seeped out of him, he had lost direction.

The telephone shrilled and he picked it up. The girl on the switchboard asked politely:

'Are you finished, Mr Lance?'

'Yes,' said Johnny. 'You might say that.'

'Is there anything else you require?' The girl sounded puzzled.

'Yes, honey, send up the hemlock.'

'I beg your pardon?'

'Two more big fat whiskies, please.'

He drank them in the bath, and while he dried himself

the doorbell tinkled. He wound the bath towel round his waist and went through to open the door.

Tracey stepped into the bedroom and closed the door behind her. They stood looking at each other for a long moment. Her eyes were big and dark, reflecting his agony faithfully.

'Johnny—' Her voice was husky, and she reached out and laid the palm of her hand on his cheek. His shoulders sagged, and he moved close to her, his forehead sinking on to her shoulder. He sighed, a ragged broken exhalation of breath.

'Come,' she said, and led him to the bed. Leaving him there she went to the windows and closed the curtains.

It was warm and safe in the half dark of the curtained room, and they held each other as they had done long years before. Clinging together, so their breathing mingled, and it was not necessary to speak.

When they became lovers it seemed that they had waited all their lives for that moment.

Afterwards he lay in her arms and he felt strength flowing back into him, drawing it from her. When he sat up in the bed the bemused, almost dazed expression had gone. His jaw was out and his eyes were bright.

'We've still got three days,' he said.

'Yes.' She sat up beside him. 'Go, Johnny. Go quickly, don't waste another moment.'

'I'll pull *Kingfisher* out of the main gully. I'll find those diamonds. They are there. I *know* they are there. I'll take her right down into the jaws of Thunderbolt and Suicide, I'll find those bloody diamonds – damned if I won't.' He swung his legs off the bed, reached for his clothes, glancing at his wrist watch as he did so. 'Four o'clock. I can get to Cartridge Bay a few minutes after dark. Will you call the communications office, ask them to radio Cartridge Bay and have a flare path set for me, and *Wild Goose* standing by to run me out?'

'I'll phone them from here. Then I'll take a bath – you go on. Don't waste time.' Tracey nodded eagerly, and Johnny let his eyes drop down over her body. He reached out and touched one big white breast almost diffidently.

'You are beautiful – I hate to go.'

'It will all be here, waiting for you, when you get back.'

'It wasn't the way I'd planned it. It wasn't good the way I'd dreamed about it.' Benedict paced angrily over the floor of the Old Man's study, swinging towards the windows and pausing to stare out at the mountain across the valley.

'You hurt him. You crushed him.' Ruby moved restlessly in her chair across the room from him, curling her long golden legs defensively under her, sitting like a cat in the big chair. She was worried, and it showed in the tiny crows' feet at the corners of her eyes and the way she held her lips pursed. She should have anticipated this reaction from him, she should have known that this moment of triumph could never match his anticipation of it – and that revenge must always be followed by sour distaste and a feeling of disappointment. She realized that her safest course was to leave him alone now, she should never have returned with him to the old house on Wynberg Hill. She stood up.

'Darling.' She crossed to him. 'I'm going home now. I want to pack his clothes and get rid of them. I want to wipe out every memory of him. From now on it's you and I – together.'

She stretched up to kiss him, but Benedict turned his face away.

'Oh! So you're going, are you?' His expression was petulant, his lips pouting spitefully.

'We're both tired, darling. Let us both rest a while – and I'll come back later this evening.'

'So now you're giving the orders, are you?' He laughed nastily.

'Darling—'

'And cut out all the darlings. We pulled a deal and it didn't work out. You were meant to be a club to break his skull – and do you know something? He didn't give a damn. I was watching him, he was pleased – yes! He was bloody well delighted to get rid of you.'

'Benedict—' She stepped back.

'Listen.' He stepped close to her, and pushed his face towards hers. 'If you're so bloody anxious to go, why don't you bloody well go – and keep going. If he doesn't want you – then I sure as hell don't want you either.'

'Benedict,' she whispered. The colour faded from her face, leaving it washed white as beach sand. She stared at him in horror, as her dreams began to fall into ruins around her. 'You don't mean that.'

'I don't? Is that so?' He threw back his head and laughed again. 'Listen, you got some nice diamonds and a mink coat. You got a big house in Bishopscourt – now, that's pretty good pay for a whore.'

'Benedict—' She gasped at the insult, but he wasn't listening.

'I proved I could have you, didn't I? I proved I could take you away from him – and that's what it was all about. Now, why don't you go on home like a good girl.'

'The machine. I know about that thing in *Kingfisher*.' It was a mistake. Until then she still had a chance. His face changed shape and the blood flooded into it. His voice when he spoke was unsteady, thick with rage for his lips seemed to have swollen.

'Try it,' he whispered back at her. 'Go on, try it. They'll give you fifteen years in a woman's prison, my beauty. And think about this also—' He showed her his hand, holding it like a blade before her eyes. 'I'll kill you. I swear before

God, I'll kill you with my bare hands. You know I'll do it – you know enough about me now.'

She backed away from him, and he followed her still holding his hand at her throat.

'You've been paid. Now get out.'

A few seconds longer she stood before him, and he was not too far gone in rage to see the fear in her eyes mingle with something else that made her eyes slit and drew her lips back to show the little white teeth.

'All right,' she said. 'I'll go.' And she walked from the room, stepping daintily, the long yellow hair swinging against her shoulders.

R uby drove slowly for her vision was blurred with her tears. Twice other drivers hooted at her but she kept both hands clenched on the wheel and stared ahead, following the De Waal Drive around the lower slopes of the mountain. Before she reached the University she swung off the road and drove up through the pine forests until she reached the car park behind the Cecil Rhodes Memorial. She left the car and walked down on to the wide paved terrace below the Greek columns and stone steps where the mounted statue eternally searched the horizon with one hand lifted to shade his eyes.

She went to the parapet and looked across to the far blue mountains of the Helderberg. She hugged herself about the shoulders for the wind through her silk summer dress was as cold as her misery.

Now the tears broke over her lids and slid down her cheeks to fall unheeded on to the silken front of her dress. They were tears of self-pity, but also the tears of an anger as searing cold as dry ice.

'The swine,' she whispered through lips that trembled.

Near her two young students sitting on the parapet, kicking their legs over the drop beneath them and hugging each other in the abandon of first love, turned to glance at her.

The boy whispered to the girl, and she giggled in unthinking cruelty – but looked away as Ruby directed a long venomous glare at her. Then in embarrassment the couple scrambled off the parapet and moved away, leaving her alone.

Never for one moment did she consider standing aside. Benedict's threats meant nothing – her only concern was to take the action which would injure him most severely. The consequences to herself were not part of her calculations. She wanted only to select the swiftest and most terrible vehicle of retribution. As the dark clouds that fogged her reason slowly cleared, the means came to her readily.

Johnny was staying at the Tulbagh Hotel.

She turned and ran back to her car, the long yellow banner of her hair floating behind her like the pennant at the tip of a cavalry lance. She drove fast until she hit the downtown rush-hour crowds. The tears dried on her face as she crawled, fuming with impatience, along the slow river of traffic.

It was after five when she parked in a loading zone outside the entrance to the Tulbagh and ran into the lobby.

'What room is Mr Lance in?' she demanded of the girl at the desk.

'Mr Lance checked out an hour ago.' Curiously the girl examined Ruby's ruined make-up.

'Did he say where he was going?' Ruby snapped at her, feeling the sickening slide of disappointment within her.

'No, Madam.' The girl shook her head. 'But he was in a hurry.'

'Damn! Damn!' Ruby swore bitterly. She turned from the desk undecided where next to look. Perhaps Johnny had gone back to the office.

Across the lobby the elevator doors slid open and Tracey

Hartford stepped out. Even in her impatience Ruby recognized in the glow that seemed to emanate from her that Tracey was a girl freshly risen from the bed of the man she loved. There was not a vestige of doubt in Ruby's mind as to the identity of that man.

The shock of it paralysed her for a moment. Then she felt the urge to cross the floor and claw that smug smile from Tracey's face. She fought it down, and instead she stepped into her path as Tracey started for the glass outer doors.

'Where is Johnny?' she demanded, and Tracey came up short. Her little gasp of guilt confirmed Ruby's suspicion.

'Where is he, damn you!' Ruby's voice was pitched low but brittle with emotion.

'He's not here.' Tracey recovered herself, quickly masking her expression.

'Where has he gone? I must see him.'

'He's flown up to Cartridge Bay.'

'When did he leave? It's important – terribly important.'

'An hour ago. He'll be airborne already.'

'Can you get a message to him?' In her impatience Ruby caught Tracey's wrist, holding her in a grip that marked the skin.

'I can radio him—' Tracey pulled her hand free.

'No,' Ruby cut in quickly. She could not have her message shouted across the ether for all to hear. 'Can you follow him – charter plane?'

Tracey shook her head. 'They won't fly to an unscheduled airfield after dark.'

'Then you must follow him – by car. You must drive up there.'

'Why?' Tracey stared at her, puzzled by this strange insistence, noticing the dried tears and the wild look in Ruby's eyes. 'It's an eight-hour drive.'

'I'll tell you. Can we use Johnny's room?'

Tracey hesitated, remembering the unmade bed. Then

the hotel manager came into the lobby and Tracey turned
to him with relief.

The Beechcraft bucked suddenly and dropped a wing,
instinctively Johnny corrected the lunge with stick
and rudder then glanced quickly at his instrument
panel for an explanation. There was none to be found there,
so he looked over the wing and for the first time noticed
the dust on the great plains below him; it was moving low
against the earth in long streamers like mist, and the setting
sun turned it to mauve and old gold. With a prickle of
alarm he scanned the horizon ahead, and saw it coming
down from the north like a great moving range of blue
mountains. Even as he watched it, it rolled across the low
sun, turning it into a sullen red orb. The light in the cockpit
changed to a weird glow as though the door to a furnace
had been thrown open.

Again the Beechcraft crabbed awkwardly as another gust
of high wind hit her, and at the same moment the radio
crackled and came alive.

'Zulu Sugar Peter Tango Baker this is Alexandra Bay
Control, come in please.'

The voice of the controller was almost unintelligible
with storm static. Johnny reached for the transmit switch of
the radio, then stopped his hand. He thought quickly. He
could guess they were trying to reach him to cancel his
flight approval. That was a big northern boiling down out
of the desert. They would abort his flight, and divert him
out of the path of the storm.

He checked his wrist watch. Twenty minutes' flying time
to Cartridge Bay. No – he was flying full into the eye of the
wind, say twenty-five or thirty minutes. Quickly he searched
the coast on his port side and saw the long white lines of

surf stretched ahead into the thickening purple gloom. The coast was still clear, it might stay that way for another thirty minutes.

'Zulu Sugar Peter Tango Baker this is Alexandra Bay. I say again – come in. Come in. Zulu Sugar Peter Tango Baker.' The agitation in the controller's voice came through over the static.

There was a fair chance of getting in to Cartridge Bay, racing the storm and winning. He could edge out to the westward and come in from the sea, pick up *Kingfisher's* riding lights as a beacon and sneak in under the leading edge of the dust clouds. If he missed he could turn and run with the wind for home. The radio was hissing and crackling angrily now, the controller's voice sometimes lost in the interference, sometimes coming through strongly.

' – Cancelled. I say again: your flight approval is cancelled. Do you read me, Zulu Sugar Peter Tango Baker. Come in, please. – Beaufort force seven. – visibility in the storm area – I say again, there is nil visibility in—'

The norther would roar for days now and with it would blow away his last chance of working the gap at Thunderbolt and Suicide.

Johnny switched off the radio, cut off contact with Control and immediately it was strangely quiet in the cockpit. He settled himself down into the bucket seat, and eased open the throttles, watching the needles creep up around the dials of the rev counters.

Now he was down to an altitude of three hundred feet and the Beechcraft was leaping about like a hooked marlin. He was flying her on instruments for outside the cockpit it was completely dark. He could not see his own wingtips, but above him the stars still showed. He was riding the vanguard of the storm, and the dust clouds were ahead, racing to meet him and blanket the flare path at Cartridge Bay.

Every few seconds he darted a quick glance ahead, hoping to pick up the lights, then his eyes flew back to the instrument panel.

'Now,' he thought grimly. 'It should be now. I should be over the grounds. Thirty seconds more and I'll know I've missed her.'

He looked up again, and there was *Kingfisher* dead ahead. All her lights were ablaze, a burning beacon of hope in the darkness. She appeared to be riding easily, for the wind had not yet had time to thrash the sea into a frenzy.

He flashed over her, seeming to graze her superstructure in passing, and now he was searching anxiously for the glow of the flare path on the land beyond.

It came up as a path of lesser darkness in the absolute blackness of the night. He steadied on course towards it, watching it change to a long double line of oil-burning flares that smoked and fluttered in the wind.

He flew her in fast, high above the stall and the shock of touchdown threatened to tear the undercarriage off her.

Then he was jolting and trundling down the earthen runway with the flares flashing past his wingtips.

'Lance, old man,' he murmured thankfully, 'that was a very shaky do!'

The wind hum against the body of the car, and the snarl of rubber on tarmac as the Mercedes snaked through the bends of the twisting mountain road were sounds to match the racing of Tracey's blood and the hammer of her heart.

She drove with an inspired abandon, watching the bends leap out at her out of the darkness, sensing the massive crags and cliffs that hung over the road and blotted out half the night sky.

The silver sheet of Clanwilliam Lake reflected the stars,

and then was left behind. Down from the mountains she went and over the Olifants River to make a brief fuel stop at Vanrynsdorp and scan the road map anxiously in the light of the gasoline pumps. She read with a sinking feeling the mileage figures printed along the little red ribbon of the road, and knew that for her each mile would be multiplied by her own urgency.

Then once more behind the wheel she faced the vast emptiness of Namaqualand – and sent the Mercedes flying across it.

' – There is some type of machine, I don't know how it works, but it filters out the diamonds. Benedict had it installed at Las Palmas—'

The headlights were puny little white shafts, and the road a long blue smear that went on endlessly. Tracey lit a cigarette with one hand, hearing Ruby's voice again in her ears.

' – There is one diamond amongst them. He called it "The Big Blue". Benedict says it's worth a million—' Tracey was not sure she believed it. It was the enormity of the treachery and deceit that she could not accept.

' – The Italian, the Captain, be careful of him. He works for Benedict. The other one also – Hugo – they are all in it. Warn Johnny.'

Benedict! Weak, spoiled Benedict, the playboy, the spendthrift. Could he have planned and carried this through?

A gust of wind hit the car from the side, taking her unawares, pushing the Mercedes off the tar on to the gravel. Tracey fought to hold the skid. Dust and gravel roared out in a cloud from under the wheels. Then she was back on the road, hurtling northwards.

'Warn Johnny! Warn Johnny!'

Benedict van der Byl sat in his father's chair, in his father's house, and he was alone. His loneliness ate deep into the fibres of his whole being. Before him on the stinkwood desk stood a crystal glass and a decanter. The brandy was no comfort, its warmth in his throat and belly seemed only to accentuate the icy cold of his loneliness. His fantasy showed him as a hollow man. He thought of himself as a husk, filled only with the cold of melancholia.

He looked about the room with its dark panelled woodwork and he smelled the musty dead smell. He wondered how many times his father had sat in this chair alone and lonely. Lonely and afraid as the cancer ate him alive.

He stood up and moved listlessly about the room, touching the furniture as if he were trying to communicate with the man who had lived and died here. He moved across and stood in front of the curtained windows. The rug was new. It replaced the other that they had been unable to clean.

'The Old Man had the right idea.' He spoke aloud, his voice sounding strange in his own ears.

Then on an impulse he crossed quickly to the cupboard that flanked the massive stone fireplace, and tried the door. It was locked.

Without passion he stood back and kicked in the panel. The wood splintered and he kicked again, smashing the door from its hinges.

The oblong leather case was on the top shelf, and he took it down and carried it to the desk. He sprang the catches and laid back the lid.

He lifted out the blue metalled double barrels of the Purdy Royal, and the gun oil was greasy on his hands.

'Jacobus Isaac van der Byl.' He read aloud the name in gold inlay set into the steel among the engraved pheasants and gundogs.

He smiled then.

'The old devil.' He shook his head smiling as though at some private joke, and began slowly to assemble the shotgun. He weighed it in his hands, feeling the sweet pure balance of the weapon.

'The old bastard made his own decisions.' And still smiling he carried the gun across to the new carpet. He placed it butt down between his feet with the barrels pointed at the ceiling and leaning slowly forward he opened his mouth and placed the muzzles between his lips, then reaching farther down he placed a thumb on each trigger and pushed them simultaneously.

Click! Click!

The firing pins fell on the empty chambers, and Benedict straightened up and wiped the taste of gun oil from his lips. He grinned again.

'That's the way he did it. Both barrels in the back of the throat. What a cure for tonsilitis!' he chuckled, and glanced across at the shattered cupboard door. The square packets of cartridges were on the second shelf.

He tucked the gun under his arm and went to the cupboard again, moving more purposefully now. He snatched down a packet of SSG and broke it open. Suddenly his hands were shaking and the fat red cartridges spilled on to the floor. He stooped and picked up two of them.

With mounting excitement and dread he broke open the shotgun and slipped the cartridges into the blank eyes of the breeches. They slid home against the seating with a solid double thunk, and he hurried back to the spot in front of the window.

His eyes were bright and his breathing quick as he pushed the safety catch on to 'Fire' and placed the butt between his feet once more.

He took the muzzles in his mouth again, in an obscene soul kiss and reached down for the triggers. They were cold and oily. He caressed them lightly, feeling the fine grooving in the curves of metal, thrilling to the touch and feel of them as he had never thrilled to the feel of a woman's body.

Then abruptly he stood up again. He was gasping for breath.

Unsteadily he carried the weapon back to the desk and laid it on the dark polished wood.

As he poured brandy into the crystal glass his eyes were fastened with perverse fascination on the beautiful glistening weapon.

The steam had fogged the mirrored walls of the bathroom, so her image was dewed and misty. Ruby Lance dried herself slowly with one of the thick fluffy towels. She was in no hurry; she wanted Tracey to have a start of at least four hours on her journey to Cartridge Bay. With a deep narcissistic pleasure she noticed in the mirrors how her whole body glowed with soft pink highlights from the hot waters of the bath.

Wrapping herself in the towel she went through into the dressing-room and picking up one of the silver-backed brushes began stroking it through her hair, moving across to the open wardrobe to select a dress for the occasion. It must be something special, perhaps the unworn full-length Louis Feraud of daffodil satin.

Still undecided she went back to seat herself at the dressing-table and began the complicated ritual of applying her make-up. She worked with meticulous care until at last she smiled at her reflection with satisfaction.

She dropped the towel, went back to the wardrobe, and stood slim and naked before it. Pouting slightly with concentration she decided against the Feraud. Then suddenly she smiled, and reached for Benedict's mink.

She wrapped herself in the pale cloud of fur, fluffing up

the collar to frame her face. It was perfect. Just the fur and a pair of golden slippers, pale gold, a perfect match for her hair.

Now suddenly she was eager to go. She ran from the house to where her car was parked in the driveway.

She switched off the headlights as she turned into the driveway that curved up to where the old house crouched on the top of Wynberg Hill. The whisper of the engine was unobtrusive and blended with the whimper of the night breeze in the chestnut trees that flanked the driveway.

She parked in the courtyard, and saw that Benedict's Rolls was still in the garage and a light burned in the window of the study, a yellow oblong behind the curtains. The front door was open. Her slippered feet made no sound along the gloomy passages, and when she tried the door to the study it swung open readily. She stepped into the room, and closed the door behind her. She stood with her back to the dark panelled wood. A single shaded lamp lit the room dimly.

Benedict sat behind the desk. The room was heavy with the smell of cigar smoke and brandy fumes. He had been drinking. His face was flushed, and the top button of his shirt was undone. On the desk in front of him lay a shotgun. Ruby was surprised at the presence of the weapon, it disconcerted her and the words she had prepared were forgotten.

Benedict looked up at her. His eyes were slightly unfocused and he blinked slowly. Then he grinned; it twisted his mouth and his voice when he spoke was slurred.

'So you've come back.'

Instantly her hatred returned in full flood. But she kept her face impassive. 'Yes,' she agreed. 'I've come back.'

'Come here.' He swivelled his chair to the side of the desk. Ruby did not move, she leaned back against the door.

'Come here.' Benedict's voice was stronger now, and suddenly Ruby smiled and obeyed.

She stood in front of him, huddled in the fur.

'Kneel down,' commanded Benedict, and she hesitated.

'Down!' his voice crackled. 'Down, damn you!'

Ruby sank to her knees in front of him, and he straightened up in the chair. She knelt in front of him in the attitude of submission, with her head forward so the golden hair hung like a curtain over her face.

'Say it,' he gloated. 'Ask me to forgive you.'

Slowly she lifted her face and looked up at him. She spoke softly.

'Tracey left for Cartridge Bay at five-thirty this evening.'

Benedict's expression changed.

'She has a start of four hours – she is half-way there already.'

He stared at her with his lips parting, soft and red and slack.

'She is going to Johnny,' Ruby went on. 'She knows about the thing in *Kingfisher*. She knows about the big blue diamond.'

He began to shake his head in disbelief.

'By dawn tomorrow Johnny will know also. So you see, my darling, you have lost again – haven't you? You can never beat him, can you, Benedict? Can you, my darling?'

Her voice was rising, ringing with triumph.

'You?' he croaked. 'You?'

And she laughed, nodding her head in agreement, unable to speak through her laughter.

Benedict lunged clumsily out of the chair, his hands going for her throat. She went over backwards with him on top of her. Her laughter died gurgling in her throat.

They rolled together on the floor. Benedict's hands locked on her neck, his voice rising in a scream of fury and despair. Her long legs kicking and thrashing, clawing at his face and hands, she fought him with the strength of a cornered animal.

They rolled back suddenly and Benedict's head struck

the solid leg of the desk with a crack that jarred his whole body. His grip on her throat loosened and she tore herself free with fresh breath hissing into her open mouth. She rolled away from him and in one fluid movement gained her feet, reeling back from him with the front of the mink torn open and her hair tangled across her face.

Benedict dragged himself up the desk on to his knees. He was still screaming, a high keening note without form or coherence, as Ruby spun away from him and stumbled to the door.

Blinded by her own hair, fighting for strangled breath, she fumbled for the door handle with her back turned to him.

Benedict reached up and lifted the shotgun off the desk. Still kneeling beside the desk he held the weapon across his hip. The recoil was a liquid pulsing jolt in his hands and the muzzle blast was thunderous in the confines of the room, the long yellow flame lighting the scene like a photographer's flash-bulb.

The heavy charge caught Ruby in the small of her back. At that range there was no spread of shot and it went through spine and pelvis in a solid shattering ball. It tore out through the front of her belly, spinning her sideways along the wall. She slid down into a sitting position, facing him with the mink flared open about her.

On his knees Benedict swung the gun to follow her fall and he fired the second barrel; again the brief thunder and flame of the muzzle blast flashed across the room.

At even closer range than the first charge it struck her full in her beautiful golden face.

B enedict stood in the garage with his forehead pressed against the cold metal of the Rolls-Royce. The shotgun was still in his hands, and his pockets were crammed with cartridges that he had picked up from the floor before leaving the study.

He was shivering violently, like a man in high fever.

'No!' he moaned to himself, repeating the single negative over and over again, leaning against the big car.

Abruptly he gagged, remembering the carnage he had created. Then he retched, still leaning against the Rolls, bringing up the brandy mingled with his horror.

It left him pale and weak, but steadier. Through the open window he threw the gun on to the back seat of the Rolls, and climbed shakily into the driver's seat.

He sat there bowed over the steering wheel, and now his instinct of self-preservation took hold of him.

It seemed to him there was but one avenue of escape still open to him. *Wild Goose* had the range to take him across an ocean – South America perhaps, and there was money in Switzerland.

He started the Rolls and reversed out of the garage, the spin of tyres against concrete burning blue smoke into the beams of the headlights.

T he Mercedes crawled through the thick sand, the headlights probing ineffectually into the bright orange fog of dust that whipped endlessly over the track ahead. The hot gritty wind buffeted the car, rocking it on its suspension.

Tracey sat forward in the driver's seat peering ahead through eyes that felt raw and swollen with fatigue and mica dust.

From the main road to the coast this Jeep track was the only land access to Cartridge Bay. It was a hundred miles of tortuous trail, made up of deep sandy ruts and broken stone where it crossed one of the many rocky ridges.

The radiator of the Mercedes was boiling furiously, over-heating in the searing wind and the slogging low-gear grind through thick sand. In places Tracey followed the track only by driving through gaps in the stunted knee-high growth of desert bush. Every few minutes a tumbleweed, driven by the wind, would bowl across the track like a frightened furry animal.

At times she was sure she had missed a turning and was now grinding aimlessly out into the desert, then reassuringly the twin ruts would show up in the lights ahead of her. Once she did drive off the road, and immediately the Mercedes came to a gentle standstill with its rear wheels spinning helplessly in the soft sand. She had to climb out of the cab and, with her bare hands, scoop away the sand from behind the wheels and stuff bundles of tumbleweed into the depressions to give the wheels purchase. She almost wept with relief when the Mercedes pulled back sluggishly on to the trail again.

The slow dawn broke through the dust clouds and Tracey switched off the headlights and drove on until suddenly, and quite unexpectedly, she reached Cartridge Bay. The depot buildings loomed suddenly before her, and she left the Mercedes and ran to the living quarters. The foreman opened the door to her insistent hammering, and stared at her in astonishment before ushering her in. Tracey cut off his questions with her own. —

'Where is *Wild Goose*?'

'She took Mr Lance out to *Kingfisher*, but she's back now lying at the jetty.'

'Hugo Kramer – the Captain?'

'He's aboard, holed up in his cabin.'

'Thanks.' Tracey left him, pushed the door open against the wind and ran out into the storm.

Wild Goose lay at her moorings, secured by heavy lines

to the bollards, but fidgeting and fretting at the push of the wind. There was a gangplank laid to her deck, and lights showed at her portholes. Tracey went aboard.

Hugo Kramer came to the doorway of his cabin in a suit of rumpled striped pyjamas. Tracey pushed past him.

'You took Lance out to *Kingfisher*?' she accused him, her voice sharp and anxious.

'Yes.'

'You idiot, didn't you realize there was something up? Good God, why otherwise would he fly in through this weather?'

Hugo stared at her, and instinctively she knew that what Ruby had told her was true.

'I don't know what you're talking about,' he blurted.

'You'll know all right when we are all sitting behind bars – we'll have fifteen long years to think about it. Lance has tumbled to it, you fool, I've got to stop him. Take me out to *Kingfisher*.'

He was confused – and afraid.

'I know nothing about—' Hugo started again.

'You're wasting time.' Brusquely Tracey brushed his protests aside. 'Take me out to *Kingfisher*.'

'Your brother – where is he? Why didn't he come?'

Tracey had anticipated the question. 'Lance beat him up – badly. He's in hospital. He sent me.'

Suddenly Hugo was convinced.

'*Gott!*' he swore. 'What are we going to do? This storm – I may be able to get you out there, but I won't be able to leave *Wild Goose*. My crew can't handle her in this sea. What can you do on your own?'

'Get me out there,' said Tracey. 'Get me aboard *Kingfisher* and you can come back. The Italian, Caporetti, he and I will take care of Lance. In this storm a man can be washed overboard very easily.'

'*Ja.*' Hugo's face lit with relief. 'That's it. The Italian!' And he a reached for his oilskins hanging on the bulkhead.

As he pulled them on over his pyjamas he looked at Tracey with new respect.

'You,' he said. 'I didn't know you were in it.'

'Did you think my brother and I would stand by and let a stranger take our birthright from us?'

Hugo grinned. 'You're a cool one, I'll say that for you. You had me fooled.' And he went out on to the bridge.

Johnny Lance and Sergio Caporetti stood shoulder to shoulder on *Kingfisher*'s bridge. The ship was taking the big green seas over her bows, solid walls of water, and the wind whipped spray that spattered the armoured glass windows of the bridge house.

Kingfisher had slipped her moorings the previous evening, leaving the big yellow buoys floating on their anchor cables and she was working free of her fetters. She was on computer navigation, holding her position over the ground against the swells and the wind by use of her engine and rudder.

'She is no good.' Sergio spoke morosely. 'We come too close to the rocks. I get sick in my heart looking at them.'

The dust clouds did not carry this far out to sea despite the vicious screeching of the wind. The visibility was a mile or more, quite enough to show the brooding twin hulks of Thunderbolt and Suicide. The storm-crazed swells burst against them, throwing white spray two hundred feet into the gloomy sky, then surging back to expose the gleaming white rock.

'Hold her,' growled Johnny. Twice during the night they had changed position, each time edging down closer on the gap between the two islands. *Kingfisher* was battling gamely to hold her ground against the insidious sucking current that added its pull to that of the swell and the wind.

Johnny was not attempting to work any one of the gullies extensively, he wanted only to sample as much of the field as possible in the time that was left to him. The storm would not stop him – for *Kingfisher* was constructed to work in worse weather than his. Her compensating hose section was keeping the dredge head on the bottom despite the lift and fall of her hull.

'Calm down, Sergio.' Johnny relented a little. 'The computer is foolproof.'

'The goddamned computer she no got eyes to see those rocks. Me, I got eyes – and it gives me a sick heart.'

Twice during the night Johnny had gone down into the control room and ordered the computer to report its recovery of diamonds. Each time the reply had been consistent – not a single stone over four carats, and a very precious few of any others.

'I'm going through to the plot. Watch her,' Johnny told Sergio, and staggering against the pitch and roll he went through the door behind the bridge.

He paused behind the repeater screen of the computer, and at a glance saw that *Kingfisher* was holding her primary operation and all departments were running normally. He passed the screen and leaned over the chart table.

The large-scale chart of the South West African coast between Luderitz and Walvis Bay was pinned down on the board. The *Wild Goose* soundings were pencilled in, and the pattern of *Kingfisher*'s sweeps were carefully plotted around the islands of Thunderbolt and Suicide.

Johnny picked up a pair of dividers and stared moodily at the chart. Suddenly a surge of anger rose in him against those two names. They had promised so much and delivered so little.

He stared at the names Thunderbolt and Suicide printed in italics among the maze of soundings, and his anger turned to blind red hatred.

With the points of the dividers he slashed at the chart, ripping the thick linen paper once, and twice, in a ragged cross-shaped tear.

This small act of violence dissipated his anger. He felt embarrassed, it had been a petty childish gesture. He tried to smooth the edges of the tear, and through the gap he felt another loose scrap of paper which someone had slipped under the chart. He probed a finger through the tear in the chart and wormed the scrap out. He glanced at the scribbled title and the lines of figures and numbers that followed.

The sheet was headed: KAMINIKOTO SECONDARY RECOVERY PROGRAMME.

He studied it, puzzled by the title but recognizing the numbers as a computer programme. The writing was in Sergio Caporetti's pointed continental style. The easiest way to resolve the mystery was to ask Sergio. Johnny started back for the bridge.

'Boss,' Sergio called anxiously, as Johnny stepped through the door. 'Look!'

He was pointing ahead into the eye of the wind. Johnny hurried to his side, the paper crumpled and forgotten in his hand.

'*Wild Goose.*' Sergio identified the small craft that was staggering and plunging towards them out of the gloom.

'What the hell is he doing here?' Johnny wondered aloud. *Wild Goose* was lost for long seconds behind the walls of green sea, then again she was lifted high into unnatural prominence, showing the red lead of her bottom as she rode the crests; water poured from her scuppers, before she shot down the steep slope of the next wave to bury her nose deep in frothing water. She came down swiftly on the wind, rounding to and beginning to edge in under *Kingfisher*'s counter.

'What the hell is he playing at?' Johnny protested, and then in disbelief he saw a slim figure dart from *Wild Goose*'s wheelhouse and run to the side nearest *Kingfisher*.

'It's Tracey,' shouted Johnny.

She reached the rail just as another swell burst over the

bows and smothered her. Johnny expected to see her washed away, but she was still there clinging to the rail.

Thrusting the page of paper into his pocket, Johnny went out through the wing of the bridge and swarmed down the steel ladder to the deck, jumping the last ten feet and running the instant he landed.

He reached the side and looked down on the drowned-kitten figure of Tracey.

'Go back,' he yelled. 'Go back. Don't try it.'

She shouted something that was lost in the next smother of spray, and when it cleared he saw her poising herself to jump the gap of surging water between the two vessels.

He flung himself over *Kingfisher*'s side and climbed swiftly down the steel rungs.

He was still ten feet above her as she gathered herself for the leap.

'Go back,' he shouted desperately.

She jumped, missed her hold and fell into the murderous stretch of water between the hulls. Her head bobbed below Johnny, and he was aware of the next swell bearing down on them. It would throw *Wild Goose* against the steel cliff of *Kingfisher*, crushing Tracey between them.

Johnny went down those last ten feet and hanging outwards by one arm he got his other arm around her, and with a heave that crackled in his muscles and joints he plucked her from the water just as the two vessels dashed together with a crunching impact that tore splinters from *Wild Goose*'s planking, and left a smear of alien paint on *Kingfisher*'s steel plating.

Wild Goose swung away, and with her diesels bellowing went bucking off into the wind.

With puddles of sea water forming around her feet from her sodden clothing, Tracey stood in the centre of *Kingfisher*'s guest cabin. Her dark hair was plastered down her face and neck, and she was shivering so violently from shock and the icy water that she could not talk. Her teeth chattered together, and her lips were blue with cold.

Desperately she was trying to form words, her eyes never leaving Johnny's face.

Quickly he stripped off her clothing and throwing one towel round her shoulders he began roughly to chafe warmth back into her with another.

'You little idiot,' he berated her. 'Are you stark staring bloody mad?'

'Johnny,' she gasped through her chattering teeth.

'Christ – that was so close,' he snarled at her as he knelt to rub her legs.

'Johnny, listen.'

'Shut up and dry your hair.'

Humbly she obeyed him, her shivers became controllable as he crossed to the locker and found a thick jersey which he pulled over her head. It hung almost to her knees.

'Now,' he said, taking her roughly by the shoulders. 'What the hell is this all about?'

And she told him in a rush of words that poured out like water from a broken dam. Then she burst into tears and stood there forlornly in the voluminous jersey with her damp hair dangling about her shoulders, sobbing as though her heart was breaking.

Johnny took her in his arms.

For a long minute Tracey revelled in his warmth and strength, but she was the first to pull away.

'Do something, Johnny,' she implored him, her voice still thick with tears. 'Stop them. You mustn't let them get away with it.'

He went back to the locker, and while he ransacked it

for clothing that might fit her, Johnny's mind was racing over the story she had told him.

He watched her pull on a pair of blue serge trousers and tie them at the waist with a length of cord. She folded back the cuffs and tucked them into thick woollen socks, before thrusting her feet into a pair of sea-boots that were only a few sizes too large for her.

'Where do we start?' she asked, and he remembered the sheet of paper. He fished it out of his pocket and flattened it on the table beside the bunk. Quickly he ran his eyes over the columns of figures. His first guess was right – it *was* a computer programme.

'Stay here,' he ordered Tracey.

'No.' Her response was immediate, and he grinned.

'Listen, I'm just going up on to the bridge to keep them busy there. I'll come back for you, I promise. You won't miss anything.'

'How is she, boss?' Sergio Caporetti's concern was genuine. Johnny realized that he must be worrying himself into a frenzy trying to guess the reason for Tracey's arrival.

'She is pretty shaken up,' Johnny answered.

'What she want – that was big chance she takes. Nearly fish food.'

'I don't know,' Johnny said. 'I want you to take over up here. Keep *Kingfisher* working. I'm going to get her to bed – I'll let you know what it's all about as soon as I find out.'

'Okay, boss.'

'Oh, and Sergio – keep an eye on those rocks. Don't let her drift down any closer.'

Johnny chose a powerful incentive to keep Sergio up on the bridge.

Johnny left him and went below, stopping only at the guest cabin.

'Come on.'

Tracey followed him, lurching unsteadily with *Kingfisher*'s antics in the high sea.

Two decks down they reached the computer control room and Johnny unlocked the heavy steel door, then locked it again behind them.

Tracey wedged herself against the bulkhead and watched as Johnny seated himself at the console and clipped the rumpled sheet into the board.

Reading from the sheet he typed the first line of figures on the keyboard. Immediately the computer registered a protest.

'Operator error,' it typed back. Johnny ignored its denial and typed the second line. This time it was more emphatic.

'No procedure. Operator error.'

And Johnny typed the next line of figures. He guessed that whoever had stored this programme in the computer's memory would have placed a series of blocks to prevent accidental discovery. Again the denial flashed back at him.

'Operator error.'

And Johnny muttered, 'Thrice before the cock crows,' striking an incongruously biblical note in the tense atmosphere of the control room.

He typed the last line of figures and the denial faded from the screen. The console clicked like a monstrous crab, then suddenly it started to print again.

'KAMINIKOTO SECONDARY RECOVERY PROGRAMME. INSTALLED OCTOBER 1969. AT LAS PALMAS BY HIDEKI KAMINIKOTO. DOCTOR OF SCIENCE. TOKYO UNIVERSITY.'

The little Japanese had been unable to resist autographing his masterpiece. Tracey and Johnny crouched over the screen, staring at it with awful fascination as the computer began spelling out its report. It began with the number of hours worked, and the weight of gravel processed during that time. Next it reported the weight of concentrates recovered from the cyclone and finally, in a series of columns, it printed out the weights and sizes of all the diamonds won from the sea. The big Blue showed up in the place of honour, and wordlessly Tracey touched the figure 320 with a forefinger. Johnny nodded grimly.

The computer ended by giving the grand total of carats recovered, and Johnny spoke for the first time.

'It's true,' he said softly. 'It doesn't seem possible – but it is.'

The click and hum of the computer ceased, and the screen went blank.

Johnny straightened up in the chair.

'Where would they put it?' he asked himself, as he ran quickly over the line of recovery. He stood up from the chair and peered through the leaded glass peephole into the X-ray room. 'It must be this side of the cyclone, this side of the drier – ' He was speaking aloud. ' – Between the drier and the X-ray room.'

Then there bobbed to the surface of memory the modification in design which he had meant to query, but which he had forgotten.

'The inspection plate on the conveyor tunnel!' He punched his fist into his palm. 'They moved the inspection plate! That's it! It's in the conveyor tunnel.'

His hands were frantic with haste as he unlocked the steel door of the control room.

Sergio Caporetti paced his bridge like a captive bear, puffing so furiously on his cheroot that sparks flew from its tip. The wind howled hungrily around the wheelhouse, and the swells still marched in from the north.

Suddenly he reached a decision and turned to the helmsman.

'Watch those goddamn rocks – watch them good.'

The helmsman nodded and Sergio shambled through the chartroom to his own cabin. He locked the door behind him, and crossed to his desk. Fumbling with his keys he opened the bottom drawer of his desk and reaching under the pile of cheroot packets he brought out the canvas bag.

Weighing it thoughtfully in his hand, he looked about the cabin for a more secure hiding place. Through the canvas he could feel the nutty irregular shape of the stones.

'That Johnny, he a clever bastard,' he muttered. 'It better be good place.'

Then he reached a decision. 'Best place where I can watch them all a time.'

He opened his jacket and stuffed the bag into his inside pocket. He buttoned the jacket and patted the bulge over his heart.

'Fine!' he said. 'Good!' And stood up from the desk. He hurried back, unlocking the door into the chartroom, and headed for the bridge. He stopped in the middle of the chartroom, and his head swung towards the repeater screen of the computer. The buzzer was going like a rattlesnake, and the red bulb that warned of a new procedure was blinking softly.

Fearfully Sergio approached the screen and stooped over it. A single glance was enough, and he rushed from it to the chart table. He saw the cross-shaped tear in the chart.

'Mary Mother!'

He ripped back the thick crackling paper and searched under it. He stepped back from the table and hit himself across the chest.

'Fool!' he said. 'Idiot!' He spent ten seconds in self-castigation, then he looked about for a weapon. The locking handle of the cabin was a twelve-inch steel bar with a heavy head. He pulled out the pin and worked it loose. He slipped it into the waistband of his trousers.

'I'm going below,' he told the helmsman curtly, and clambered down the companionway. Swiftly he moved through the ship, balancing easily to her roll and pitch.

When he reached the lowest deck he became more stealthy, creeping silently forward. Now he carried the steel bar in his right hand. Every few paces he stopped to listen, but *Kingfisher*'s hull was groaning and popping as she worked in the swells.

He could hear no other sound. He crept up to the door of the control room and cautiously peered through the small armoured glass window. The control room was empty. He tried the handle, and found it locked.

Then he heard voices – from the open doorway of the conveyor room behind him. Quickly he crossed to it and flattened himself against the jamb.

Johnny's voice came muffled and indistinct:

'There's another hatch in here. Get me a half-inch spanner from the tool cupboard.'

'What's a half-inch spanner look like?'

'It's a big one. The size is stamped on it.'

Sergio glanced one-eyed around the door jamb. The cover was off the inspection hatch in the conveyor tunnel, and Tracey's head was thrust into the opening.

It was clear that Johnny Lance was in there, and that he had found the secret compartment.

Tracey drew her head out of the hatch, and Sergio ducked back and looked down the passageway. The tool cupboard was bolted to the bulkhead under the stairs from the deck above. He turned and darted around the corner of the passageway. Tracey came out of the conveyor room, and went to the cupboard. She opened the doors on the glittering array of tools, each clipped securely to its rack.

While she stood before the cupboard, completely absorbed in her search for a half-inch spanner, Sergio came from around the corner and crept up silently behind her.

He lifted the steel bar over his shoulder and came up on his toes, poised to strike.

Tracey was muttering softly to herself, head bowed slightly, handling the spanners – and Sergio knew the blow would crush her skull.

He closed his mind to the thought, and aimed carefully at the base of her skull. He started the blow, and then checked it. For a second that seemed to last for a long time he remained frozen. He couldn't do it.

With an exclamation of satisfaction Tracey found what she was searching for. As she turned away from the cupboard Sergio shrank back behind the angle of the bulkhead, and Tracey hurried back into the conveyor room.

'I've got it, Johnny,' she shouted into the hatch.

'Bring it to me. Hurry, Tracey. Sergio will be getting suspicious,' he shouted back, and Tracey hitched up her voluminous trousers and wriggled into the hatch.

On hands and knees she crawled up beside him. It was cramped and hot in the narrow tunnel. He took the spanner from her.

'Hold the flashlight.' She took it from him, holding the beam on the panel while he unscrewed the retaining bolts and lifted off the cover.

Lying on his side he peered into the opening.

'There's a container of sorts,' he grunted, and reached in. For a minute he struggled with the clamps, then slowly he lifted out the stainless steel cup.

At that moment *Kingfisher* reared and plunged to a freak wave and the cup slipped from Johnny's fingers, and from it spilled the diamonds. They cascaded over both of them, a glittering shower of stones of all sizes and colours. Some lodged in Tracey's damp hair, the rest rolled and bounced and scattered about them, catching the light from the torch and throwing it back in splinters of sunshine.

'Yipes!' gasped Tracey and laughed at Johnny's whoop of triumph.

Lying side by side they scrabbled and snatched at the treasure scattered around them.

'Look at this one,' exulted Tracey.

'And this.' They were crazy with excitement, hands filled with diamonds. They hugged each other and kissed ecstatically, laughing into each other's mouths.

Johnny sobered first, 'Come on. Let's get out of here.'

'What about the diamonds?'

'Leave them. There'll be plenty of time later.'

They crawled backwards down the tunnel, still laughing and exclaiming, and one after the other emerged into the conveyor room. While they straightened their clothing, and regained their breath, Tracey asked, 'What now?'

'First thing is to get young Sergio safely under lock and key, his crew also.' Johnny's face hardened. 'The bloody bastards,' he added angrily.

'Then?' Tracey asked.

'Then we'll pull up the hose, and sail *Kingfisher* back into Cartridge Bay. Then we'll call up the police on the radio. There's going to be an accounting with the whole gang of the bastards – your darling brother included.'

Johnny started for the door, asking as he crossed the deck:

'Why did you close the door, Tracey?'

'I didn't,' she replied as she hurried after him, and Johnny's expression changed. He ran to the heavy steel door and threw his weight on it. It did not move, and he swung round to face the door that led into the cyclone room.

It was closed also. He charged across the room and grabbed the handle, heaving at it with all his strength.

He stood back at last, and looked wildly about the long narrow cabin. There was no other opening, no hatch or porthole – nothing except the tiny square peephole in the centre of the steel door that led into the cyclone room beyond. The peephole was covered with three-inch armoured glass that was as strong as the steel that surrounded it. He looked through it.

The tall cyclone reached from floor to roof, dominating the room. Beyond it the steel pipe that carried the gravel from the sea bed pierced the roof from the deck above, but the cyclone room was deserted.

Johnny turned slowly back to Tracey and put an arm around her shoulders.

'We've got problems,' he said.

After closing and locking both the doors that led into the conveyor room, Sergio climbed quickly back to his bridge. The helmsman looked at him curiously.

'How's the lady?'

'Fine,' Sergio snapped at him. 'She's safe.' And then with unnecessary violence, 'Why you no mind your own business, hey? You think you Captain for this ship?'

Startled, the helmsman quickly transferred his attention back to the storm which still raged lustily about them. Sergio began to pace up and down the bridge, balancing easily and instinctively to her exaggerated motion. His smooth baby face was crumpled into a massive scowl, and he puffed on one of his cheroots. With all his soul Sergio Caporetti was lamenting his involvement in this business. He wished that he had never heard of *Kingfisher*. He would have traded his hopes of a life hereafter to be sitting on the seafront at Ostia, sipping *grappa* and watching the girls go by.

Impulsively he pulled open the storm doors at the angle of the bridge and went out on to the exposed wing. The wind buffeted him and set his soft hair dancing and flickering.

From inside his jacket he pulled the canvas bag.

'This is the trouble,' he muttered, looking at the bag in his hand. 'Bloody little stones.'

He threw back his arm like a baseball pitcher, set to hurl the bag out into that hissing green sea below him, but again he could not make the gesture. Swearing quietly to himself, he stuffed the stones back into his jacket, and went back into the wheelhouse.

'Call the radio operator,' he ordered, and the helmsman reached quickly for the voice tube.

The radio operator reached the bridge still owl-eyed with sleep and buttoning his clothing.

'Get on to *Wild Goose*,' Sergio told him.

'I won't be able to raise her in this,' the man protested, glancing out at the storm.

'Call her.' Sergio stepped towards him threateningly. 'Keep calling until you get her.'

*W*ild Goose staggered and wallowed through the turbulence at the entrance to Cartridge Bay, then fought her way into the sanctuary of the channel.

Hugo relaxed perceptibly. It had been a long hard run back from Thunderbolt and Suicide. Yet there was an uneasy feeling that still persisted. He hoped that the girl was able to handle Lance. He was a tough cookie that Lance, he wished that he had been able to go along with her and make sure of the business. Fifteen years was one hell of a long time – he would be almost fifty years old at the end of it.

Hugo followed the channel markers that appeared like milestones out of the dust clouds, until ahead he made out the loom of the jetty and the depot buildings.

There was a figure on the jetty, crouched beside the mountain of dieseline drums. With a prickle of alarm, Hugo strained his eyes in the bad visibility.

'Who the hell is it?' he puzzled aloud. The figure straightened and came forward to stand on the edge of the jetty. Bare-headed, dressed in rumpled dark business suit, the man carried a shotgun in one hand – and it was another few seconds before Hugo recognized him.

'Christ! It's the boss!' Hugo felt alarm flare in his stomach and chest, it tightened his breathing.

Benedict van der Byl jumped down on to the deck of *Wild Goose* at the moment she touched the jetty.

'What's happened?' Benedict demanded as he barged into the wheelhouse.

'I thought you were in hospital,' Hugo countered.

'Who told you that?'

'Your sister.'

'You've seen her? Where is she?'

'I took her out to *Kingfisher*. Like you said. She went out to deal with Lance.'

'Deal with Lance! She's with him, you idiot, she's not with us. She knows the whole deal. Everything!'

'She told me—' Hugo was appalled. But Benedict cut him short.

'The whole thing's blown up. We've got to clear out. Get your crew to load those drums of dieseline into the hold. How are your water tanks?'

'Full.'

'Food?'

'We are stocked up.'

189

'For how long?'

'Three weeks – at a push, four.'

'Thank God for that.' Benedict looked relieved. 'This storm will blow another three days – we'll have that much start. They'll never find us in this. By the time it clears we'll be well on our way.'

'Where to – Angola?'

'God, no! We have to get well clear. South America.'

'South America!'

'Yes – we can do it, carrying extra fuel.'

Hugo was silent a moment, becoming accustomed to the idea.

'We can do it,' Benedict repeated.

'Yes.' Hugo nodded. 'We can do it,' he agreed thoughtfully. For the first time he examined Benedict closely. He saw that he was in an emotional and physical mess, his bloodshot eyes were sunk into deep plum-coloured hollows, dark new beard covered his jowls, and there was a gaunt hunted look to him – like some fugitive animal.

He was filthy with dust, and there was a streak of something that could have been dried vomit down the front of his jacket.

'But what do we do when we get there?' For the first time since he had known Benedict he felt in control. This was the time to deal, to make bargains.

'We'll get ashore on some deserted spot, and then we split up and disappear.'

'What about money?' Hugo spoke carefully. He glanced down at the shotgun. Benedict's hands were fidgety and restless on the weapon.

'I've got money.'

'How much?' Hugo asked.

'Enough.' Benedict blinked cautiously.

'For me also?' Hugo prodded him, and Benedict nodded.

'How much for me?' Hugo went on.

'Ten thousand.'

'Pounds?'

'Pounds,' Benedict agreed.

'That's not enough.' Hugo shook his head. 'I'll need more than that.'

'Twenty.' Benedict increased his bid, but he knew he was playing from weakness into strength. Ruby was lying mutilated in his study, the net was probably being spread for him already.

'Fifty,' said Hugo decisively.

'I haven't that much.'

'Who are you kidding, Buster!' Hugo snorted. 'You've been stacking it away for years.'

Benedict let the barrels of the shotgun swing towards Hugo's belly suggestively.

'Go ahead,' Hugo grinned at him, screwing up his pale albino eyes. 'That'll leave you to paddle this canoe – you want to try it? You'd pile her up on the bar at the entrance – that's how far you'd get.'

Benedict swung the barrels aside.

'Fifty,' he agreed.

'Right!' Hugo spoke briskly. 'Let's get the hell out of here.'

*W*ild *Goose* was clear of the land, and of the towering blinding dust clouds. The following seas came sweeping up under her stern urging her on her westward flight, while the high-pitched shriek of the wind in her rigging cried to her to hasten.

'Why don't you get down below and grab some sleep?' Hugo said. He found Benedict's restless haunting presence in the crowded wheelhouse disconcerting.

Benedict ignored the suggestion. 'Switch on the radio,' he said.

'What for? You'll get nothing on the set.'

'We are out of the dust,' Benedict replied. 'We might pick up a police message.'

The image of Ruby was so clear in his mind. He wanted to know if they'd found her yet. He felt his gorge rising again. That head – oh God – that head! He crossed quickly to the radio set and switched it on.

'They won't be on to us yet,' said Hugo, but Benedict was manipulating the dials – searching the tortured radio waves. The static wailed and gibbered and shrieked like a maniac.

'Turn it off,' snapped Hugo, and at that moment a voice cut in on them.

' – *Wild Goose*,' said the voice from the loudspeaker quite clearly. Benedict crouched eagerly over the set, his hands busy on the dials, and Hugo came up beside him.

' – Come in, *Wild Goose*. This is *Kingfisher*. I repeat, come in *Wild Goose*—'

Benedict and Hugo looked at each other. 'Don't answer,' said Hugo, but he made no move to intervene as Benedict lifted the microphone off its hook.

'*Kingfisher*, this is *Wild Goose*.'

'Stand by, *Wild Goose*.' The answer came back immediately. 'Stand by for Captain Caporetti.'

'*Wild Goose* standing by.'

Hugo caught Benedict's shoulder and his voice was angrily uncertain.

'Leave it, don't be a fool.'

Benedict shrugged off the hand, and Sergio's voice boomed out of the speaker.

'This is Caporetti – who dat?'

'No names,' Benedict cautioned him. 'Where are your guests?'

'They safe – battened down nicely.'

'Safe? Are you certain? Both of them safe?'

'*Si*. I have them safe and sure.'

'Stand by.' Benedict crouched over the set, and his mind

was racing. Johnny Lance was in his power. This was the last chance he would ever have. Plans began to form, gelling quickly in his mind.

'The diamonds. Caporetti has the diamonds. That big Blue is worth a million on its own,' said Hugo. 'If Caporetti has taken care of the others – it would be worth the risk.'

'Yes.' Benedict turned to him, he had been puzzling how he could make Hugo turn back. He had forgotten the diamonds. 'It would be worth it,' he agreed.

'Just a quick pass alongside *Kingfisher* – pick up Caporetti with the diamonds and we'd be on our way.'

'I have to go aboard.' Benedict qualified the suggestion.

'Why?' Hugo asked.

'Wipe out the reel on the computer that carries the programme – it's got the Jap's name on it. They could trace him. I paid him on my Swiss bank. They'll find the account.'

Hugo hesitated. 'No killing – or anything like that. We've got enough trouble without that.'

'You think I'm crazy?' Benedict demanded.

'Okay, then,' Hugo agreed.

'*Kingfisher*,' Benedict spoke into the microphone. 'We are coming to you. I'll be coming on board to finalize matters.'

'Fine.' Through the static they could hear the relief in Sergio's voice. 'I'll be standing by.'

It took nearly two hours for *Wild Goose* to slug her way back to where *Kingfisher* lay beneath the ghostly white shapes of Thunderbolt and Suicide, and it was after midday before Hugo began manoeuvring *Wild Goose* into the big ship's lee.

'Don't waste time,' Hugo cautioned Benedict. 'The sooner we get on our way – the better for all of us.'

'I'll be about half an hour,' Benedict answered. 'You lay off and wait for us.'

'Are you taking that bloody shotgun?' Benedict nodded.

'What for?' But Benedict did not reply, he looked up at the sky. The sun was merely a luminous patch of silver light through the ceiling of sea-fret and wind-driven mist, and still the storm hunted hungrily across the sea.

'It will slow you up on the ladder.' Hugo harped on the shotgun. He wanted very much to part Benedict from it, he wanted it over the side – for its presence aboard would prejudice the plans that Hugo had been forming during the last few hours – plans that took into account the ready market for diamonds in South America, and the undesirability of sharing the proceeds with two partners.

'I'll take it.' Benedict tightened his grip on the stock of the weapon. Without it he would feel naked and vulnerable – and it was part of his own private plans for the future. Benedict's brain had also been busy during the last two hours.

'Suit yourself.' Hugo resigned himself to Benedict's refusal; there would be an opportunity later, during the long passage across the Southern Atlantic. 'You better get up for'ard.'

This time Hugo's approach was neatly executed; in a lull between the colossal swells he touched *Wild Goose*'s bows to the steel side of the factory ship. Benedict stepped across the gap and was up the landing ladder and standing at *Kingfisher*'s rail before the next wave came marching down on them.

He waved Hugo off, then hanging on to the rail, made his way aft to *Kingfisher*'s bridge works.

'Where is Lance?' he demanded of Sergio the moment he stepped on to the bridge, but Sergio glanced significantly at the inquisitively listening helmsman and led Benedict through into his cabin.

'Where is Lance?' Benedict repeated the moment the door was locked.

'He and your sister they are in the conveyor room.'

'The conveyor room?' Benedict was incredulous.

'Si. They find out about Kammy's machine. They open the hatch and go inside. I close both doors. Lock them good.'

'They are in there now?' Benedict asked to gain time to reconstruct his plans.

'Si. Still there.'

'All right.' Benedict reached his decision. 'Now listen, Caporetti, this is what we are going to do. The whole thing has blown up on us. We are going to wipe out as much of the evidence against us as possible, then we are clearing out. We are going to run for South America in *Wild Goose*. You have got the diamonds – haven't you?'

'Si.' Sergio patted the breast of his jacket.

'Give them to me.' Benedict held out his hand, and Sergio grinned.

'I tink I look after them. They keep my heart warm.'

A frown of annoyance narrowed Benedict's eyes, but he let the moment pass.

'All right.' His tone was still friendly. 'Now, what you have to do is get down to the control room and wipe out Kaminikoto's programme. Get his name off that reel. He showed you how to do that?'

'Si.' Sergio nodded.

'How long will it take?'

'Half an hour, not longer,' Sergio answered, and Benedict checked his wrist watch, sure that this would give him time enough to do what he had to do.

'Good! Get cracking.'

'Boss.' Sergio hesitated at the cabin door. 'What about my boys, my crew? They good boys, no trouble for them?'

'They're clean,' Benedict pointed out irritably. 'I'll get

them together now, and explain that you have to go ashore. They can keep *Kingfisher* hove to waiting for you to come back. After the storm blows out they are bound to radio base and find out we have disappeared. They'll be all right.'

Sergio nodded his satisfaction.

'I'll call them all to the bridge now. You talk to them.'

The five crew members were gathered on *Kingfisher*'s bridge, and Sergio had disappeared down below.

'Any of you speak English?' Benedict demanded, and two of them affirmed that they did.

'Right,' Benedict addressed them. 'You will have been wondering about all the coming and going in this weather. I want you all to be ready to leave the ship. I want you to get all your valuables – now!'

Quickly they translated to the others, who looked apprehensively at Benedict. He was a strange wild-eyed figure with the shotgun tucked under his arm.

'Right – let's go.' And there was no dissent from any of them as they trooped to the companionway.

Benedict followed them along the passageway towards the crew quarters, and glanced quickly at his wrist watch. Seven minutes had elapsed. He looked at the men ahead of him.

The backs of their heads formed a solid target. He had shot guineafowl like that in Namaqualand when they were on the ground running away from him in a thick file, down on one knee and aim for the thicket of heads, knocking down half the flock with both barrels.

He knew he could take all five of these men with two shots. Just let them get a little further ahead so the shot could spread. But he remembered Ruby and his stomach heaved. The other way was just as sure.

'Stop!' he commanded as the five men came level with

the paint store. They obeyed and turned back to face him. Now he held the shotgun so that there was no mistaking its menace. They stared at the gun fearfully.

'Open that door.' He pointed at the paint store. Nobody moved.

'You.' Benedict picked on one of those who spoke English. Like a man in a trance he went to the steel door and spun the locking handle. He pulled the door open.

'In!' Eloquently Benedict gestured with the shotgun. Reluctantly the five of them filed into the small windowless cubicle, and Benedict slammed the door on them. He spun the lock, throwing all his weight on the handle to set it.

Now he had a clear field, and his wrist watch gave him another twenty minutes. He hurried for'ard, he wanted to keep well clear of the control room and Sergio Caporetti.

Using the forward companionway he dropped down to the working deck, fumbling out his duplicate set of keys.

WARNING. EXPLOSIVES. NO UNAUTHORIZED ENTRY.

He unlocked the door, and laying the shotgun flat on the deck he lifted a twenty-five pound drum of plastique down from its rack.

In his haste he tore a fingernail on the lid of the drum, but hardly felt the pain. He uncoiled a six-foot length of the soft dark toffee-coloured material and slung it around his neck. Next he selected a cardboard box of pencil time fuses. He read the label.

'Fourteen-minute delay. That's about right.'

Blood from his torn nail left brown blotches on the cardboard as he took four of the pencils from the box, picked up the shotgun and hurried aft. The jet engine whine of the cyclone mounted deafeningly as he came closer to it.

T racey was curled on the bare steel plating of the deck with Johnny's jacket folded under her head. She was in a fatigue-drugged sleep, so deep as to be almost deathlike.

Every few minutes Johnny interrupted his restless patrol of the conveyor room to stand over her and look down on her unconscious form. His worried expression softened a little each time he studied her pale lovely face. Once he stooped over her and tenderly lifted a strand of dark hair from her cheek, before resuming his pacing up and down the narrow cabin.

Each time he reached the door of the conveyor room he glanced through the tiny window. The glass had resisted his attempts to smash it with one of the spanners. He had wanted to open the window to call for help, but his efforts had not marked the thick armoured glass.

There was no way out of the cabin. Johnny had tried every possible outlet. The apertures for the conveyor system were guarded at one end by the furnace, and at the other by moving machinery which would ferociously chew to tatters anyone who became entangled in it. They were caged securely, and Johnny paced his cage.

Again he stopped before the peephole, but this time he flung himself at the door with clenched fists. The steel plate smeared the skin from his knuckles as he hammered on it and the pain sobered him. He pressed his face to the glass and through it watched Benedict van der Byl enter the conveyor room and, without glancing at the window, cross to the cyclone.

Benedict laid aside the shotgun he carried and for a moment stood looking up at the thick steel pipe that carried the gravel down from the deck pumps above. As he lifted the thick rope of plastique from around his neck, Johnny knew exactly what he was going to do.

He watched in fascination as Benedict mounted the steel ladder up the side of the cyclone. Hanging with one hand to the ladder, Benedict reached out with the other and clumsily tied the rope of plastique around the gravel pipe. It hung there like a necklace about the throat of some obscene prehistoric monster.

'You bastard! You murdering bloody swine!' Johnny shouted, and again he beat on the steel door with his fists. But the thickness of the door and the whine of the cyclone drowned his voice. Benedict showed no sign of hearing him – but Tracey sat up and looked about her blearily. Then she came to her feet and staggering to the roll and pitch of the ship she went to Johnny and pressed her face to the window beside her.

Benedict was sticking the time pencils into the soft dark explosive. He used all four fuses, taking no chances on a misfire.

'What's he doing?' Tracey asked after she had recovered from the surprise of recognizing her brother.

'He's going to cut the pipe, and let *Kingfisher* pump herself full of gravel.'

'Sink her?' Tracey's voice was sharp with alarm.

'She'll pump water and gravel into herself at pressures that will tear away all the inner bulkheads.'

'This one?' Tracey patted the steel plate.

'It'll pop like a paper bag. God, you have no idea of the power in those pumps.'

'No.' Tracey shook her head. 'He's my brother. He won't do it, Johnny. He couldn't murder us.'

'By the time he's finished – ' Johnny contradicted her grimly, ' – *Kingfisher* will be lying in 200 feet of water. Her hull will be packed so tightly with gravel that it will be like a block of cement. We, and everything in her, including his little machine, will be so flattened as to be unrecognizable. It would cost millions to salvage *Kingfisher* – and no one will care that much.'

'No, not Benedict.' Tracey was almost pleading. 'He's not that bad.'

Johnny interrupted her brusquely. 'He could get away with it. It's a good try – his best chance. Encase all the evidence against him in concrete, and bury it deep.'

'No, Benedict.' Tracey was watching her brother as he climbed down the cyclone ladder and picked up the shotgun. 'Please, Benedict, don't do it.'

Almost as if he had heard her, Benedict turned suddenly and saw the two faces at the window. The shock of guilt held him rigid for a moment as he stared at them – Tracey's pale lips forming words he could not hear, Johnny's eyes burning with accusation.

Benedict dropped his eyes, he made a gesture that was indecisive, almost pathetic. He looked up at the fused and charged rope of explosive – and then he grinned. A sardonic twitching of the lips, and he stumbled out of the cyclone room and was gone.

'He'll come back,' whispered Tracey. 'He won't let it happen.'

'I wouldn't bet on that – if I were you,' said Johnny.

B enedict reached *Kingfisher*'s rail and clung to it. He looked out to where *Wild Goose* bobbed and hung on the swells. He saw Hugo's face as a white blob behind the wheelhouse window, but as the little trawler began closing in for the pick-up Benedict waved it away. He glanced at his watch again, then looked back anxiously at the bridge.

The long minutes dragged by. Where the hell was the Italian? Benedict could not leave him – not while he still had that diamond; not while he could stop the dredge pumps and release the prisoners locked below.

Again Benedict checked his watch, twelve minutes since he had set the time pencils. He must go back and find Caporetti. He started back along the rail, and at that moment Sergio appeared on the wing of the bridge. He shouted a question at Benedict that was lost in the wind.

'Come on!' Frantically Benedict beckoned to him. 'Come on! Hurry!'

With another last look about the bridge, Sergio ran to the ladder and climbed down to deck level.

'Where my boys?' he shouted at Benedict. 'Why nobody at the con? What you do with them?'

'They are all right,' Benedict assured him. He had turned to the rail and was signalling *Wild Goose* to come alongside.

'Where they?' Sergio demanded. 'Where my boys?'

'I sent them to—' Benedict's reply was cut off as *Kingfisher*'s deck jarred under their feet. The explosion was a dull concussion in her belly, and Sergio's jaw hung open. Benedict backed away from him along the rail.

'Filth!' Sergio's jaw snapped closed, his whole body appeared to swell with anger.

'You kill them, dirty pig. You kill my boys. You kill Johnny – the girl.'

'Keep away from me.' Benedict braced himself against the rail, leaving both hands free to use the gun.

Not even Sergio would advance into the deadly blank eyes of those muzzles. He paused uncertainly.

'I'll blow your guts all over the deck,' Benedict warned him, and his forefinger was hooked around the trigger.

They stared at each other, and the wind fluttered their hair and tore at their clothing.

'Give me those diamonds,' Benedict commanded, and when Sergio stood unmoving, he went on urgently, 'Don't be a hero, Caporetti. I can gun you down and take them anyway. Give them to me – and our deal is still on. You'll come with us. I'll get you out of here. I swear it.'

Sergio's expression of outrage faded. A moment longer he hesitated.

'Come on, Caporetti. We haven't got much time.' It may have been his imagination, but to Benedict it seemed that

Kingfisher's action in the water had altered, she was sluggish to meet the swells and her roll was more pronounced.

'Okay,' said Sergio, and began unbuttoning his jacket. 'You win. I give you.'

Benedict relaxed with relief, and Sergio thrust his hand into his jacket and stepped towards him. He grasped the canvas bag by its neck, and brought it out held like a cosh.

Sergio was close to him, too close for Benedict to swing the shotgun on to him. Sergio's expression became savage, his intentions blazed in his dark eyes as he lifted the canvas bag and poised himself to deliver a blow at Benedict's head, but he had not reckoned with the extraordinary reflexes of the natural athlete he was facing.

As Sergio launched the blow, Benedict rolled his shoulders and head away from it, lifting the butt of the shotgun as a guard. Sergio's wrist struck the seasoned walnut, and he grunted with the pain. His fingers opened nervelessly and the canvas bag flew from his grip, glanced off Benedict's temple and flew on down the deck, sliding to stop against one of the compressed air tanks thirty feet away.

Benedict danced back, dropping the barrels of the shotgun until Sergio looked into the muzzles.

'Hold it, you bastard,' Benedict snarled at him. 'You've made your choice. Now let's see what your guts look like.'

Sergio was hugging his injured wrist to his belly, crouching over it. Benedict was backing away to where the bag lay against the tank. His face was flushed and hectic with anger, but he kept darting side glances at the canvas bag.

At that moment *Kingfisher* took another wave over her bows, and the water came swooshing down the deck, picking up the bag and washing it towards the scuppers.

'Look out!' Sergio shouted. 'The bag! It's going.'

Benedict lunged for it, sprawling full length. With his free hand he grabbed the sodden canvas as it was disappearing over the side. But he was thirty feet away from Sergio, and he still held the shotgun in his other fist. Sergio could not hope to reach him without getting both charges of buckshot in his belly.

Instead Sergio spun round and sprinted back along the deck towards the bridge.

Benedict was on his knees frantically stuffing the bag of diamonds into the side pocket of his jacket and shouting after Sergio.

'Stop! Stop or I'll shoot!'

Sergio did not look back nor check his run, and Benedict had the bag in his pocket and now both hands were free. He lifted the shotgun, and tried to balance himself against *Kingfisher*'s wallowing motion as he aimed.

At the shot, Sergio stumbled slightly but kept on running. He reached the ladder and went up it.

Again Benedict aimed, and the shotgun clapped dully in the wind. This time a spasm of pain shuddered through Sergio's big body, and he froze on the ladder.

Benedict fumbled in his pocket for fresh shells, but before he could reload Sergio had begun climbing again. Benedict broke the gun and thrust the shells into the breech. He snapped the gun closed and looked up just as Sergio disappeared through the storm doors – and the two shots that Benedict loosed after him merely pockmarked the paintwork and starred the glass of the wheelhouse.

'The stupid bastard.' Hugo watched from the wheelhouse of *Wild Goose*. 'He's gone berserk.'

Hugo had heard the explosion and seen the shooting.

'Fifteen years is enough – but not the rope as well.'

He swung the wheel and *Wild Goose* sheered in towards

Kingfisher's side. Peering through the spray and salt-smattered windows, he saw Benedict drag himself to his feet and start after Sergio along the deck.

Hugo snatched the electric loudhailer from its bracket and pulled open the side window of the wheelhouse, holding the hailer to his lips.

'Hey! You stupid bastard, have you gone mad? What the hell you doing?'

Benedict glanced down at the trawler, then ignored it to give all his attention to reloading the gun. He kept going back along the deck, following Sergio to finish him off.

'You'll get us all strung up, you fool,' Hugo called through the loudhailer. 'Leave him. Let's get out of here.'

Benedict kept scrambling and slipping towards *King-fisher*'s bridge.

'I'm leaving – now! Do you hear me? You can stew in your own pot. I'm getting out.'

Benedict checked and looked down at the trawler. He shouted and pointed at the bridge. Hugo caught one word: 'Diamonds.'

'All right, friend! Do what you like – I'll see you around,' Hugo hailed, and hit the trawler's throttle wide open. The roar of the diesels and the churning of her propeller convinced Benedict.

'Hugo! Wait! Wait for me, I'm coming.' He scampered back to the ladder and started down it.

Hugo throttled back and brought *Wild Goose* in neatly under the ladder.

'Jump!' he shouted through the hailer, and obediently Benedict jumped to hit the foredeck heavily. The shotgun flew from his hands to fall into the water alongside. Benedict cast one longing glance after the gun, then crawled to his feet and limped back to the wheelhouse.

Already *Wild Goose* was plunging away into the wind, but as Benedict entered the wheelhouse Hugo turned on him with his pink albino face set in a snarl of rage.

'What the hell have you done, you bastard? You lied to me. What was that explosion?'

'Explosion – I don't know. What explosion?'

Hugo hit him a stinging open-handed blow across the cheek.

'We agreed no killing – and you put us all on the spot.' Hugo's attention was focused completely on Benedict who had backed into the furthest corner of the wheelhouse. He massaged the dark red finger marks that stained his cheek.

'You set scuttling charges in *Kingfisher* – didn't you, you dirty son of a bitch. God, I hate to think what you've done with Lance and the girl.'

Outside the storm was nearing its climax. A rain squall swept down on *Wild Goose* – a sure sign that the wind must soon drop.

Automatically Hugo switched on the rotating wipers to clear the rain from the screen, as he continued to harangue Benedict.

'I saw you trying to murder the Italian. Christ! What for? He's one of us! Am I next on your list?'

'He had the diamonds,' mumbled Benedict. 'I was trying to get them from him.'

And Hugo's expression changed; he turned away from the wheel and stared at Benedict.

'You haven't got the diamonds? Is that what you're saying?' His tone was almost hurt.

'I tried – he wouldn't—'

And Hugo left the wheel and was across the wheelhouse like a white leopard. He grabbed the front of Benedict's coat, and screamed into his face.

'You left the diamonds! You stick my head in a noose – and I get nothing out of it.'

He was trembling with rage and his pale eyes bulged from their sockets.

Looking into those eyes Benedict realized his own danger. In the time it had taken him to leave *Kingfisher*'s deck and reach the wheelhouse of the trawler he had decided to let Hugo think that Sergio still had the diamonds. Squeamish as Hugo appeared to be about drowning Johnny and Tracey, despite his repeated demands for 'No killing', Benedict knew intuitively that Hugo had no intention of splitting a million pounds' worth of diamonds with him.

Once Hugo was certain that Benedict had the stones on board, Benedict knew there was no chance that he would reach South America alive.

The crossing might take weeks, the crew of the trawler were in Hugo's pay and loyal only to him. Benedict must sleep, and they would take him in the night.

On the other hand, of course, Benedict had no intention of splitting a million pounds' worth of diamonds with Hugo Kramer. He let his voice whine as he cringed in Hugo's grip.

'I tried. Sergio had them. He wouldn't – that's why I shot him.'

Hugo drew back his hand to slap Benedict again. Benedict twisted slightly, and drove his knee into Hugo's crutch, sending him staggering back across the wheelhouse, clutching himself between the legs and whimpering with the pain.

'Right, Kramer,' Benedict spoke softly. 'That's a little lesson for you. Behave yourself, and you'll get your fifty grand on the other side of the Atlantic.'

They stared at each other. Hugo Kramer weak and pale with agony, Benedict standing tall and arrogant again.

'Treat me gently, Kramer. I'm your meal-ticket. Remember it.'

Hugo gaped at him. The positions had reversed so swiftly. He pulled himself upright and his voice was thick with agony, but humble.

'I'm sorry, Mr van der Byl, I lost my temper. It's been a hell of a—'

'Skipper! Ahead!' The warning was shouted by the coloured crewman, Hansie.

Hugo stumbled to the untended wheel, and peered out into the storm.

Wild Goose was shooting down another slope of green water, and just ahead of her bows Hugo saw one of the huge yellow buoys that *Kingfisher* had laid down and then abandoned. It was held captive in the trough of the swells by the anchor cable. The cable was drawn as tight as a rod of steel across the trawler's bows, lifted just above the surface of the water; shivering drops of water flew from it under the tension of the buoy's drag.

'Oh God!' Hugo spun the wheel and threw *Wild Goose*'s engine into reverse – but she was racing down the swell, and her speed was unchecked as the cable scraped harshly along her keel.

Then came the harsh banging and clattering of the drive shaft as the cable fouled the propeller – followed by a crack as the shaft snapped. *Wild Goose*'s engine screamed into overrev as the load was lifted from it.

Hugo shut the throttle, and there was silence in the wheelhouse. *Wild Goose* swung beam on to the seas which came boiling in over her deck. Without her propeller she was transformed from a husky little sea creature to a piece of driftwood at the mercy of each current and the whim of the wind.

Hugo's head swung slowly until he was looking downwind to where the massive shapes of Thunderbolt and Suicide just showed through the rain squall.

'Cover your ears – tight!' Johnny Lance pressed Tracey against the bulkhead as far from the cyclone room as they could get. 'There are twenty-five pounds of plastique in there – it will blow like a volcano. He will have used short fuse, fourteen minutes. We won't have long to wait.'

Johnny set Tracey's shoulders squarely against the steel plating, and crouched over her – trying to shield her with his own body.

They stared into each other's eyes, teeth clenched, the heels of their palms jammed hard over their ears and they cowered away from the blast that must come.

The minutes passed, the longest minutes of Tracey's life. She could not have borne them without screaming hysteria except for that big hard body covering her – even with it she felt her fear mounting steadily during the molasses drip of time.

Suddenly the air lunged at her, driving the breath from her lungs. Johnny was thrown heavily against her. The blast sucked at her eardrums, and burst in her head so that bright lights flashed across her vision and she felt the steel plates heave under her shoulders.

Then her head cleared, and although her eardrums buzzed and sang, she found with a leaping relief that she was still alive.

She reached out for Johnny, but he was gone. In panic she groped, then opened her eyes. He was lurching down the long conveyor room, and when he reached the locked door at the far end he pressed his face to the peephole.

The fumes of the explosion still filled the cyclone room, a swirling bluish fog, but through them Johnny could make out the shambles that was the aftermath.

The huge cyclone had been torn from its mountings, and now sagged against the far bulkhead – crushed. It was worth only a single glance before Johnny froze into rigidity at the true horror.

The gravel pipe had been severed cleanly just below its juncture with the upper deck. It protruded for six feet, but now the force of the jet through it was flicking and whipping it about as though it were not steel but a rubber garden hose.

The jet was a solid eighteen-inch column, a pillar of brown mud and yellow gravel and sea water that beat against the steel plates of the hull with a hollow drumming roar.

In the few seconds since the explosion the cyclone room was already half-filled with a slimy shifting porridge that rushed from wall to wall with the movement of the ship. It was like some monstrous jelly fish which each second gathered weight and strength.

Tracey reached Johnny's side and he placed his arm around her shoulders. She looked through the armoured glass and he felt her body stiffen.

At that moment the yellow monster spread over the window, obscuring it completely. Johnny felt the first straining of the steel plates under his hands. They fluttered and bulged, then began to protest aloud at the intolerable pressure. A seam started, and a fine jet of filthy water hissed from the gap and soaked icily through Johnny's jersey.

'Get back.' Johnny dragged Tracey away from the squeaking, groaning bulkhead. Back along the narrow conveyor room they stumbled, moving with difficulty for the deck beneath their feet was slanting as *Kingfisher* began to lean under the increasing weight in her belly.

Still holding Tracey, he reached the locked door and resisted the futile desire to attack it with his bare hands. Instead he forced his brain to work, tried to anticipate the sequence of events that would lead to the final destruction of *Kingfisher* – and all those aboard her.

Benedict had left the other entrance to the cyclone room wide open. Already that viscous mass of mud and water must be spreading rapidly through the lower levels of the hull, following always the avenue of least resistance – finding the weak spots and bursting through them.

If the walls of the conveyor room held against the pressure, the rest of the hull would be filled and they would be enfolded in the tentacles of that great yellow monster – a small bubble of air trapped within it and taken down with it when it returned to the depths from which it had come.

Would the bulkheads of the conveyor room hold? The answer came almost immediately in the squeal of metal against metal, and the crackle of springing rivets.

The monster had found the weak spot, the aperture through the drying furnace into the conveyor, ripping away the fragile baffles, bursting through the furnace in a cloud of steam, it gushed into the conveyor room bringing with it the sewage stench of deep-sea mud.

Kingfisher made another sluggish roll, so different from her usual spry action, and the mud came racing down the tunnel in a solid knee-high wall.

It slammed both of them back against the steel door with a shocking strength, and the feel of it was cold and loathsome as something long dead and putrefied.

Kingfisher rolled back and the mud slithered away, bunched itself against the far bulkhead then charged at them again.

Waist-deep it struck them, and tried to suck them back with the next roll.

Tracey was screaming now, nerves and muscles reaching their breaking-point. She was clinging to Johnny, coated to the waist in stinking ooze, her eyes and mouth wide open in terror as she watched the mud building up for its next assault.

Johnny groped for some hold to anchor them. They must keep on their feet to survive that next rush of mud. He found the locking handle of the door and braced himself against it, holding Tracey with all his strength.

The mud came again, silently, murderously. It burst over

their heads and punched them with stunning force against the plating.

Then it sucked back once more, and left them down on their knees, anchored only by Johnny's grip on the locking handle.

Tracey was vomiting the foul mud and it filled her ears and eyes and nostrils, clogging them so that it bubbled at her breathing.

Johnny could feel her weakening in his arms, her struggles becoming more feeble as she tried to regain her feet.

His own strength was going. It needed his last reserve to drag them both upright.

The locking handle turned in his fingers, spinning open. The steel door against which he was braced fell away, so that he staggered backwards without support but still clutching Tracey.

There was just a moment to recognize the big, reassuring bulk of Sergio Caporetti beside him and feel an arm like the trunk of a pine tree steady him before the rush of mud down the conveyor room hit them and knocked all three of them down, sending them swirling and rolling end over end before its strength dissipated in the new space beyond the conveyor room door.

Johnny pulled himself up the bulkhead. He had lost Tracey. Dazed but desperate he looked for her, mumbling her name.

He found her swilling aimlessly in the waist-deep mud, floating on her face. He took a handful of muddy hair and lifted her face out, but the mud had hold of his legs, pulling him off balance as it surged back and forth.

'Sergio. Help!' he croaked. 'For God's sake, Sergio.'

And Sergio was there, lifting her like a child in his arms and wading to the ladder that led to the deck above. The mud knocked Johnny down again, and when he surfaced Sergio was climbing steadily up the ladder.

Despite the mud and water that blurred Johnny's eyesight, he could see that Sergio's wide back, from shoulders to hips, was speckled with dozens of punctures as though he had been stabbed repeatedly with a knitting needle. From each tiny wound oozed droplets of blood that spread like brown ink on the blotting-paper of his sodden jacket.

At the head of the companionway Sergio turned, still holding Tracey in his arms; he stood like a Colossus looking down at Johnny wallowing and slipping in the mud below.

'Hey, Lance – go switch off your bloody machine. She drown my ship. I sail her myself now – the right way. No bloody fancy machine.'

Johnny steadied himself against the bulkhead and called up at him:

'Sergio, what happened to Benedict van der Byl, where is he?'

'I think he go with *Wild Goose* – but first he shoot the hell out of me, not half. Fix your machine, no time for talk.'

And he was gone, still carrying Tracey.

Another rush of mud carried Johnny down the flooded passage and threw him against the door to the control room. Already his body seemed to be one aching bruise, and still the battering continued as he tried to unlock and open the control room door.

At last, using the suck of the mud to help him, he yanked it open and went in with a burst of yellow slime following him and flooding the compartment shoulder deep.

Clinging to the console of the computer he reached up and punched the master control buttons.

'Dredge Stop.'

'Dredge engines Stop.'

'Main engines manual.'

'Navigation system manual.'

'All programmes abort.'

Instantly the roar from the severed dredge pipe, which

had echoed through the ship during all their strivings, dwindled as though some vast waterfall had dried. Then there was silence. Though only comparative silence, for the hull still groaned and squeaked at the heart-breaking burden it now carried and the mud slopped and thudded against the plating.

Weak and sick, Johnny clung to the console. He was shivering with cold, and every muscle in his body felt bruised and strained.

Suddenly the ship changed her motion, heaving under his feet like a harpooned whale as she swung broadside to the storm. Johnny roused himself with alarm.

The journey back through the flooded passages to the companionway was an agony of mind and body – for *Kingfisher* was now behaving in a strange and unnatural way.

The scene that awaited Johnny as he dragged himself on to the bridge chilled his soul as the icy mud had chilled his body.

Thunderbolt and Suicide lay less than a furlong off *Kingfisher*'s starboard quarter. Both islands were wreathed in sheets of spray that fumed from the surf that was breaking like cannon-fire on the cliffs.

The maniacal flute of the wind joined with the drum of the surf to produce a symphony fit for the halls of Hell, but above this devil's music Sergio Caporetti bellowed, 'We got no power on port main engine.'

Johnny turned to him. Sergio was hunched over the wheel, and Tracey lay on the deck at his feet like a discarded doll.

'The water, she kill port main.' Sergio was pumping the engine telegraph. Then abandoning the effort, he looked over the side.

The reeking white cliffs were closer now, much closer – as though you could reach out a hand to them. The ship was drifting down rapidly on the wind.

Sergio spun the wheel to full port lock, trying to bring *Kingfisher*'s head round to meet the sea and the wind. She was rolling as no ship was ever meant to roll, hanging over at the limit of each swing, so that the wheelhouse windows seemed but a few feet from the crests of the green waves. She hung like that as though she meant never to come upright again. Then sluggishly, reluctantly, she swung back, speeding up as she reached the perpendicular and the great mass of mud and water in her hull shifted and slammed her over on her other side, pinning her like that for eternal seconds before she could struggle upright again for the cycle to be repeated.

Sergio held the wheel at full lock, but still *Kingfisher* wallowed down towards the cliffs of Thunderbolt and Suicide. The wind had her the way a dog carries a bone in its teeth. Under half power and with her decks awash *Kingfisher* could not break that grip.

Johnny was a helpless spectator, held awe-bound so he could not break away even to succour Tracey who was still lying on the deck. He saw everything with a supernatural clarity – from the dribbling little shot holes in Sergio's back, to the ponderous irresistible rush of the white water up the cliffs that loomed so close alongside.

'She no answer helm. She too sick.' Sergio spoke now in conversational tones which carried with surprising clarity through the uproar of the elements. 'All right then. We go the other way. We take the gap.'

For a moment Johnny did not understand, then he saw it. *Kingfisher*'s bows were coming up to the narrow opening between the two islands.

A passage less than a hundred yards wide at its narrowest point, where the vicious cross-currents met head-on and leapt fifty feet into the air as they collided. Here the surface was obscured by a thick froth of spindrift that heaved and humped up as though the ocean were fighting for breath under the thick cream-coloured blanket.

'No.' Johnny shook his head, staring at that hideous passage. 'We won't make it, Sergio. We won't do it.'

But already Sergio was spinning the wheel from lock to lock, and unbelievably *Kingfisher* was responding. Helped now by the wind she came around slowly, seeming to brush her bows across the white cliff of Thunderbolt, and she steadied her swing and aimed at the gap. It was then Johnny saw it for the first time.

'Christ, there's a boat dead ahead!'

The steep swells had hidden it up to that moment, but now she bobbed up on a crest. It was a tiny trawler, flying a dirty scrap of canvas as a staysail at her stubby mast, and struggling piteously in the granite jaws of Thunderbolt and Suicide.

'*Wild Goose!*' roared Sergio, and he reached for the handle of the foghorn that hung above his head.

'Now we have some fun.' And he yanked the handle. The croaking bellow of the foghorn echoed off the cliffs that were closing on either side of them.

'Kill my boys – hey? Shoot me – hey? Trick me – hey? Now I trick you – but good!' Sergio punctuated his triumphant yells with blasts on the foghorn.

'Christ, no! You can't do it!' Johnny caught urgently at the big Italian's shoulder, but Sergio struck his hand away and steered directly for the trawler as it lay full in the narrow passage.

'I give him plenty warning.' Sergio sent another blast echoing off the cliffs. 'He no give me warning when he shoot me – the bastard.'

There was a group of men on the trawler's foredeck. Johnny could see that they were manhandling an inflatable escape raft, a thick mattress of black rubber, towards the nearest side of the trawler. But now they were frozen by the bellow of *Kingfisher*'s foghorn. They stood looking up at the tall cliff of steel that bore down on them. Their faces were pale blobs in the gloom.

'Sergio. It's murder. Turn away, damn you, you can miss them. Turn away!' Again Johnny lunged across the wheel-house and grabbed at the wheel.

Sergio swung a backhanded blow that cracked against Johnny's temple and sent him reeling back half-stunned against the storm doors.

'*Who* Captain for this bloody ship!' There was blood on Sergio's lips, the shout had torn something inside him.

Kingfisher's bows were lifting and swinging down like an executioner's axe over the trawler. They were close enough now for Johnny to recognize the men on the trawler's deck – but only one of them held his full attention.

Benedict van der Byl cowered against the trawler's rail, gripping it with both hands. His hair fluttered, soft and dark, in the wind. His eyes were big dark holes like those of a skull in the bone-white face, and his lips a pink circle of terror.

Then suddenly the trawler disappeared under *Kingfisher*'s massive bows, and immediately after that came the splinter-ing crunching sound of her timbers shattering. *Kingfisher* bore on down the passage between the cliffs without a check in her speed.

Johnny fumbled with the catch of the storm doors, and the wind tore it open. He staggered out on to the exposed wing of the bridge and reached the rail.

He stood there with the storm clawing at his clothing and looked down at the wreckage that dragged slowly along *Kingfisher*'s hull, and then was left behind.

There were human heads bobbing among the wreckage, and the wash from *Kingfisher*'s propeller pushed them towards the cliffs of Suicide.

A wave picked up one of the men and carried him swiftly on to the cliff, sweeping him high and then swirling back to leave the body stranded on that smooth white slope of granite.

The man was still alive, Johnny saw him clawing at the

smooth rock with his bare fingers, trying to drag himself above the reach of the sea.

It was Hugo Kramer; even through the fog of spray there was no mistaking that head of pale hair and the lithe twisted body.

The next wave reached up and dragged him back over the rock, tearing the nails from his hooked fingers as he tried to find a hold.

He was swirled and flung about in the turbulence below the cliff before another wave lifted him and hurled him on to the granite. One of his legs was broken at the knee by the force of the impact and the lower part of the leg spun loosely like the blade of a windmill as the water tugged at it.

Once again Hugo was left stranded but now he made no movement. His arms were flung wide, and his leg stuck out at a grossly unnatural angle from the knee.

Then from among these mighty waves there rose up a mass of green water which dwarfed all the others.

It reared up with slow majesty and hung poised over the granite cliff before it fell on Hugo's broken body with a boom that seemed to shake the very rock.

When the giant wave drew back, the cliff was washed clean. Hugo was gone.

The same wave that destroyed him came down the passage between the cliffs and, in contrast to its treatment of Hugo Kramer, it was tender as a mother as it lifted *Kingfisher* and carried her out into the open sea beyond the reach of those cruel cliffs.

Looking back into the gap between the islands, the last trace that Johnny saw of the *Wild Goose* was the black rubber escape raft tossing and leaping high on the turmoil of broken water and creamy spindrift.

'They'll have no use for that,' he said aloud. He searched for a sight of any survivor, but there was none. They were chewed to pulp in the jaws of Thunderbolt and Suicide, and swallowed down into the cold green maw of the sea.

Johnny turned away and went back into the wheelhouse. He lifted Tracey from the deck and carried her through to Sergio's cabin.

As he laid her on the bunk he whispered to her, 'I'm glad. I'm glad you didn't see it, my darling.'

At midnight the wind still howled about the ship, hurling sheets of solid rain against the windows of the bridge. Forty minutes later the wind had veered through a hundred and eighty degrees and become a light south-easterly air. The black sky opened like a theatre curtain, and the full moonlight burst through so brightly as to pale the stars. Though the tall black swells still marched in martial ranks from the north, the gentle wind was soothing and lulling them.

'Sergio, you must rest now. I will take the con. Let Tracey dress your back.'

'You take the con!' Sergio snorted scornfully. 'I save the ship – and you sink her for me. Not bloody likely.'

'Listen, Sergio. We don't know how badly you are hurt. You are killing yourself.'

The same argument spluttered and flared intermittently during the long night hours while Sergio clung stubbornly to the helm and coaxed the labouring vessel back towards Cartridge Bay. He insisted on detouring far out to sea to avoid the islands, so that when the bright dawn broke, the land was only a low brown line on the horizon and the mountains of the interior were a distant blue.

An hour after dawn Johnny made radio contact with the very agitated operator at Cartridge Bay.

'Mr Lance, we've been trying to raise you since yesterday evening.'

'I've been busy.' Despite his fatigue Johnny grinned at his own understatement. 'Now, listen to me. We are coming into Cartridge Bay. We'll be there in a couple of hours. I want you to have a doctor, Doctor Robin Sutherland, flown up from Cape Town – also I want you to have the police standing by. I want somebody from both the Diamond police and the Robbery and Murder squad – have you got that?'

'The police are here already, Mr Lance. They are looking for Mr Benedict van der Byl. They found his car here – they have a warrant . . .' The operator's voice broke off and Johnny heard the mumble of background voices, then – 'Mr Lance, are you there? Stand by to speak to Inspector Stander of the CID.'

'Negative!' Johnny cut in on his transmission. 'I'm not talking to anybody. He can wait until we get into the Bay. Just you have Doctor Sutherland ready. I've got a badly wounded man on board.'

Johnny leaned over the radio set and shut off the main switch, then he stood and made his way slowly back to the bridge. Every muscle in his body felt stiff and bruised, and he was groggy with tiredness, but he took up the argument with Sergio where they had left off.

'Now listen to me, Sergio. You must lie down. You can take us in over the bar; but now you must get an hour or two's rest.'

Still Sergio would not relinquish the wheel, but he consented to strip to the waist and let Tracey examine his back.

In the expanse of white muscle were little black holes each set in its own purple bruise. Some of the holes had sealed themselves with black clotted blood, from others fluid still oozed – clear or pink in colour – and there was a faint sweetish smell from the wounds.

Johnny and Tracey exchanged worried looks before Tracey reached into the first aid box and set to work.

'How she look, Johnny?' Sergio's jovial tone was belied by his face which was a lump of bread dough touched with greenish blue hues.

'Depends if you like your meat rare.' Johnny matched his tone, and Sergio chuckled but cut it short with a wince.

Johnny put a cheroot between Sergio's lips and held a match for him. As Sergio puffed the tip into a glow, Johnny asked casually, 'What made you change your mind?' And Sergio looked up at him quickly, guiltily, through the cloud of cheroot smoke.

'You had us cold. You could have got away with it – perhaps,' Johnny persisted quietly. 'What made you come back?'

'Listen, Johnny. Me, I've done some damned awful bloody things – but I never killed a man or a woman – ever. He said no killing. Fine, I go along. Then I hear the plastique blow. I know you two in conveyor room. I think the hell with it. Now, I climb off the wagon – but she's going too fast. I get bum full of buckshot.'

They were silent for a while. Tracey was absorbed in patching the shot-wounds with adhesive tape.

Johnny broke the silence. 'Was there a big diamond, Sergio? A big blue diamond?'

'Si.' Sergio sighed. 'Such a diamond you will never see again.'

'Benedict had it?'

'Si. Benedict had it.'

'Did he have it on him?'

'In his coat. He put it in his coat pocket.'

Tracey stepped back. 'That's all we can do for now,' she murmured and caught Johnny's eye, shaking her head slightly and frowning with worry. 'The sooner we get him to a doctor the happier I'll be.'

A little before noon Sergio took Kingfisher in through the entrance to Cartridge Bay, handling the mud-filled ship with all the aplomb of the master mariner, but as they approached the first turning in the channel he sagged gently to the deck and the wheel spun out of his hands.

Before Johnny could reach the helm, *Kingfisher* had yawed wearily across the channel. She had so little way on her that when she went up on the sand bank there was only a small jolt and she listed over a few degrees.

Johnny pulled the engine telegraph to 'STOP'.

'Help me, Tracey.' He stooped over Sergio and took him under the armpits. Tracey grasped his ankles. Half dragging, half carrying, they got him through to his cabin and laid him on his bunk.

'Hey, Johnny. Sorry, Johnny,' Sergio was mumbling. 'First time I put ship on bank – ever! Idiot! So close – then *wap*! Sorry, hey, Johnny.'

The motor launch left the jetty and came down the channel towards the sand bank on which *Kingfisher* lay stranded. The launch was crowded, and the whine of the outboard engine raised a storm of water fowl into a whirlwind of frightened wings.

As it drew closer Johnny recognized some of the occupants. Mike Shapiro and with him Robin Sutherland, but there were also two uniformed policemen and another person in civilian clothes who stood up in the launch as it came within hail and cupped his hands about his mouth.

'I am a police officer. I have a warrant for the arrest of Benedict—'

Mike Shapiro touched the man's arm, and spoke softly to him. The officer hesitated and glanced up at Johnny again, before nodding agreement and settling back on to his seat.

'Robin, get up here as quick as you can,' Johnny shouted down at the launch, and when Robin came over the side Johnny hustled him towards the bridge, but Mike Shapiro hurried after them.

'Johnny, I must talk to you.'

'It can wait.'

'No, it can't.' Mike Shapiro turned to Tracey. 'Won't you take care of the doctor, please? I must speak to Johnny before the police do.'

Mike led Johnny down the deck and offered him a cigarette, while the three policemen hovered at a discreet distance.

'Johnny, I have some dreadful news. I want to break it to you myself.'

Johnny visibly braced himself. 'Yes?'

'It's about Ruby—'

Johnny made his statement to the police inspector in *Kingfisher*'s guest cabin. It took two hours for him to relate the full story, and during that time one of the uniformed policemen discovered the crew locked in the paint store below decks. They were half poisoned with paint fumes but able to make their statements to the police.

The inspector kept them waiting in the next-door cabin while he finished his interrogation of Johnny.

'Two more questions for now, Mr Lance. In your opinion was the collision between the two ships accidental or deliberate?'

Johnny looked into the steel-grey eyes and lied for the first time.

'It was unavoidable.'

The inspector nodded and made a note on his pad.

'Last question. The survivors from the trawler, what were their chances?'

'In that storm they had none. There was no hope of effecting a rescue with *Kingfisher* almost disabled, and considering the condition of the surf in the passage between the islands.'

'I understand.' The inspector nodded. 'Thank you, Mr Lance. That is all for the present.'

Johnny left the cabin and went quickly to the upper deck. Tracey and Robin were still working over Sergio's bunk, but Robin looked up and came immediately to Johnny as he stood in the doorway.

'How is he, Robin?'

'He hasn't a chance,' Robin replied, keeping his voice low. 'One lung has collapsed, and there appear to be perforations of the bowel and intestine. I suspect a massive peritonitis. I can't move him without risking a secondary haemorrhage.'

'Is he conscious?'

Robin shook his head. 'He's going fast. God knows how he has lasted this long.'

Johnny moved across to the bunk and placed his arm about Tracey's shoulders. She moved closer to him and they stood looking down at Sergio.

His eyes were closed, and a dark pelt of new beard covered the lower part of his face. His breathing sawed and hissed loudly in the quiet cabin, and the fever lit bright spots of colour in his cheeks.

'You magnificent old rogue.' Johnny spoke softly, and Sergio's eyes blinked open.

Quickly Johnny stooped to him.

'Sergio. Your crew – your boys are safe.'

Sergio smiled. He closed those dark gazelle eyes, then opened them again and whispered painfully, 'Johnny, you give me job when I come out of prison?'

'They won't have you in prison – you'd lower the tone of the place.'

Sergio tried to laugh. He managed one strangled chuckle, then he came up on his elbows in the bunk with his eyes bulging, his mouth gaping for breath. He coughed once, a harsh tearing sound, and the blood burst from his lips in thick black clots and a bright red spray of droplets.

He fell back on the pillows, and was dead before Robin reached his side.

Tracey was asleep in the bedroom next door. Robin had sedated her heavily enough to keep her that way for the next twelve hours.

Johnny lay naked on the narrow bunk in the second guest room of the Cartridge Bay depot, and when he switched on the beside lamp his wrist watch showed the time as 2.46 in the morning.

He looked down at his own body. The bruises were dark purple and hot angry red across his ribs and flanks from where the mud had battered him against rough steel plating. He wished now that he had accepted the sleeping pills Robin had offered him, for the ache of his body and the whirl of his thoughts had kept him from sleep all that night.

His mind was trapped on a nightmare roundabout, revolving endlessly the two deaths which Benedict van der Byl must answer for in the dark places to which he had surely gone.

Ruby and Sergio. Ruby and Sergio. One he had seen die, the other he could imagine in all its gruesome detail.

Johnny sat up and lit a cigarette, seeking a distraction from the tortured images with which his overexcited brain bombarded him.

He tried to concentrate on reviewing the practical steps that would be necessary to clear up the aftermath of these last disastrous days.

He had spoken that evening by radio to Larsen, and received from him a promise of complete financial support during the time it would take to clear the mud from *Kingfisher*'s hull and recover the diamonds in the conveyor tunnel, and to tide over the period of salvage and repair before the dredger was ready to begin once more harvesting the rich fields of Thunderbolt and Suicide.

A salvage team would fly in tomorrow to begin the work on *Kingfisher*. He had cabled IBM requesting engineers to check out the computer for water damage.

Six weeks, Johnny estimated, before *Kingfisher* was ready for sea.

Then his unruly imagination leapt suddenly ahead to Ruby's funeral. It was set for Tuesday next week. Johnny rolled restlessly on his bunk, trying to shut his mind against the thoughts that assaulted it – but they crowded forward in a dark host.

Ruby, Benedict, Sergio, the big blue diamond.

He sat up again, stubbed out his cigarette and reached across to switch out the bedside lamp.

He froze like that, as a new thought pressed in on him. He heard Sergio's voice in his memory.

'*Such a diamond as you will never see again.*'

Now he felt the idea come ghosting along his spine so that the hair at the nape of his neck and on his forearms prickled with excitement.

'The Red Gods!' he exclaimed, almost shouting the name. And again Sergio's voice spoke.

'*In his coat. He put it in his coat pocket.*'

Johnny swung his legs off the bunk, and reached for his clothes. He felt the pounding of his heart beneath his fingers as he buttoned his shirt. He pulled on slacks and sweater, tied the laces of his shoes and snatched up a sheepskin jacket as he ran from the room.

He was shrugging on the jacket as he entered the deserted radio room and switched on the lights. He crossed quickly to the chart table and pored over it.

He found the name on the map, and repeated it aloud.

'The Red Gods.'

North of Cartridge Bay the coast ran straight and featureless for thirty miles, then abruptly the line of it was broken by the out-thrust of red rock, poking into the sea like an accuser's finger.

Johnny knew it well. It was his job to find and examine any such natural feature that might act as a barrier to the prevailing inshore currents. At such a place diamonds and other seaborne objects would be thrown ashore.

He remembered the red rock cliffs carved by wind and sea into the grotesque natural statues which gave the place its name, but more important he remembered the litter of ocean debris on the beaches beneath the cliff. Driftwood, waterlogged planking, empty bottles, plastic containers, scraps of nylon fishing-net and corks – all of it cast overboard and carried up by the current to be deposited on this promontory.

He ran his finger down the chart and held it on the dots of Thunderbolt and Suicide. He read the laconic notation over the tiny arrows that flew from the islands towards the stark outline of the Red Gods.

'Current sets South South-West. 5 knots.'

Above the chart table the depot keys hung on their little cuphooks, each labelled and numbered.

Johnny selected the two of them marked 'GARAGE' and 'LAND-ROVER'.

The moon was full and high. The night was still and without a trace of wind. Johnny swung the double doors of the garage open and switched on the parking lights of the Land-Rover. By their glow he checked out the vehicle; petrol tank full, the spare five-gallon cans in their brackets full, the can of drinking-water full. He dipped his finger into the neck of the water container and tasted it. It was clean and sweet. He lifted the passenger seat and checked the compartment beneath it. Jack and tyre spanner, first aid kit, flashlight, signal rockets and smoke flares, water bottle, canvas groundsheet, two cans of survival rations, towrope, tool kit, knapsack, knife and compass. The Land-Rover was equipped to meet any of the emergencies of desert travel.

Johnny climbed behind the wheel and started the engine. He drove quietly and slowly past the depot buildings, not wanting to awaken those sleeping inside, but when he hit the firm sand at the edge of the lagoon he switched on the headlights and gunned the engine.

He cut across the sand dunes at the entrance to the bay, and swung northwards on to the beach. The headlights threw solid white beams into the sea mist, and startled sea-birds rose on flapping ghost wings before the rush of the Land-Rover.

The tide was out and the exposed beach was hard and shiny wet, smooth as a tarmac road. He drove fast, and the white beach crabs were blinded by the headlights and crunched crisply beneath the tyres.

The dawn came early, silhouetting the mystic shapes of the dunes against the red sky.

Once he startled a strand wolf, one of the brown hyenas which scavenged this bleak littoral. It galloped, hunch-shouldered, in hideous panic for the safety of the dunes. Even in his urgency Johnny felt a stir of revulsion for the loathsome creature.

The cold damp rush of the wind into his face refreshed Johnny. It cooled the gritty feeling of his eyes, and eased the throb of sleeplessness in his temples.

The sun burst over the horizon, and lit the Red Gods five miles ahead with all the drama of stage lighting. They glowed golden red in the dawn, a procession of huge half-human shapes that marched into the sea.

As Johnny drove towards them the light and shadow played over the cliffs and he saw a hundred-foot tall figure of Neptune stooping to dip his flowing red beard into the sea, while a monstrous hunchback with the head of a wolf pranced beside him. Ranks of Vestal Virgins in long robes of red rock jostled with the throng of weird and fantastic shapes. It was eerie and disquieting. Johnny curbed his fancy and turned his attention to the beaches at the foot of the cliffs.

What he saw started his skin tingling again, and he

pressed the accelerator flat against the floorboards, racing across the wet sand to where a white cloud of seabirds circled and dived and hopped about something that lay at the water's edge.

As he drove towards them a gull flew across the front of the Land-Rover. A long ribbon of something wet and fleshy dangled from its beak, and the gull gulped at it greedily in flight. Its crop was distended and engorged with food.

The seabirds scattered raucously and indignantly as the Land-Rover approached, leaving a human body lying in the centre of an area of sand that was dappled by the prints of their webbed feet, and fouled with dropped feathers and excreta.

Johnny braked the Land-Rover and jumped out. He took one long look at the body, then turned quickly away and braced himself against the side of the vehicle.

His gorge rose in a hot flood of nausea, and he gagged it back.

The body was nude but for a few sodden tatters of clothing and a sea boot still laced on to one foot. The birds had attacked every inch of exposed flesh – except for the scalp. The face was unrecognizable. The nose was gone, the eye sockets were empty black holes. There were no lips to cover the grinning teeth.

Above this ruined face the shock of colourless albino hair looked like a wig placed there as an obscene and tasteless joke.

Hugo Kramer had made the long voyage from Thunderbolt and Suicide to the Red Gods.

Johnny took the canvas groundsheet from under the passenger seat of the Land-Rover. Averting his eyes from the task, he wrapped the corpse carefully, tied the whole bundle with lengths of rope cut from the tow line, then laboriously dragged it up the beach well above the high-water mark.

The thick canvas would keep off the birds, but to make doubly certain Johnny collected the driftwood and planking that was scattered thickly along the high-water line and piled it over the corpse.

Some of the planking was freshly broken and the paint on it was still bright and new. Johnny guessed this was part of the wreckage of *Wild Goose*.

He went back to the Land-Rover, and drove on towards the Red Gods which lay only a mile ahead.

The sun was well up by now, and already its heat was uncomfortable. As he drove he struggled out of the sheepskin jacket without interrupting his search of the beach ahead.

He was looking for another gathering of seagulls, but instead he saw a large black object stranded in the angle formed by the red stone cliffs.

He was fifty yards from it before he realized what it was.

He felt his stomach jar violently and then clench at the shock.

It was a black rubber inflatable life raft – and it had been dragged up the beach *above the high-water line*.

As he climbed out of the Land-Rover Johnny felt his legs trembling beneath him, as though he had just climbed a mountain. The hard knotted sensation in his chest shortened his breathing.

He went slowly towards the raft, and there was a story to read in the soft sand.

The smooth drag mark of the raft, and the two sets of footprints. One set made by bare feet; broad, stubby-toed and with flattened arches, the prints of a man who habitually went barefooted.

These tracks had been made by one of the coloured crew of *Wild Goose*, Johnny decided, dismissed them and turned his whole attention to the other set of footprints.

Shod feet, long and narrow, smooth leather soles; the

imprints were sharp-edged suggesting new shoes little worn, the length of the stride and the depth of prints were those of a tall heavily built man.

Johnny realized with mild surprise that his hands were shaking now, and even his lips quivered. He was like a man in high fever; light-headed, weak and shaking. It was Benedict van der Byl. He knew it with complete and utter certainty. Benedict had survived the maelstrom of Thunderbolt and Suicide.

Johnny balled his fists, squeezing hard and he thrust out his jaw, tightening his lips. Still the hatred washed over his mind in dark hot waves.

'Thank God,' he whispered. 'Thank God. Now I can kill him myself.'

The footprints had churned the sand all about the raft. Beside them lay a thick piece of planking which had been used as a lever to rip the emergency water container and the food locker from the floor-boards of the raft.

The food locker had been ransacked and abandoned. They would be carrying the packets of iron rations in their pockets to save weight, but the water container was gone.

The two sets of prints struck out straight for the dunes. Johnny followed them at a run and lost them immediately in the shifting wind-blown sands of the first dune.

Johnny was undismayed. The dunes persisted for only a thousand yards or so, then gave way inland to the plains and salt flats of the interior.

He ran back to the Land-Rover. He had his emotions under control again. His hatred was reduced to a hard indigestible lump below his ribs, and he contemplated for a few seconds lifting the microphone of the Land-Rover's R/T set and calling Cartridge Bay.

Inspector Stander had the police helicopter parked on the landing-strip behind the depot buildings. He could be here in thirty minutes. An hour later they would have Benedict van der Byl.

Johnny dismissed the idea. Officially Benedict was dead, drowned. No one would look for him in a shallow grave in the wastes of the Namib desert.

The crewman with him would be a complication; but he could be bribed and frightened or threatened. Nothing must stand in the path of his vengeance. Nothing.

Johnny opened the Land-Rover's locker and found the knife. He went to the raft and stabbed the blade through the thick material at a dozen places. The air hissed from the holes, and the raft collapsed slowly.

Johnny bundled it into the back of the Land-Rover. He would bury it in the desert; there must be no evidence that Benedict had come ashore.

He started the engine, engaged the four-wheel drive, and followed the spoor to the foot of the dunes.

He picked his way through the valleys and across the knife-backed ridges of sand.

As he descended the last slope of the dunes he felt the oppressive silence and immensity of the land enfold him. Here, only a mile from the sea, the moderating influence of the cold Benguela current did not reach.

The heat was appalling. Johnny felt the sweat prickling from the pores of his skin and drying instantly in the lethal desiccating air.

He swung the Land-Rover parallel to the line of the dunes and crawled along at walking speed, hanging over the side of the vehicle and searching the ground. The bright specks of mica in the sand bounced the heat of the sun into his face.

He cut the spoor again where it came down off the dunes and went away on it, headed arrow straight at the far line of mountains which were already receding into the blue haze as the heat built up towards noon.

Johnny's progress was a series of rushes where the spoor ran true, broken by halts and painstaking casts on the rocky ridges and areas of broken ground. Twice he left the Land-

Rover to work the spoor through difficult terrain, but across one of the flat white salt pans he covered four miles in as many minutes. The prints were strung like the beads of a necklace, cut clearly through the glistening crust of salt.

Beyond the pan they ran into a maze of black rocks, riven by gullies, and guarded by the tall misshapen monoliths.

In one of the gullies he found Hansie, the little old coloured crewman from *Wild Goose*. His skull had been battered in with the blood-caked rock that lay beside him. The blood had dried slick and shiny, and Hansie stared with dry eyeballs at the merciless sky. His expression was of mild surprise.

The story of this new tragedy was written in the sandy bottom of the gully. In an area of milling, confused prints the two men had argued. Johnny could guess that Hansie had wanted to turn back for the coast. He must have known that the road lay beyond the mountains, a hundred miles away. He wanted to abandon the attempt, try for the coast and Cartridge Bay.

The argument ended when he turned his back on Benedict, and returned on his old tracks.

There was a depression in the sand from which Benedict had picked up the rock and followed him.

Standing over Hansie, and looking down at that pathetic crushed head, Johnny realized for the first time that he was following a maniac.

Benedict van der Byl was insane. He was no longer a man, but a raging demented animal.

'I will kill him,' Johnny promised the old white woolly head at his feet. There was no need for subterfuge now.

If he caught up with Benedict and did it, no court in the world would question but that it was self-defence. Benedict had placed himself beyond the laws of man.

Johnny took the deflated rubber raft and spread it over

Hansie. He anchored the edges of the rubber sheet with rocks.

He drove on into the dancing, shimmering walls of heat with a new mood on him; murderous, elated expectation. He knew that at this moment in time he was part animal also, corrupted by the savagery of the man he was hunting. He wanted payment in full from Benedict van der Byl in his own coin. Life for life, and blood for blood.

A mile farther on he found the water container. It had been flung aside violently, skidding across the sand with the force of its rejection; the water had poured from its open mouth, leaving a dried hollow in the thirsty earth.

Johnny stared at it in disbelief. Not even a maniac would condemn himself to such a horrible ending.

Johnny went across to where the five-gallon brass drum lay on its side. He picked it up and shook it, there was the sloshy sound of a pint or so of liquid in it.

'God!' he whispered, awed and feeling a twinge of pity despite himself. 'He won't last long now.'

He lifted the container to his lips and sucked a mouthful. Immediately his nostrils flared with disgust, and he spat violently, dropping the can and wiping at his lips with the back of his hand.

'Sea water!' he mumbled. He hurried to the Land-Rover and washed out his mouth with sweet water.

How the contamination had occurred he would never know. The raft might have lain for years in *Wild Goose* without its stores being checked or renewed.

From that point onwards Benedict must have known he was doomed. His despair was easy to read in the blundering footsteps. He had started running, with panic driving him. Five hundred yards further on he had fallen heavily into the bed of a dry ravine, and lain for a while before dragging himself up the bank.

Now he had lost direction. The spoor began a long curve

to the northwards, running again. It came round full circle, and where it crossed itself, Benedict had sat down. The marks of his buttocks were unmistakable. He must have controlled his panic here because once more the spoor struck out with determination towards the mountains.

However, within half a mile he had tripped and fallen. Now he was staggering off course again, drifting southwards. Once more he had fallen, but here he had lost a shoe.

Johnny picked it up and read the printed gold lettering on the inner sole. 'BALLY OF SWITZERLAND, SPECIALLY MADE FOR HARRODS. That's our boy Benedict, all right. Forty-guinea black kid,' he muttered grimly, and climbed back into the Land-Rover. His excitement was climaxing now. It would be soon, very soon.

Farther on Benedict had wandered down into the bed of an ancient watercourse, and turned to follow it. His right foot was lacerated by the razor flints in the river bed, and at each pace he had left a little dab of brown crumbly blood. He was staggering like a drunkard.

Johnny zigzagged the Land-Rover through the boulders that choked the watercourse. The gully deepened, and spiky cockscomb ridges of black rock hedged it in on either hand. The air in the watercourse was a heavy blanket of heat. It seared the throat, and dried the mucus in Johnny's nostrils brick hard. A small noon breeze came off the mountains, a sluggish stirring of the heavy air, that provided no relief but seemed only to heighten the bite of the sun and the suffocating oppression of the air.

Scattered along the river bed were bushes of stunted scrub. Grotesque little plants, crippled and malformed by the drought of years.

From one of the bushes ahead of the Land-Rover a monstrous black bird flapped its wings lethargically. Johnny screwed up his eyes, uncertain if it was reality or a mirage of the heat and the tortured air.

Suddenly the bird resolved itself into the jacket of a dark

blue suit. It hung in the thorny branches, the breeze stirring the folds of expensive cloth.

'In his coat. He put it in his coat pocket.'

With eyes only for the jacket, recklessly he pressed down the accelerator and the Land-Rover surged forward. Johnny did not see the knee-high boulder of ironstone in his path. He hit it at twenty miles an hour, and the Land-Rover stopped dead with the squeal of tearing metal. Johnny was flung forward against the steering-wheel, the impact driving the breath from his lungs.

He was still doubled up with the pain of it, wheezing for breath, as he hobbled to the jacket and snatched it out of the bush.

He felt the heavy drag of the weighted pocket.

Then the fat canvas bag was in his hands, the contents crunched nuttily as he tore at the drawstring. Nothing else in the world felt like that.

'Such a diamond as you will never see again.'

The drawstring was knotted tightly. Johnny ran back to the Land-Rover. Frantically he scrabbled in the seat locker and found the knife. He cut the drawstring and dumped the contents of the bag on to the bonnet of the Land-Rover.

'Oh God! Oh sweet God!' he whispered through cracked lips. His eyesight blurred, and the big blue diamond glowed mistily, distorted by the tears that flooded his vision.

It was a full minute before he could bring himself to touch it. Then he did so reverently – as though it were a sacred relic.

Johnny Lance had worked all his life to take a stone such as this.

He held it in both hands and sank down into the scrap of shade beside the body of the Land-Rover.

It was another five minutes before the hot cloying smell of engine oil reached the conscious level of his mind.

He turned his head and saw the slowly spreading pool of it beneath the Land-Rover chassis. Quickly he rolled on to his stomach and, still clutching the diamond, crawled under the vehicle. The ironstone boulder had shattered the engine sump. The Land-Rover had bled its lifeblood into the hot sand of the river bed.

He wriggled out from under the body of the Land-Rover and leaned against the front tyre. He looked at his wrist watch and was surprised to see it was already a few minutes after two o'clock in the afternoon.

He was surprised also at the conscious effort it required to focus his eyes on the dial of the watch. Two days and two nights without sleep, the unremitting emotional strain of those days and nights, the battering his body had taken, the long hours in the heat and the soul-corroding desolation of this lunar landscape – all these had taken their toll. He knew he was as light-headed as in the first stages of inebriation, he was beginning to act irrationally. That sudden reckless charge down the boulder-strewn river bed, which had wrecked the Land-Rover, was a symptom of his present instability.

He fondled the great diamond, touching the warm smooth surface to his lips, rubbing it softly between thumb and forefinger, changing it from hand to hand, while every fibre of his muscles and the very marrow of his bones cried out for rest.

A soft and treacherous lethargy spread through his body and reached out to numb his brain. He closed his eyes for a moment to shut out the flare, and when he opened them again with an effort the time was four o'clock. He scrambled to his feet. The shadows in the gully were longer, the breeze had dropped.

Although he moved with the stiffness of an old man, the sleep had cleared his mind and while he wolfed a packet of biscuits spread with meat paste and washed it down with a mugful of lukewarm water he made his decision.

He buried the canvas bag of rough diamonds in the sand

beneath the Land-Rover, but he could not bring himself to part with the big blue. He buttoned it securely into the back pocket of his slacks. Into the light knapsack from the seat locker he packed the two-pint water bottle, the first aid kit, a small hand-bearing compass, two of the smoke flares and the knife. He checked his pockets for his cigarette lighter and case.

Then without another glance at the radio set on the dashboard of the Land-Rover he turned away and hobbled up the gully on the spoor of Benedict van der Byl.

Within half a mile he had walked the stiffness out of his body, and he lengthened his stride, going well now. The hatred and hunger for vengeance which had died to smouldering ash since he had found the diamonds now flared up again strongly. It gave power to his legs and sharpened his senses.

The spoor turned abruptly up the side of the gully and he lost it on the black rock of the ridge, but found it again on his first cast.

He was closing fast now. The spoor was running across the grain of the land, and Benedict was clearly weakening rapidly. He had fallen repeatedly, crawled on bloody knees over cruel gravel and rock, he had blundered into the scrub bushes and left threads of his clothing on the hooked red-tipped thorns.

Then the spoor led out of the ridges and scrub into another area of low orange-coloured sandhills and Johnny broke into a jog trot. The sun was sliding down the sky, throwing blue shades in the hollows of the dunes and the heat abated so that Johnny's sweat was able to cool him before drying.

Johnny was intent on the staggering footprints, beginning to worry now that he would find Benedict already dead. The signs were those of a man in extreme distress, and still he was driving himself on.

Johnny did not notice the other prints that angled in from the dunes and ran parallel to those of Benedict, until they closed in again and began overlaying the human prints.

Johnny stopped and went down on one knee to examine the broad dog-like pug marks.

'Hyena!' He felt the sick little flutter of revulsion in his stomach as he spoke. He glanced around quickly and saw the other set of prints out on the left.

'A pair of them! They've smelt the blood.'

Johnny began to run on the spoor now. His skin crawled with what he knew could happen when they caught up with a helpless man. The filthiest and most cowardly animals in Africa, but with jaws that could crunch to splinters the thigh bone of a full-grown buffalo, and their thick stubby fangs were coated with such a slime of bacteria from a diet of putrid carrion that their bite was as deadly as that of a black mamba.

'Let me be in time; please God, let me find him in time.'

He heard it then. From beyond the crest of the next dune. The horror of the sound stopped him in mid-stride. It was a shrill giggling gibbering cry that sobbed into silence.

Johnny stood listening, panting wildly from his run.

It came again. The laughter of demons, excited, blood-crazy.

'They've got him.'

Johnny flung himself at the soft slope of sand. He reached the crest and looked down into the saucer-shaped arena formed by the crescent of the dune.

Benedict lay on his back. His white shirt was open to the waist. The blue trousers of his suit were ripped and shredded, exposing his knees. One foot was a bloody lump of sock and congealed dirt.

The pair of hyenas had trampled a path in the sand around his body. They had been circling him for hours, while greed overcame their cowardice.

One hyena sat ten feet from him, squatting obscenely

with its flat snakelike head lowered between humped shoulders. Brown and shaggy, spotted with darker brown, its round ears pricked forward, its black eyes sparkling with greed and excitement as it watched its mate.

The other hyena stood with its front paws on Benedict's chest. Its head was lowered, and its jaws were locked into Benedict's face. It was leaning back, bracing its paws on his chest, tugging viciously as it sought to tear off a mouthful of flesh. Benedict's head was jerking and twitching as the hyena worried it. His legs were kicking weakly, and his hands fluttered on the sand like maimed white birds.

The flesh of his face tore. Johnny heard it distinctly in the utter silence of the desert evening. It tore with the soft sound of silk – and Johnny screamed.

Both hyenas bolted at the scream, scrambling over the far crest of the dune in horrible clownish panic, leaving Benedict lying with a bloody mask for a face.

Looking down at that face Johnny knew he could not kill him now, perhaps could never have killed him. He could not revenge himself on this broken thing with its ruined face and twisted mind.

He dropped on to his knees beside him, and loosened the flap of the knapsack with clumsy fingers.

Benedict's one ear and cheek were hanging over his mouth in a thick flap of torn flesh. The teeth in the side of his jaw were exposed and the blood dribbled and spurted in fine needle jets.

Johnny tore the paper packaging off an absorbent dressing and with it pressed the flap back into place. Holding it there with the full pressure of his spread fingers. The blood soaked through the dressing, but it was slowing at the pressure.

'It's all right, Benedict. I'm here now. You'll be all right,' he whispered hoarsely as he worked. With his free hand he stripped the packaging off another dressing, and substituted it neatly for the sodden one. He maintained the pressure on the clean dressing while he lifted Benedict's head and cradled it in his lap.

'We'll just dry this bleeding up, then we'll give you a drink.' He reached into the first aid kit for a piece of cotton wool and tenderly began to clean the blood and sand from Benedict's nostrils and lips. Benedict's strangled breathing eased a little but still whistled through the black lips. His tongue was swollen, filling his mouth like a fat purple sponge.

'That's better,' Johnny muttered. Still without relaxing pressure on the compress dressing, he got the screw top off the water bottle. Holding his thumb over the opening to regulate the flow, he let a drop of water fall into the dark dry pit of a mouth.

After another ten drops he propped the water bottle in the sand, and massaged Benedict's throat gently to stimulate the swallowing reflex. The unconscious man gulped painfully.

'That's my boy,' Johnny encouraged him, and began again feeding him a drop at a time, crooning softly as he did it.

'You're going to be all right. That's it, swallow it down.'

It took him twenty minutes to administer half a pint of the warm sweet water, and by then the bleeding was negligible. Johnny reached into the kit again and selected two salt and two glucose tablets. He placed them in his own mouth and chewed them to a smooth thin paste then he bent over the mutilated face of the man he had sworn to kill and pressed his own lips against Benedict's swollen dry lips. He injected the solution of salt and glucose into Benedict's mouth, then straightened up and began again dripping the water.

When he had given Benedict another four tablets and half the contents of the water bottle, he stoppered it and returned it to the knapsack. He soaked the compress with bright yellow acriflavine solution, and bandaged it firmly into place. This was a more difficult task than he had anticipated and after a few abortive attempts he passed the bandage under the jaw and over the eyes, swathing Benedict's head completely except for the nose and mouth.

By this time the sun was on the horizon. Johnny stood up and stretched his back and shoulders as he watched the splendid gold and red death of another desert day.

He knew he was delaying his next decision. He reckoned it was five miles to where he had abandoned the Land-Rover in the gully. Five miles of hard going, a round trip of four hours – probably five in the dark. Could he leave Benedict here, get back to the vehicle, radio Cartridge Bay, and return to him?

Johnny swung round and looked up at the dunes. There was his answer. One of the hyenas was squatting on the top of a dune watching him intently. Hunger and the approach of night had made it unnaturally bold.

Johnny shouted an obscenity and made a threatening gesture towards it. The hyena jumped up and loped over the back of the ridge.

'Moon rise at eight tonight. I'll rest until then – and we'll go in the cool,' he decided and lay down on the sand beside Benedict. The lump in his back pocket prodded him, and he took the diamond out and held it in his hand.

In the darkness the hyenas began to cackle and shriek, and when the moon rose it silhouetted their evil shapes on the ridge above the saucer.

'Come on, Benedict. We're going home. There are a couple of nice policemen who want to talk to you.' Johnny lifted him into a sitting position, draped Benedict's arm over his shoulder and came up under him in a fireman's lift.

Johnny stood like that a moment, sinking ankle deep into the soft sand, dismayed at the dead weight of his burden.

'We'll rest every thousand paces,' he promised himself, and began plodding up the dune, counting softly to himself, but knowing that he would not be able to perform that lift again without a rock shelf or some support, against which to brace himself. He had to make it out of the sandhills in one go.

' – Nine hundred and ninety nine. One thousand.' He was counting in his mind only. Husbanding his strength, bowed under the weight, his shoulders and back locked in straining agony, the sand hampering each pace. 'Another five hundred. We'll go another five hundred.'

Behind him padded the two hyenas. They had gobbled the bloody dressings that Johnny had left in the saucer, and the taste of blood was driving them hysterical.

'Right. Just another five hundred.' And Johnny began the third count, and then the fourth, and the fifth.

Johnny felt the drip, drip on the back of his legs. Benedict's head-down position had restarted the bleeding, and the hyenas warbled and wailed at the smell.

'Nearly there, Benedict. Stick it out. Nearly there.'

The first cluster of moon-silver rocks floated towards them and Johnny reeled in amongst them and collapsed face forward. It was a long time before he had regained enough strength to shift Benedict's weight off his shoulders.

He readjusted Benedict's bandages, and fed him a mouthful of water which he swallowed readily. Then Johnny washed down a handful of salt and glucose tablets with two carefully rationed swallows from the water bottle. He rested for twenty minutes by his watch, then using one of the rocks as an anchor he got Benedict across his shoulder again and they went on.

Johnny rested every hour for ten minutes. At one o'clock in the morning they finished the last of the water, and at two o'clock Johnny knew beyond all possibility of doubt that he had missed the watercourse and that he was lost.

He lay against a slab of ironstone, numb with fatigue and despair, and listened to the cackling chorus of death among the rocks nearby. He tried to decide where he had gone wrong. Perhaps the watercourse curved away and he was now moving parallel to it, perhaps he had already crossed it without having recognized it. That was possible, he had heard of others stumbling blindly across a tarmac road without realizing it.

How many ridges had they climbed and descended? He could not remember. There was a place where he had stumbled into a scrub thorn and ripped his legs. Perhaps that was the watercourse.

He crawled across to Benedict.

'Brace up, bucko. We're going back.'

Johnny fell for the last time a little before dawn. When he rolled his head and squinted sideways at his wrist watch it was light enough to read the dial. The time was five o'clock.

He closed his eyes and lay for a long time, he had given up. It had been a good try – but it hadn't worked. In an hour the sun would be up. Then it was finished.

Something was moving near him, soft and stealthy-footed. It was of no interest, he decided. He just wanted to lie here quietly, now that it was finished.

Then he heard the sniffing, the harsh sniffing of a hungry dog. He opened his eyes. The hyena was ten feet away, watching him. Its bottom jaw hung open, and the pink tongue lolled loosely from the side of its mouth. He could smell it, a stink like an animal cage at the zoo, dung and offal and rotting carrion.

Johnny tried to scream, but no sound came from his mouth. His throat was closed, and his tongue filled his mouth. He struggled on to his elbows. The hyena drew back, but without the ludicrous panic of before.

Leisurely it trotted away, and then turned to face him again from a distance of twenty yards. It grinned at him, slurping the pink tongue into its mouth as it gulped saliva.

Johnny dragged himself to where Benedict lay, and looked down at him.

Slowly the blind bandaged head turned towards him, the black lips moved.

'Who's there?' A dry husky whisper. Johnny tried to answer but his voice failed him again. He hawked and chewed painfully, working a trace of moisture into his mouth. Now that Benedict was conscious Johnny's hatred flared again.

'Johnny,' he croaked. 'It's Johnny.'

'Johnny?' Benedict's hand came up and he touched the bandages over his eyes.

'What?'

Johnny reached across, lying on his side, and untied the knot at Benedict's temple. He peeled the bandages from his eyes, and Benedict blinked at him. The light of dawn was stronger now.

'Water?' Benedict asked.

Johnny shook his head.

'Please.'

'None.'

Benedict closed his eyes and then opened them, staring in terror at Johnny.

'Ruby!' Johnny whispered. 'Sergio! Hansie!'

A spasm of guilt twisted Benedict's face, and Johnny leaned closer to him to hiss a single word into his ear.

'Bastard!'

Johnny rested on his elbows, swallowing thickly, then he spoke again.

'Up!' He crawled behind Benedict and pushed and dragged him into a sitting position.

'Look.'

Twenty yards away the two hyenas sat expectantly, leering idiotically and bright-eyed with impatience.

Benedict began to tremble. He made a mewing whimpering sound. Johnny worked him slowly backwards until he had him propped against a rock.

He rested again, leaning on the rock beside Benedict.

'I'm going,' he whispered. 'You stay.'

Benedict made that mewing sound again, shaking his head weakly, staring at the two slobbering animals ahead of him.

Johnny slung the knapsack about his neck. He closed his eyes and called upon the last reserves of his strength. With a heave he got to his knees. Darkness and bright lights obscured his vision. They cleared and he heaved again and he was on his feet. His knees buckled and he grabbed at the rock to steady himself.

'Cheerio!' he whispered. 'Have fun!' And he went lurching and staggering away into the wilderness of black rock.

Behind him the mewing whimper rose to a bubbling scream.

'Johnny. Please, Johnny.'

Johnny closed his mind to that cry, and staggered on.

'Murderer!' screamed Benedict. The accusation checked Johnny. He leaned against another rock for support, and looked back.

Benedict's face was convulsed, and a thin line of bloody froth rimmed his lips. The tears were pouring unashamedly down his cheeks to soak into the blood and antiseptic stained bandages.

'Johnny. My brother. Don't leave me.'

Johnny pushed himself away from the rock. He swayed and almost fell. Then he staggered back to Benedict and slipped down into a sitting position beside him.

From the knapsack he took out the knife and laid it on his lap. Benedict was sobbing and moaning.

'Shut up. Damn you!' whispered Johnny.

T he sun was well up now. It was burning directly into Johnny's face. He could feel the skin of his cheeks stretching to bursting-point. The veils of darkness kept passing over his vision, but he blinked them away. The flutter of his eyelids was the only movement he had made in the last hour.

The hyenas had closed in. They were pacing nervously back and forth in front of where Johnny and Benedict sat. Now one of them stopped and stretched its neck out, sniffing eagerly at Benedict's blood-clotted foot, creeping inch by inch closer.

Johnny stirred and the creature jumped back, bobbing its head ingratiatingly, grinning as if in apology.

The time had come to fall back on their last line of defence. Johnny hoped he had not left it too late. He was very weak. His eyes and ears were tricking him, his vision jumped and blurred and there was a humming sound in the silence as though the desert was an orchard filled with bees. He spun the cog-wheel of his cigarette lighter and the flame lit. Carefully he applied it to the fuse of the smoke flare, and it spluttered and caught.

Johnny lobbed the flare towards the hyenas, and as the clouds of pink smoke spewed out, they fled in shrieking terror.

An hour later they were back. Slinking out of the rocks, cautious again. Johnny saw them only in flashes, between the bursts of darkness in his head. The insect drone in his ears was louder, it was confusing, making it difficult for him to think clearly.

It took him ten minutes to light the second flare. His throw was so weak that the flare pitched only a few inches beyond his own feet. The pink smoke spread over them.

Johnny felt the blood humming in his ears as the swirling pink clouds engulfed him. The sulphurous bite of the smoke in his throat choked him. The sound in his ears became a drumming roar, a rushing clattering hissing bellow. Then there was a wild wind in the stillness of the desert. Miraculously the smoke cloud was ripped away by the wind.

Johnny looked up into the sky from which the great wind came. Twenty feet above him, hanging on the glistening dragon-fly wing of its rotor, was the police helicopter.

Tracey's face was framed in the cabin window of the helicopter. He saw her lips form his name before he fainted.

Visit **www.panmacmillan.com** to read more about all our books and to buy them. You will also find features, author interviews and news of any author events, and you can sign up for e-newsletters so that you're always first to hear about our new releases.

www.panmacmillan.com

GIFT SELECTOR
YOUR ACCOUNT
WISH LIST
WAITING LIST

HOME | ABOUT US | IMPRINTS | TRADE/MEDIA | CONTACT US | ADVANCED SEARCH | SEARCH | GO

BOOK CATEGORIES | WHAT'S NEW | AUTHORS/ILLUSTRATORS | BESTSELLERS | READING GROUPS

Coming Soon...

Reading Groups

Competitions
Feeling Lucky?

Extracts
Sneak Previews

Interviews

Events
Meet Our Stars

Reviews
What The Critics Say

News & Awards

Editor's Choice
What We're Reading